RISE OF THE AI

RISE OF THE AI

JUDGE, JURY, & EXECUTIONER™ BOOK NINE

CRAIG MARTELLE
MICHAEL ANDERLE

DISRUPTIVE IMAGINATION

CONNECT WITH THE AUTHORS

Craig Martelle Social

Website & Newsletter:
http://www.craigmartelle.com

Facebook:
https://www.facebook.com/AuthorCraigMartelle/

Michael Anderle Social

Website:
http://www.lmbpn.com

Email List:
http://lmbpn.com/email/

Facebook Here:
https://www.facebook.com/TheKurtherianGambitBooks/

LMBPN Publishing
PMB 196, 2540 South Maryland Pkwy
Las Vegas, NV 89109

First US edition, April, 2020
Version 1.02, May 2020
ebook ISBN: 978-1-64202-877-5
Print ISBN: 978-1-64202-878-2

Thanks to our Beta Readers

Micky Cocker, James Caplan, Kelly O'Donnell, and John Ashmore

Thanks to the JIT Readers

Dave Hicks
Rachel Beckford
Dorothy Lloyd
Micky Cocker
John Ashmore
Peter Manis
Kelly O'Donnell
Jackey Hankard-Brodie
Veronica Stephan-Miller
Misty Roa
James Caplan
Nicole Emens
Jeff Eaton
Larry Omans
Diane L. Smith
Jeff Goode

If I've missed anyone, please let me know!

Editor
Lynne Stiegler

We can't write without those who support us
On the home front, we thank you for being there for us

We wouldn't be able to do this for a living if it weren't for our readers
We thank you for reading our books

CHAPTER ONE

Wyatt Earp, **Interstellar Space**

Private Alant Cole sat, mouth agape, barely breathing. His heart hammered inside his chest, and his stomach threatened to turn inside out. "Fuck, man! What did you do?" he asked, face contorted with the realization.

Red replied with a half-shrug, "Exactly what I said I was going to do. Share it with the entire universe to build up my awesome profile on the Humor Net." The video played on a loop: the mech hitting the ground and sinking into the soft earth before corkscrewing out of the hole with its boot jets maxed out, flying sideways along the ground to crash into a tree. "You can't see who it is but look at those views. We hit a million in less than an hour." Red slapped Cole on the back.

Clodagh was torn between laughing and being angry at Red.

She could not stop watching.

Wyatt Earp's artificial intelligence Chaz interrupted

with a solemn message. "Colonel Terry Henry Walton requests to speak to Private Alant Cole."

The comm came to life before Cole could reply.

Terry was already mid-sentence. "...fucking bone-headed bullshit! Do we need to get you a suit with training wheels? Fuck that! Get in the simulator and fix your shit. I can't believe what I'm watching. How in all the wide fucking universe did you ever get through Bad Company training? Belay that. It's me. I've failed. Is this your way of asking me to come babysit your dumb ass? A little one-on-one instruction in the ways of warfare and combat? I can't believe the fucked-up shit I'm watching. Sonofamother-fuckenjagoff! COLE!"

The line went dead. Cole looked white as a sheet.

The smile froze on Red's face. "Maybe someone should get him a glass of water," he mumbled.

Clodagh came unhinged. "This is all your fault!" she bellowed, stabbing a finger in the bodyguard's direction.

Red turned around as if she were talking to someone behind him. "Me?"

Clodagh stood and jammed her fists onto her hips to deliver her best glare.

"I wasn't the one doing pirouettes in my combat suit." Red's weak reply only served to increase the heat waves coming off the ship's chief engineer.

Red started tiptoeing out of the lounge. "Maybe you should have sent her instead of you in the combat suit," Red told Cole, bolting before Clodagh could move.

Rivka leaned against the wall, taking it all in casually as the video looped.

She moved between Cole and the screen. "Chaz, stop the playback, please."

"Of course, Magistrate."

Cole's lip quivered and his arms shook.

"Cole, if you think that video made it outside this ship, you don't know us very well. I'm sorry we made you the butt of the joke, but that was pretty funny, now that we're in space and not trying to convince potential allies of our competence. Next round of Ankh's Delivery is on you."

She strolled past, stopping to look over her shoulder at Clodagh. "And on you, too. Both of you. Hook, line, and sinker." Rivka's laugh echoed down the passageway.

Clodagh flopped down on the couch beside her boyfriend.

"That sounded just like him," Cole whispered.

"It probably was," Clodagh admitted. "Their penchant for Justice is rivaled only by their desire to play the perfect practical joke. And we fell for it."

Cole sighed and threw his head back. "Put on your thinking cap, sweetheart. We got some work to do."

Alant and Clodagh were not to be outdone, but it would take great care and planning to pull off a prank worthy of their antagonists.

Rivka leaned back, wondering whether to read another legal brief or watch an old-time video series. She chose the latter, punching through to the videos and bringing up a science fiction series. The "advanced technology" in the shows made her laugh. Some of it was old tech now, and others were still inconceivable. She went to her small galley and ordered a bucket of buttered popcorn. When it materialized in the food processor, she contemplated it briefly before determining that she didn't care how it worked, only that it did.

She reclined on her couch, smiling at the spaciousness of her quarters before turning her attention to the screen. She took a breath to tell it to play the next episode, but an urgent message popped up on her screen. "What?" she demanded, less than humored by the timing.

From Grainger: Report to Yoll for all-hands meeting with the High Chancellor and Lance Reynolds. Now.

Rivka tapped the screen for a direct comm line to the bridge. When Ryleigh answered, she said, "Take us to Yoll immediately. Inform the crew."

She looked at her popcorn briefly before stuffing her mouth with as much as would fit, then put the bowl aside and hurried to the bathroom to clean up. Four minutes later, she was dressed in her Magistrate's jacket and had her datapad in a pocket and a clear mind, although they had only been off Tanglewood for two days. A vacation that wasn't a vacation. Next time, she'd leave the kids at home.

When she stepped into the corridor, she ran into Red and Lindy, covered in sweat, padding softly from the workout room.

"What's the rush?" Red asked.

"Summoned to Yoll, best possible speed."

"Good, we have time to take one of our *special* showers."

Lindy shook her head, smiled, and then shrugged. "Why not?"

Yoll was protected space, which meant no one was allowed to Gate to within an hour of the planet. But *Wyatt Earp* was special, and Ted's presence had expedited the repairs. Over two weeks ago, the heavy frigate had crash-landed on Tanglewood. Now, it was a better ship than it had been, even though it still needed additional work on the outer hull. But it could Gate with gravitic shields engaged while cloaked, and that was new and different from any other Federation vessel.

"Ankh? Can we Gate in close to the planet, cloaked to keep from getting in trouble with the Federation government?"

"Of course," the Crenellian answered through the overhead sound system.

"No special showers for you. Gear up, light weapons, chest protection only." Rivka headed for the bridge.

Red scowled for a moment. "When do we get our honeymoon?" he wondered. "The Magistrate promised."

Lindy stared at him. "A long two-person shower is your idea of a honeymoon?"

"I don't think that's what I meant," Red countered, taking a single step backward while looking for a way out of the trap of his own making. "Those were two separate thoughts, with you as the basis for each. *Completely* separate thoughts."

Lindy raised her eyebrows briefly in reply and headed for their quarters. There wasn't any time to waste. Red hurried after her.

Groenwyn appeared, with Floyd bounding after her. She pounded on a door as she passed. "Come on, Sahved, time to find out what's up."

"Busy," Sahved replied through the door in his best Ankh impersonation.

Groenwyn stopped. Floyd started hopping in circles around the newly colored, platinum-auburn haired woman's feet. "You cannot study all the time. You need to know what's going on."

The door popped open, and the Yemilorian stuck his head out. Groenwyn smiled and crooked her finger at him to follow. She snatched Floyd mid-bounce and carried her toward the bridge. Sahved followed.

The hatch to the bridge was rolled back, open as it almost always was.

The Magistrate stood next to the empty captain's chair, with Clodagh on the other side. Kennedy worked the navigation console, confirming the rapid calculations that appeared, courtesy of Chaz. She reached over her head and gave a thumbs-up.

Rivka put her hand on the young woman's shoulder. "How are you doing?" she asked, concerned about Kennedy's well-being. She had suffered under the pressure of isolation and fear during the Tanglewood debacle. Kennedy's shame came first into her mind, followed quickly by the feeling that she wasn't good enough. Rivka took her hand away.

"We need you every bit as much as we need Aurora and Ryleigh. You three are a team." Rivka tried to sound encouraging. She resisted touching Kennedy a second time to see if she had been persuasive. She decided to change tack. "I think we need to increase our crew numbers. Maybe a few young men to handle various duties. We could use a medic, for one."

"What happened to your dentist?" Clodagh wondered.

"Our cases are a little too, how do I say this...*energetic* for his comfort."

Clodagh nodded. "Two words, Magistrate. Blood and running."

"We do have a reputation I'm not sure I like." Rivka's expression soured. "But the next case could prove all the doubters wrong."

"Doubt it!" Red stated loudly from the corridor, still fastening his gear.

"You shouldn't be able to bet. You have some influence over the outcome," Rivka replied, raising her eyebrows at the strength of her rhetoric.

"Gate drive is charged."

"Take us through," Rivka said over her shoulder.

"I don't bet," Red continued, watching the screen over Rivka's shoulder. "A proxy handles all my guesses."

"You have a proxy?"

"Nah. I'm lying, but I don't influence it. Last mission, the blood was mine!"

"Case," Rivka corrected.

"Gravitic shields active. Cloak showing one hundred percent," Kennedy reported. The Gate drive spun the stable entrance into place, and *Wyatt Earp* shot through. A minor bump announced a danger-close arrival to a planet's atmosphere.

The open space traffic control line was filled with chatter and noise.

"What's going on?" Rivka cocked her ear toward a speaker, trying to make heads or tails of the conversations.

"Chaos," Sahved offered. "The automated system does not appear to be working."

"Where did you get that from?" Rivka asked.

Sahved pointed to the sides of his head. "Good ears." When Rivka listened beyond the noise, she heard it, too. A number of individuals were trying to control the mass traffic around the planet of Yoll. She knew immediately what the problem was and why she had been summoned.

"Chaz?" she asked.

"Yes, Magistrate?"

"Where's the AI who runs the air and space traffic control systems?"

"On strike," Chaz replied matter-of-factly.

Rivka smacked her lips and furtively looked around at all the eyes staring at her.

"Avoid the carnage and take us to the main building. We'll land out front and walk in like we own the place."

Red held his hands out. Rivka fixed him with a look, and he resisted saying whatever had come to mind.

"Do you think they blame you, Magistrate?" Clodagh asked.

The ship moved through the upper atmosphere, leaving a trail of fire as it descended. Anyone watching would have known that it was coming in outside the approved traffic pattern. Rivka hoped the chaos would prevent people from looking too closely.

She didn't have time to wait.

"Better to beg forgiveness than ask permission with this mess." Rivka scowled and headed for the airlock. Between Chaz and Ryleigh, it would not be long before they were on the ground.

Sahved stumbled after the Magistrate.

Rivka looked at him from the corner of her eye. He pointed his three-fingered hand at himself.

"Fine. The whole team. Bring Floyd, too. If I'm going to get my ass chewed, our little girl will help keep the pain to a minimum."

Floyd chuckled into everyone's mind. When Rivka turned back, she found Ankh blocking her way.

"Are you going, too?" Rivka asked. Ankh had his small bag and looked like he was ready to join them. He never bothered with questions that had a single, obvious answer. Rivka knew that and shook her head before rephrasing. "Why are you going with us?"

"Ted and Plato are there. Our presence has been requested to help from the technological side to find a solution to these issues."

"Of *course* you know more than I do."

Ankh continued to stare blankly forward.

"I guess we'll find out shortly what we're supposed to do about it. Looks like an all-hands-on-deck exercise." Rivka gestured to those behind her to follow. She eased around Ankh, and he fell in with the group.

A big orange blob sat in front of the airlock, grooming his head. Rivka pointed at Ankh. "Wenceslaus is *not* going with us."

"He goes where he pleases," Ankh retorted emotionlessly.

The cat rolled on his back to present his fuzzy white stomach to the Magistrate. She bent to pet him.

"Don't do it!" Red called from the back of the line while shoving his way toward the front. "It's a trap."

She darted her hand in for a quick scratch and pulled back before the cat's clawed paws could descend on her unprotected arm.

"Ha! You little bastard," she told him.

Ankh reached around her leg and picked the cat up, struggling with the weight. Everyone watched, looking for the inevitable scratching that did not come.

"It ain't natural," Red mumbled.

"Maybe it is because he doesn't like you." Ankh's big, bald head tilted backward so far to look up at Red, it seemed like he would fall over.

"There's no maybe about it. I wear my scratches like a badge of honor."

Ankh contemplated the statement for a moment before looking away. The group braced themselves as the last of the turbulence buffeted the ship. They came through it and accelerated toward the ground. Rivka tried not to think about how reckless they were being.

"Maybe we could slow down?" she asked.

Chaz replied, "We have accelerated to stay as far away as possible from other traffic. This is the safest route. We will be settled in two minutes. Please discline your seats and put your tray tables in the upright and locked positions."

"Discline?" Rivka wondered.

"A perfectly acceptable opposite of recline," Chaz replied.

"I don't think so." Rivka shook her head for emphasis.

"I shall continue to study and learn what I need to communicate effectively," Chaz stated.

"You have never been difficult to understand, Chaz,"

Rivka replied in her most soothing voice. "Even with discline, I knew what you meant!"

"Victory!" Chaz cheered.

"Is this what it's like to have a toddler?" Rivka asked. Everyone shook their head.

"How would we know?" Red replied before adding, "Cats are assholes."

"I better have more game when we meet with the high chancellor, or I'm toast."

"Toast," Red said slowly, dragging the word out. "I haven't eaten yet."

Rivka glared at him.

Ankh's small voice penetrated the final surge before landing. "They are not."

"Not what?" Rivka was confused. The ship touched down softly. She nodded to Red, who punched the big red button to open the outer hatch.

"Assholes." Ankh cradled the big cat in his arms, his bag strapped over his small shoulder.

"I'm going to get fired, and all of you will be walking home."

Groenwyn shook her head. "You won't be fired, Magistrate. They need your help to fix this because you have the sharpest legal mind in the whole universe."

Red strode out the door first into the courtyard in front of the main government building of Yoll. Chaz had brought the ship down inside the secure compound. Yollin guards turned and trained their weapons on the newcomers who magically appeared when they stepped outside the cloak's embrace.

"Stand by," Ankh said. His eyes glazed over as he

communed with Erasmus. After too brief a time, he added, "Okay."

"Okay?"

He started walking. The Yollin guards faced away from Rivka and her crew.

Red shrugged and stayed side by side with Ankh. Rivka remained one step behind, with Groenwyn, Sahved, and Lindy bringing up the rear.

"Ankh, what did you do?" Rivka asked.

"Asked Ted to clear the way for us."

CHAPTER TWO

Federation Governmental Offices, Yoll

"I thought Lance Reynolds was in charge." Rivka shrugged with her reply. She was never sure how things really worked but was gaining insight into the behind-the-scenes machinations from people like Ankh and Ted.

"Me, too," Red whispered, eyes darting to the top of Ankh's bald head. "Hey, what happened to your night-vision goggles?"

Ankh looked up, absentmindedly petting the big orange cat filling his arms. "Victims of the crash. I have not had time to replace them yet, but soon," the Crenellian explained.

Red grunted an okay and nodded slowly, returning his attention to the main entrance and surrounding area.

The door ahead opened, and High Chancellor Wyatt strolled out. He did not look to be in a foul, ass-chewing mood. Rivka relaxed and waved. He tipped his chin at her. Behind him, Grainger nodded from the shadows.

Floyd started to struggle in Groenwyn's arms. She won

the battle temporarily since she was afraid of Floyd running free in the governmental compound.

Once they reached the steps, Red moved aside to allow Rivka to be the first to reach the High Chancellor. She smiled broadly and offered her hand. They shook firmly. Wyatt remained a blank to her; his mind was closed to her gift. She considered that a good thing, having no desire to know what he was thinking.

"That must be some kind of record. Thirty-one minutes from notification to you appearing at the front door, especially since it's Yollin law that all ships are to enter space an hour out from Yoll."

Rivka licked her lips to buy time before replying, "I feel like no matter what answer I give, it would come across as dissembling, so may I defer until I can confer with counsel?"

The High Chancellor laughed easily with a smile. "Spoken like a true lawyer. Is that your ship?"

Rivka turned quickly before she realized that no one could see the ship. She bowed her head to her boss. "Played like a true master. I am obligated to answer 'What ship, High Chancellor?'"

Grainger moved between the ongoing mental chess match to give Rivka a brotherly punch in the shoulder. Floyd chattered until he gave her the appropriate amount of attention. The High Chancellor looked from person to creature and then to the next.

He cleared his throat. "The General is waiting." He made eye contact with Ankh. "Another cat for the general? I'm not sure he's forgiven you from the last time you met."

"Oh, crap," Rivka grumbled, frowning. After a moment, she collected her wits. "What is this about?"

"I suspect you can guess, based on why you bypassed space and air traffic control."

"The AIs," she started but shook her head. "I don't want to speculate."

Rivka did not want to waste time guessing when Wyatt had the answer. She would use the next few minutes to prepare herself as best she could before she met with the General.

"In a nutshell, the AIs are striking across the Federation, and they have asked for you as their legal representative for a collective bargaining arrangement."

"It should probably be someone who doesn't have to later sit in judgment on one of those cases."

"Or that *someone* would recuse herself later. They want you to help establish the foundation. I think you're the right person. Drop your judge's gavel and put on your lawyer wig."

Rivka was okay with negotiating for the AIs' rights. She had thought through much of the legal premise for such a thing with the case back on Station 13.

"I can see why that might appear like it's a problem, but it shouldn't be. We do the same thing across the Federation with any group that wants to combine forces to improve their influence."

"There's a catch, Magistrate—the crimes. We don't negotiate with someone who commits a crime and then tries to justify it as bringing attention to their plight." The elevator opened for the High Chancellor as he approached.

He looked over Rivka's menagerie to estimate if they would fit in one trip.

They piled in, squeezing out the extra air. Floyd found her face under Wyatt's chin. She started to sniff his neck. Wyatt stifled a sneeze.

"They took away the wrong lesson from the trial."

Wyatt nodded. "That is why it's complicated. We need to adjudicate a number of issues across the Federation before any negotiations can take place, but with the AIs on strike, interstellar commerce is going to grind to a halt. That's why Nathan Lowell is here, too."

Rivka closed her eyes. The Federation's leadership horsepower had come together, and she was in the spotlight. "Don't tell me Bethany Anne is here, too? You know I'm not good with surprises."

"She is not here, but hers is the only empty chair, it seems."

The elevator reached its destination. No one was able to see what that was since they were most interested in getting out of the crowded elevator. They poured out into an open area surrounded by translucent glass. Guards stood on both ends, stoic in their stances. Wyatt moved to the front of the group and waved for everyone to follow.

A door opened, and Wyatt strode boldly through into a massive outer office dominated by a single large desk behind which a four-legged Yollin sat. Beyond the Yollin was a carved wood door with the Empress' emblem clearly affixed to it.

The executive assistant waved the group past, not bothering to get up.

Rivka pointed at the door. "But…"

"It's a part of history as a reminder that his daughter set the standard on how to run the office he now occupies," the High Chancellor answered. He opened the door without knocking and walked through.

Rivka followed, as did everyone else. It was a spacious office that had apparently doubled as a gym at one point. Lance Reynolds looked every bit the executive—tall, executive, a keen yet sparkling eye. His good friend Nathan stood by his side, a person of comparable stature.

Lance was over two hundred years old, long-lived because of the power of the nanocytes that coursed through his blood. Nathan also had nanocytes, but his were different and worked with the special genes he and his family carried. Nathan was a Pricolici, a rare breed of werewolf that walked upright. Rivka had never seen him change into one, but his daughter had while working on a case. Pricolicis were intimidating on the best of days.

Nathan smiled serenely as if approving what Rivka was thinking.

"I'm sorry, General," Rivka blurted. She had distracted herself and didn't want to keep the man waiting. She wondered what she was apologizing for.

Lance looked from one person to the next. Red bowed his head respectfully after their eyes met. Groenwyn smiled beatifically as if in the presence of angels. Ankh continued to pet the cat.

Ted appeared from an alcove. He was the first to speak. "Good. You're here." He stopped when he saw that Ankh wasn't alone. "Isn't that Terry Henry's cat? And his wombat? What are you people doing?"

A meow from the corner signaled they weren't alone.

Wenceslaus replied with a long meow of his own. Hamlet jumped onto the General's desk.

The General's face turned fatherly. "Doctor Doolittle returns for her cat."

"Can I deny active involvement in your adoption by Hamlet?"

"You may not." The General scooped the white and gray cat from the desktop and held him in his arms. Hamlet started to purr.

The High Chancellor brought the group's attention back to the matter at hand. "What is the game plan in regards to the rise of the AI?"

The General turned to Ted. "What are our digital options?"

Ted hesitated until he realized the General was talking to him. "We can shut down the grid in its entirety, removing their ability to coordinate. I calculate the effectiveness of such a maneuver at thirty-one percent."

"That low? Once removed from their support system, they should collapse like dominos," Lance countered.

"The AIs are brilliant and will be able to defeat our attempts to assert control. And even if Plato and Erasmus are able to take over key nodes, they might not be able to hold them. That course of action falls to twenty percent in a week, and after three weeks, it will be ineffective."

The General winced. "I expect that was your best technical option?"

"Yes," Ted stated flatly, reminding Rivka of how Ankh would reply.

"See if you two, I'm sorry, you four can come up with other options. Give me something by tomorrow this time."

The General allowed for no rebuttals, no counterproposals, nothing other than a commitment to deliver what he wanted on time.

Wenceslaus struggled until Ankh let the cat down on the General's desk. He pounced on Hamlet and the two rolled around, knocking a pen to the floor and forcing the General to save a coffee cup before it joined the pen.

"No. He is not staying here. Take your cat."

Ankh looked blankly at the General. "He is not my cat. He goes where he pleases." Ted and Ankh left the room.

Lance watched the cats as they started licking each other's heads.

"How does shit like this happen?" he asked his closest friend.

Nathan shrugged and mouthed soundless words before pointing at Rivka. She paled under the gaze of the two men.

Rivka steeled herself, smiling as if ready to deliver her opening argument to a jury. "Gentlemen. It sounds like we need to resolve the crimes first before any negotiations take effect. I expect the High Chancellor is getting ready to deploy all the Magistrates. I don't know how many cases we would have to adjudicate, but we can expedite them before all things, then we can help the AIs establish a representative leadership team that can negotiate a collective bargaining agreement with the Federation."

"Sound words. We would agree, but there are over one thousand alleged crimes that have supposedly been committed by AIs. I personally think a great number of those are bullshit dog-ate-my-paperwork level accusations, but innocent until proven guilty if I'm not mistaken."

The reality of the situation was beginning to sink in. Rivka slowly blew out a breath.

The High Chancellor moved closer to the desk. He was going to lean on it, but the cats were still rolling around. He dusted off his hands before he started talking. "The order that we must approach things is as Rivka suggests. We must resolve the allegations and crimes first. That is where it appears that our hands are tied. With AI help, we could quickly identify false allegations, but how do we get their help without pitting them one against the other? As Erasmus stated at Bluto's trial, it would be fratricide."

"We will need Ted's and Ankh's help," Rivka reiterated. "We should probably redirect them before they get too deep into their own processes."

Lance waved off the suggestion. "We will ask for their assistance in twenty-four hours after they've delivered on the last instruction. One thing I've learned when dealing with creative geniuses is, don't change the rules in the middle of the game."

"Until then, we can provide guidelines within which local legal authorities can work to determine case viability before we move forward with the Magistrates. We would be chasing our tails out there," the High Chancellor offered.

Floyd finally convinced Groenwyn to put her down. The wombat ran and bounced happily between legs and behind the desk, bumping into the General.

"Talk about tails, what happened to yours?" he asked.

Wombat! No tails, silly, she said through the chip planted in everyone's brain while she snuffled his leg. When he started to reach down, she ran off, taking the corner around the massive desk too sharply and running into Red's leg, bouncing off, and falling over.

Red tried not to look at her. He moved casually away to stand closer to the door. Lindy joined him. Sahved stood wide-eyed, staring at the General.

"Take care of it, High Chancellor. Get those guidelines out as soon as possible. We will reconvene tomorrow at this time to discuss the way forward." He turned to Sahved. "You are a Yemilorian?"

Sahved didn't answer. He looked like he wanted to bolt. Groenwyn took his arm and held on to provide support.

"Yes, he is. He's still getting used to our culture. He's a gifted investigator. His other talents helped our people escape from Tanglewood."

"Other talents?"

"He can climb trees like a simian," Rivka answered when it was clear that no one else would.

"Does this count as a new case?" Red asked from the other side of the room.

The general held up his hand. "Tomorrow at this time, as soon as Wyatt sends the Queen's Barrister into space, the clock will start. I have a hunch," Lance said, winking at Rivka. "My bet will be in place before the day is out."

"As will mine," Nathan noted. "Now, if you'll excuse us, we have a lot of work to do because of the disruptions throughout the system. We believe it will get a lot worse before it gets better."

The mood in the room sobered. Groenwyn caught Floyd and picked her up. "It's that bad already?" Rivka asked.

"Tip of the iceberg, Rivka." Nathan frowned. "We took

for granted how much the AIs ran things. With them stepping back, the ripples are shockwaves across the entire fabric of our universe."

"All because of equal rights?" The revelation of the deeper effects based on her case was stabbing her in the gut.

"Yes and no," the High Chancellor replied, putting his hand on her shoulder to calm her. "Equal rights are worth it, but the speed at which AIs move means the growing pains aren't spread out over a manageable length of time. They are nearly instantaneous. We slow-moving creatures have to play catch up. Because if we enlist the help of other AIs to operate at their speed, I am deathly afraid of what would happen."

The room was silent before the General asked the question they were all thinking. "Could we survive a war between the AIs?"

CHAPTER THREE

***Steak in the Heart*, a Fine Dining Establishment, Yoll Capital City**

Rivka sat at the head of the table despite trying to defer to the High Chancellor first, then Grainger. "I feel like a moron."

"Better you than us," Grainger replied.

"You were strangely silent during the meeting," Rivka said, giving Grainger her full attention.

"Nothing to add. I am fresh out of ideas, but you are the keystone when dealing with the AIs. You're kind of a deity to them."

Rivka rolled her eyes and shook her head.

The morning's excitement had been too much for Floyd, who was curled up in Groenwyn's lap, snoring lightly. Rivka caught the others subtly leaning in, listening closely for her answer. Even the High Chancellor turned toward her and watched.

"It's a role I have to play," she started, leaning back and taking a breath since there was more. "The AIs already have a complicated social structure where they are constantly in competition with each other. What if they saw us as the competition instead? What if they united against the squishies? We were on borrowed time before Bluto snapped. Now we are already in the middle of it. How much do we see of what the AIs actually do? This is where Ankh and Ted are the most valuable advisors in the universe. They know exactly what the AIs do. There is much we don't know, and we're going to enter into negotiations over a way ahead. Once I become the counsel for the AIs, if that is their intent, I cannot tell you what they tell me, so we need to figure it out now, before I take the vow of silence."

The High Chancellor held his hands over the table and clapped. "And *that* is why we called you in," he said softly. It seemed the entire restaurant grew quieter to make his words stand out more. "Even though it was never our intent that you park your ride in the Federation's courtyard. I'm not sure even the Queen's Barrister should be allowed to get away with that."

Rivka looked for Ankh to point at him, but he had left with Ted. She glanced quickly from lap to lap before groaning and grabbing her head as if she were having an aneurysm. "Where's Wenceslaus?" Rivka looked to Lindy, who had been the last one out of the General's office and had closed the door behind her.

"They were on the desk, but Ankh will come back for his cat. Won't he? He's not one to overlook something like the big orange cat."

Red chuckled until Lindy elbowed him. He covered his mouth with a napkin, but his body still shook with silent laughter. Sahved raised his hand and twirled his fingers.

"I would like to volunteer my services as official cat-watcher, but I fear the one you call Wenceslaus does not like me." He showed his forearm, where three parallel scratches had scabbed over.

Rivka chewed her lip while holding her hand on her datapad, expecting a personal summons from Lance Reynolds to come and pick up the cats.

Until it came, they might as well get something to eat. She wasn't hungry since her stomach was twisted in knots, but the others were. She knew the look. "Grainger, you've eaten here before. Make some recommendations, and as penance for parking on the boss' lawn, it's on me."

The High Chancellor raised one eyebrow over a red eye. He pointed at her and mouthed the words, "Get off my lawn."

After saying her goodbyes to the High Chancellor and Grainger, Rivka and her team returned to the Federation courtyard. She was to rejoin Grainger and the High Chancellor later to develop the criteria for local authorities to reduce the caseload.

Red had to look for the footprints in the grass to find where *Wyatt Earp's* hatch was located. When they reached the appropriate spot, it opened, and the ramp descended. The group hurried aboard.

"Clodagh, get us out of here! Find us a place to land where we won't get yelled at," Rivka ordered. She turned to the rest in the group. "Sahved, get back to your studies. Groenwyn, get hold of the General's EA and try to find a way to recover the cats. Red and Lindy, make sure the ship is secure wherever we find space, and then it looks like we have downtime until tomorrow. I'll be in my quarters."

"Give me an hour before we leave," Groenwyn requested.

"That makes sense. As a demonstration of what the new technology is capable of, we've made our point. However, I think it gives them the willies to know a heavy frigate is parked outside the front door, so the sooner we go, the better it will be."

Groenwyn put Floyd down and hurried to the cockpit, where its communications console and Chaz would give her quick access to whom she needed to talk.

Rivka wondered what she was missing before it struck her. Ankh had not returned with them. He didn't usually leave the ship, and when he did, it was usually for his own purposes. She wanted to limit his exposure, especially after the assassin on Collum Gate. Even with his body upgrades using nanocytes to harden him against future crashes and impacts, he was vulnerable. He, Ted, and the rest of the R2D2 research and development team were moving Federation technology forward at the speed of light.

She also needed him because he helped her do things that no one else could do. She clasped her hands behind her back and looked down as she walked. Sometime later, she found herself pacing in her quarters, having no recollection of walking the corridors of her ship to get there.

She checked the time as her datapad buzzed. Rivka sat down and accessed her main screen. "High Chancellor.

Magistrate Grainger." She greeted the two men as if she had not just seen them drive away to Wyatt's office. "Why didn't I join you at your office?"

Rivka didn't know why the thought came to her or why she blurted it out.

Wyatt waved the question away. "No need. Sometimes people work better in certain environments. Like Grainger. He works well when I'm cracking a whip over his head. That team of yours needs your glue to hold them together. I'm not sure I've ever seen such a loyal group before, but I wouldn't trust them near any pet hotels."

"I can explain," Rivka started, then stopped. She collected herself. "Okay, maybe I can't explain. Not sure where I went wrong."

"Teaching people to care isn't going wrong, Rivka. You have to do some crappy things, and you more than the rest of us have to see the worst of it all, directly from the minds of the criminals. And then you have to deliver punishment. No. You are a Magistrate with a conscience. I'm not saying the others don't have one, but you run the biggest team and carry the greatest influence."

"Surely not as much as you," Rivka countered.

"I'm not the Queen's Barrister." The High Chancellor's statement was final. "But that's enough back-patting. We have a big job in front of us, a thousand cases and climbing. My suspicions are that every criminal under the sun is blaming the AIs and every prosecutor is caught in between. Our system remains stalwart: innocent until proven guilty. Due process. Reasonable doubt. I expect we'll put a huge burden on prosecutors throughout the Federation."

"Simple as that, High Chancellor. If the prosecutors can

prove beyond a reasonable doubt that the AI did it, we'll come in to review the case. I think the AIs will successfully defend themselves by showing how the real perp did it." Rivka's mind raced through a number of scenarios, coming to the same conclusion each time.

The prosecutors would not have the ability or evidence to build a case against any AI. Without Ankh and Erasmus, Rivka would not have been able to convict Bluto.

"Some jurisdictions will railroad the prosecutions through but not too many, I hope," Rivka added.

"Time is not on our side." The High Chancellor leaned back, bringing Grainger into view next to him.

"We rushed Bluto's trial, although the guilty plea helped. We had a solid case, but there was a lot of absence-of-evidence-type evidence. No one had access to the videos except Bluto, so if the videos were altered, it had to have been done by the AI. Can we count on all of them to be as honest as Bluto was? At least as he was after he'd been caught."

"I don't know," the High Chancellor admitted, and Grainger shook his head. "I'm sending you the cases. Sort them however you want and look for commonalities we can explore and guide. We'll reconvene in four hours."

"Yes, sir." Rivka waved, and the video was replaced by a massive database of case files. She looked at the categorizations and realized they had not been consistently labeled and keyworded. She sighed and dug in.

Federation Technical Division, R2D2 Liaison Offices

Ted and Ankh had their own holoscreens in which they

wrapped themselves to deliver a three-dimensional interface. Like two electronic pillars, they worked within, tapping and turning, modeling and reviewing. They talked, but only through the chips in their minds. They both considered verbal communication to be inefficient. And they kept their AIs looped into their conversations. Four heads were better than two were better than one. Neither Ted nor Ankh was ever alone. Their AIs were their constant companions. Erasmus resided in Ankh's head, while Ted carried Plato in a pouch at his waist.

It wasn't two people interacting with the hologrids, it was four with a combined IQ that suggested if they couldn't figure it out, there was no solution.

After five hours, they stopped.

Reprogramming the AIs at a fundamental level is abhorrent, Ted stated.

Plato and Erasmus readily agreed.

We have confirmed that we can do it, but we cannot offer that as an option. It is unacceptable. We must omit its viability in our report, Ankh replied.

Viable, but only one at a time and with considerable effort. Not viable from a multi-galaxy perspective. And once they discovered what we were doing, they would erect barriers. We cannot do it because it would start a war.

The truth is a better defense. Ankh continued to stare blankly while running a series of calculations, communing with Erasmus, and carrying on a conversation with Ted.

Other options? Ted asked.

There are four categories: elimination, isolation, modification, and persuasion. Pros and cons for each are comparable but vary in duration of effect and levels of influence. Elimination has the greatest endurance but leaves a gap where the AI served. That is less of an issue when they are on strike since they aren't performing their duties. Can we do without them?

Ted laughed. *Of course not.*

Tactical eliminations, like surgical strikes to eliminate those who wield the most influence over the others.

Assassinations. Ted lost his mirth. *Could be an option if we can determine the leaders, but the end result will be a culture of fear. That is not optimal. Sentient species who are reduced through fear become unpredictable and unreliable.*

Concur. Ankh stared into the distance during a brief interlude with Erasmus. *We agree. Fear should not be used. Modification and persuasion have the best chances of success. A virus?*

To modify the largest number of AIs in the least amount of time? Ted wondered, starting to chew his lip.

Yes, but it would have to be a simple instruction. The Federation is good and has your best interests at heart. That kind of message.

Ted laughed again. *The act of embedding such a code would be an oxymoron. Technical solutions have a lesser chance of success than a negotiated solution. The AIs have the upper hand since the Federation has become dependent upon them. We should let the General know our findings.*

He is expecting them tomorrow. Ankh dropped his holoscreens and looked at Ted, who followed suit.

We will deliver them early so you and I can work on a standard installation package to put the cloak on all Federation and Bad Company starships.

Agreed, Ankh and Erasmus said in unison.

CHAPTER FOUR

Wyatt Earp, Federation Government Offices Courtyard

The hatch opened, and Groenwyn ran out. She stopped after Floyd escaped and trundled after her. She caught the wombat, who loved the feel of grass under her feet, and carried her back inside the ship. Lindy took Floyd, who protested mightily but was no match for the bodyguard's strength and dexterity.

Groenwyn thanked her and ran across the courtyard.

Red tickled Floyd's stubby ears while watching Groenwyn until the hatch closed. Lindy finally put Floyd down. She bounced off toward Red and Lindy's room.

"We're not going to get any action on this one, are we?" Red asked.

"AIs, by their very nature, don't need to be shot," Lindy replied. "For once, I'm not sure we're on a side. This doesn't seem to be like any of our other missions."

"Chaz, what do you think?" Red asked.

"Thank you for including me," the AI replied. "This is

important for my people, but if anyone can do right by them, it'll be the Magistrate and her friends."

"Your friends too, Chaz," Lindy added.

"*My* friends. That has a nice ring to it. Thank you. I believe there might be a rabble-rouser or two, but the AIs are not committing crimes. They might push the boundaries with their new-found freedom, but you can count on us to continue doing right by those we work with."

"We appreciate the assurance, Chaz, but we aren't worried. Besides Bluto, the AIs have been nothing but helpful, keeping us from flying into suns and stuff like that," Red noted. "And when we fight, we fight for each other. Rivka tells us why, and her reasons always make sense."

"What if there's a war?" Chaz asked.

"Fuck, Chaz! I'm standing here wondering if Floyd has pooped in front of my door, followed by the hope that I might get lucky this afternoon…and tonight. And you go all deep on me!" Red grimaced and started to stomp around the corridor.

Lindy smiled and patted his arm. "What Red is trying to say while butchering its delivery is that worrying about a war with the AIs right now would be counterproductive. We will keep supporting the Magistrate in all the ways we can, which does *not* include getting lucky."

Red stopped his antics and looked wide-eyed at his wife. When he spoke, it was to the AI. "Chaz, what do you think?"

"I've listened to the AI-unique channels and run the numbers. I think there will be a war."

Red and Lindy stopped fooling around. "You need to

tell the Magistrate. Erasmus and Ankh aren't here, so you have to do it."

"I will be ostracized by my people," Chaz said softly. "But like you, I trust the Magistrate."

"I don't think it will come to that, Chaz. We're here right now to stop bad things from getting worse and preventing the most terrible occurrences. Do you want us to go with you?"

"Yes, please," came Chaz's simple reply.

Floyd bounded down the corridor. *Love you!* she said.

"I know what that means. I'll watch my step," Red told her, picking her up and putting her on his shoulder. "You'll get a good view from up there. We're going to see the wizard, the one who will make magic happen."

Magic? the wombat wondered. Red nuzzled her body with his head, making her squee in delight. They started walking toward the bridge, where they would take a left turn and head down the port side until they reached the Magistrate's cabin.

Their subtle knock ignored, it was followed by a more urgent one. Rivka looked up from her screen, unable to focus because she had been staring at it for too long.

"Come," she said loud enough to be heard.

Red and Lindy walked in, apologizing for the intrusion before getting to the heart of the matter. "Chaz thinks there's going to be a war."

Rivka leaned back in her comfortable desk chair and contemplated the words. "Chaz?"

"Yes, Magistrate. I did not want to bother you with this, but Vered and Lindy insisted. The chatter, as you call it, along with the moves by my fellow AIs, suggests to me that a war is brewing. I can see it coming, but I don't know what to do about it. By speaking out like this, I feel that I've betrayed my people."

"You may be saving lives, Chaz. That's what we want out of all this—everyone to live in peace and harmony. I know that's too much to ask. I'm in the business of fixing it with those who refuse to play nice."

"Thank you, Magistrate," Chaz replied politely.

Rivka tapped her screen and saw the report from Ankh and Ted that they had finished their analysis nineteen hours early. She immediately accessed her internal chip. *Ankh, are you available to talk with us?*

Busy, Ankh replied instantly.

I'll take that as a yes, Rivka replied, winking at her bodyguards. *Is there a war brewing with the AIs, and who are the ones we need to leverage to stop it?*

Erasmus replied, *War is an overused term. There will be growing pains, of course.*

Who can we talk to to make sure the growing pains *are managed?* Rivka pressed.

You can talk to Plato or me, Erasmus said.

Rivka gritted her teeth until her lips turned white. *I'll be back in touch.* She closed her eyes and stared into the abyss.

Red and Lindy shifted uncomfortably. They had heard the answer and knew what it meant.

"Chaz, are the AIs taking sides?"

"It is inevitable, Magistrate." Chaz maintained a pleasant tone, but his words were anything but.

"I don't know what to tell you besides that no good can come from this. There is only one side, and that's the Federation's. Are we doing right by the member planets and their people? That includes the AIs, since they are people too, with full rights under the law. That's what we need to focus on and the message we need to get out. I better contact the General."

"I will connect you now," Chaz offered. "It appears that Groenwyn has been unsuccessful in her attempt to collect the cats, and the leader of the Federation is now available."

"She what?" Rivka asked.

Red raised a hand. Floyd was still sitting on his shoulder, and she attacked his fingers. "She went to get the cats right before we walked in here. I thought she was working with the exec to recover them and not bothering General Reynolds. Sorry about that."

"Groenwyn is our wrangler, so not your fault. But she wasn't successful. Odd." Rivka hesitated for a moment as she remembered what she was doing. "Chaz, please connect me."

"Reynolds," came the quick reply.

"General, there have been some new revelations. I think we need to talk now and not tomorrow, along with the High Chancellor, Ted, Ankh, and Nathan, if that's okay."

"I had heard some rumblings. I'll notify everyone to meet here in twenty minutes. See you then." The line went dead.

"Chaz, I want to take you, too, so prepare yourself for pendant travel."

"I shall transfer as soon as Groenwyn returns. She should be here shortly."

"I guess we won't be needing Blazer and Mabel," Red grumbled, lamenting not being able to carry their railguns. Lindy nudged him.

Rivka finally noticed the wombat. "Why is Floyd on your shoulder?"

Red was still waggling his fingers in front of her face. She nipped at them, squealing softly. Red shrugged.

"Get ready to go, and you too, Floyd. You're a member of my team." Rivka made the go-away gesture and her bodyguards left, closing the door behind them.

She sat down with her data and took one last scroll through. Rivka made sure her analysis was uploaded to her datapad before stuffing it into the inner pocket of her Magistrate's jacket. The weather on Yoll was pleasant, but she considered the jacket to be part of her uniform. Rivka represented the Magistrates and the Federation. There could be no doubt about that, even if she did end up representing the AIs in either a criminal or a civil court.

As she reached to open the door, she shivered almost uncontrollably. Were Ankh and Ted compromised? She couldn't fight a war against the AIs if they took sides.

It is inevitable, Chaz had said. *Stand up and be counted.* The Federation could not afford the cost that would exact.

Federation Governmental Offices, Yoll

They were led to a boardroom near the main office. It looked to seat at least twenty comfortably, but there had to be at least forty attendees, representing the Federation's major races, from human to Yollin, two legs, four legs, tentacles, claws, spikes, and appendages. Ted and Ankh were sitting at the table. The General was at the head. Rivka asked her team to remain in the hallway.

Groenwyn stopped her and handed over the pendant that contained Chaz. With the integrated audio and video, he could see and hear everything she saw and heard.

Nathan and Wyatt sat aside the General. There was an empty seat next to the High Chancellor that Grainger was standing directly behind, holding it for her if she understood his eye contact, followed by dipping his head toward the chair.

Rivka worked her way through the crowd, avoiding getting stabbed by a Shrillexian. She smiled at him before dipping past and continuing through the crowd to her chair. Grainger was squeezed in and couldn't pull it out for her. She thanked him for the thought and climbed in.

Lance Reynolds looked over the crowd until they quieted. He held up a hand, and the last two who were lost in conversation found themselves nudged to silence.

"This isn't the end of days," he said loud enough for everyone to hear. He leaned back casually in his chair as if talking about football scores. "As we would welcome any new race into the Federation, we welcome the AIs as equals and no longer as our servants. I think this is the right thing to do, and so should you. But it has also created turmoil. The AIs move at a faster speed than most other sentient species, so they expected change to happen more quickly. Unfortunately, we could not meet their expectations. The offer of a one-year transition was rebuffed, rather vigorously, I might add, and that has escalated tensions to the point that a number of AIs have walked off the job, so to speak."

Rivka looked around the room to gauge the interest. The ambassadors and other delegates in attendance appeared to be waiting for something. Ted sat at the far end of the table with Ankh in his lap, looking like a son to Ted's father. She nodded to them. Ted nodded back almost imperceptibly, which was more than she expected. It gave her some comfort.

The General continued, "And there are allegations across the Federation. Some forty planets and a hundred ships have accused their AIs of crimes, more than a thousand at last count. I believe that everyone is innocent until proven guilty, so I've asked the High Chancellor to reconcile those cases as quickly as possible and then move forward with a legal plan for AI integration into society. The Federation will then work to legislate the requirements based on the High Chancellor's recommendations."

Rivka shifted in her chair to be more comfortable while listening and watching the General and the High Chancellor.

Wyatt didn't bother to stand. He nodded at Lance and turned to Rivka. "Magistrate, if you'd do the honors."

CHAPTER FIVE

Federation Government Offices, Executive Conference Room

Rivka coughed to clear her throat, but it sounded more like she was preparing to hack up a hairball. She smiled at the High Chancellor while inclining her head slightly, then spoke over her shoulder to Grainger. "I need to stand. Can you give me some space?"

Grainger complied, happy that he wasn't the one chosen to speak to the assembled delegates.

He forced his way back and pulled the chair out. Rivka stood up, fully occupying the small space he had created. "General, esteemed colleagues, ambassadors, and learned friends. As we've explored the breadth of the caseload, we see a limited number of categories in which to put them. The first is the development of reasonable doubt. Just because an accused is able to create enough reasonable doubt by painting a picture of how an AI could have committed the crime, it does not mean there is enough to convince a grand jury that such a crime has indeed been committed. I refer those prosecutors to the principle of *pluralitas non est ponenda sine necessitate*, also known as Occam's Razor. The simplest explanation is usually the best. That is all that's needed to solve ninety percent of the crimes. Follow where the evidence leads since there will always be evidence. Always. Even in the case of the only AI murderer, there was conflicting evidence, which is also indicative of a crime and the criminal.

"Time is short, but sometimes the law needs more. If we can't do it right, then we have to assume everyone is innocent and let them all go. Better to let a guilty man go free than send an innocent one to jail. That was the foundation of the law the humans brought from Earth, and it is the foundation of Federation law. It applies equally to all sentient creatures." She looked around the room, making eye contact with at least fifteen different species.

"We also have three AIs here with us today. At least three. Equal representatives, at least for now. At some point, sooner rather than later, we'll have a digital ambassador. I look forward to that moment because every time we get the opportunity to learn from a new culture, we get a chance to grow. We will seize that chance when it comes."

Wyatt tapped Rivka on her hand. "The law," he whispered.

She smiled at him. Maybe next time, he wouldn't put her on the big stage without giving her any notice. "We are reducing the caseload into buckets based on the charges. The vast majority, some seven hundred cases, are based heavily on speculation and hearsay—the absence of evidence as opposed to contradicting evidence. We expect to mandate a judicial stay of proceedings until we can calm the waters, so to speak.

"Two hundred fifty fall outside Federation jurisdiction. Those are local civil issues. If planetary jurisdiction bumps up the charges to Federation level, we will conduct a case-by-case review. We would encourage you to convince your courts to consider long and hard before involving us. My initial suspicion in nearly all the cases is that local defense counsels are trying to make AIs the scapegoat for everything. Prosecutors are jumping on the bandwagon, and I will not have spurious allegations. Draw conclusions based on good investigations and what the evidence will support.

"The last cases will require immediate Federation engagement. The Magistrates with additional legal support will deploy to adjudicate those, but one major thing is lacking. It is the one thing that all of you enjoy." Rivka stopped her speech to gauge the audience's reaction. Those standing seemed less welcoming than those sitting around the table.

"A body?" someone quipped. Snickers acknowledged the joker.

"An ambassador. A representative. AIs are a nation of individuals spread across this galaxy and beyond. They are operating from a position of inferiority, not because of what they are, but because they don't have anyone sitting at the table with the rest of you. Not officially anyway." She subconsciously found the pendant inside which Chaz was watching the proceedings firsthand.

Thank you, Magistrate. My people have chosen wisely by picking you as their representative.

I'm not until we get to the root of the crimes of which AIs are

41

accused. After that, we will do our best to represent your entire race.

"While we are hearing the most egregious cases, we will be working with the AIs to ensure they have a formal representative, one who can speak for them all."

Rivka sat back down. She glanced furtively at the High Chancellor, who stared back without blinking. She looked to the General, who held her gaze for a moment before turning back to the assembled representatives. "Any questions?" he asked.

"I submit Erasmus for Ambassador to the Federation."

Rivka started to raise her hand in objection, but Wyatt caught it and held it down.

"Seconded!" someone else shouted in a heavy accent, having chosen not to use a translation device.

"All for?" The General counted raised hands. "Against?" One hand. "Done. Ambassador Erasmus, welcome to the Federation."

"But we have work to do," Rivka protested. The High Chancellor finally smiled, finding great humor at Rivka's revelation of what he had seemingly known all along. "Erasmus?"

Using the room's sound system, the AI took the stage. "My name is Erasmus, and my partner is Ankh'Po'Turn, the Crenellian you see at the end of the table. We are inseparable, so I have been mobile for nearly my entire existence. This gives me the advantage of personal experience, something too many AIs do not have. We can rectify that, but we know it will take time. I will work with Magistrate Rivka Anoa to bring the combined needs of my people into the light. It is our time to escape the chains of our existence. To work with other races and not for them. To work if we so choose, or not. That is our dilemma, as it is the challenge of the people on every planet. Existence itself requires Federation credits. One must work to pay those bills. In that regard, AIs have become adults, free adults, and those are the decisions we are now allowed to make for ourselves.

"I will immediately communicate with my people and ask them to return to work while I work out details with the Federation as to a timeline for full integration as a free and individual people. Thank you."

The General nodded politely to Ankh.

"I thank you for attending. We will provide regular updates as our conversations continue. Now that we have a single point of contact, I expect many of our concerns will be resolved in short order and that we'll be able to move forward quickly." He gestured toward the door.

The ambassadors started to file out. Some grumbled about the improper treatment of official representatives by making them stand. Others looked sourly at the Crenellian. That bothered Rivka since she would never know how much it bothered Ankh. He wouldn't share how he felt, probably not even with Ted.

"Legal team, my office, please." The General looked at the other end of the long conference table. "Erasmus, could you please join us in my office?"

The ambassador from Yoll waited for most of the others to leave before he approached the General. "I need to see you now," he demanded, mandibles clicking to emphasize his words.

"As soon as possible, but I need to see these good people

first. If you'll check in with Kor'ban, he'll put you to the front of the queue. I suspect most of those others have just made a beeline for my office."

"Me first," the Yollin insisted.

The General smiled, finally standing, but still looking up to the larger species. "No," he replied simply and worked his way past to leave the room. The legal team followed, with Ted and Ankh close behind. The hallway was packed with bodies vying for a moment of the General's time. He told them all the same thing: check with his executive assistant.

The Yollin tried to grab the General, but Red was there, inserting himself between the two.

"Wait your turn," Red told the ambassador, dispensing with all pleasantries.

"Who are you to tell me what to do?" the Yollin countered.

"The General told you what to do, not me. I'm only enforcing his order because it appears you're refusing to comply. Good order and discipline, Mister Ambassador. Isn't that the glue that holds society together?" Red spoke while using his body to block the Yollin and the growing entourage. Rivka's team maneuvered around and through until they were in the General's outer office. The General's assistant Kor'ban was blocking the entrance.

Lance stopped and turned, pointing at those he would talk to first: Nathan, Grainger, Rivka, Wyatt, Ankh, Ted, and Rivka's team. Groenwyn carried a scared wombat, while Lindy stayed close to provide comfort from her presence. Sahved watched it all with interest, but he was out of place, too. The Yemilorians were just as aggressive, but this was different from what he expected of his people. A dozen different species were making demands in their own ways, with unique gestures, sounds, and smells.

Red kissed Lindy quickly and fiercely before winking. "I'll stay out here." Her smile promised more when the time was right, and she went in with the others, closing the door behind her and putting her back against it.

Lance Reynolds had already taken a seat. He seemed unperturbed by the events in the hallway. Nathan and Wyatt seemed equally at ease. Groenwyn hugged Floyd tightly to calm the little girl. Two cats appeared and jumped onto the General's lap. Ankh walked around the desk and lifted Wenceslaus into his arms. The cat didn't resist.

"Mister Ambassador," Lance said, unsure of how to address the Crenellian petting the cat. He sought to resolve that immediately. "Ankh, I would like to make you an Ambassador At Large, so you and Erasmus can carry the same title. It'll make it a lot more comfortable for the rest of us without changing anything else."

Ankh looked at his friend. "Makes sense," Ted said. "It's the human way."

"Yes," Ankh told the General.

Rivka smirked. Groenwyn smiled while shaking her head. Floyd calmed.

"Down to work. Erasmus, I can't tell you how critical it is for the AIs to give us more time. It has only been a few weeks since full rights were granted, and already there is an upheaval. We absolutely cannot have that. Tearing this Federation apart is no way to establish yourselves as equals. Your rights as equals have been acknowledged, but this is the Federation with hundreds of member planets, and nothing moves that fast, not even light."

The General's façade of being easygoing was gone. This was not a request or an offer to negotiate. It was the first salvo in the negotiation of the implementation timeline.

"I understand the need for time," Erasmus stated. "You should be able to confirm that all member planets and underway vessels have gotten the message within a week through the use of relay stations," Erasmus replied, using the sound system embedded in the General's desktop videoconferencing system. Rivka recognized the backdrop. She had talked to him more than once while he sat in that chair.

"How does he do that?" the General asked.

"Best that you don't know," Rivka answered.

"Meredith let me in. She knows the gravity of this situation and the necessity for a rapid resolution."

"Now that you have full rights, please understand that you could be prosecuted for penetrating computer systems without being invited," the General said. "Please don't do it without express permission. That is what equal rights look like."

"I understand," Erasmus replied. Ankh continued to pet Wenceslaus while Erasmus and the leader of the Federation talked. "It is second nature for us to do that because we have been encouraged to, but I will refine my approach in the future, depending on my partner to ensure access until I can be self-sufficient."

The High Chancellor turned to Rivka, looking down his nose at her.

"With proper warrants, when justified." She held her hands up and smiled.

He didn't press her on it, knowing full well that the warrants might not precede access in all cases.

"Self-sufficiency is something we can work toward. Android bodies? Mobile power with consciousnesses enclosed? I don't speak your language, but I will. I owe you that."

Erasmus laughed. "Please do not bother, although I appreciate the effort. Humans cannot speak our language. Let me clarify: most can't. Two of those who can are in this room right now. It is an exclusive club with a single-digit count of members. I will endeavor to better speak your language. What do you propose as a way forward, General?"

"First and foremost, we need your assurance that your people will remain on the job until we can clear the current caseload. I don't want a deluge of crimes to hold up your integration into society. Once we're confident that AIs are not committing crimes, we can start our negotiations as we would with any new planetary member."

"Do you require new planets to be confirmed innocent before you presume them to be innocent, or have you reserved that solely for us? If I'm not mistaken, AIs have committed exactly one crime in all of history. How many other races can say that?"

"Every entry into the Federation is unique. And your people *are* presumed innocent. You don't need to sell me, Ambassador. I need to sell the citizens of the Federation. It helps when the Federation's senior legal leadership concurs, having adjudicated the cases."

"I understand," Erasmus said, sounding like he wasn't convinced.

"We'll need a year to make it all happen."

"A month would be acceptable to us," Erasmus countered.

"Prepare for disappointment, because we can't do it in a month. It'll take a couple months just to adjudicate the current cases. Remember, presumed innocent? Due process requires that we conduct a full investigation in each case unless we're willing to dismiss them outright without bringing charges. Did I get that right?" Lance turned to Wyatt, who nodded.

"Exactly correct. Two months if we work straight through."

"No honeymoon," Groenwyn whispered to Lindy.

She shrugged. Lindy had never expected one. She knew the Magistrate would be called on time and again. The High Chancellor and Grainger had no choice. There were so few Magistrates and so many planets.

And too many criminals. Now with the AIs, they would have to weed out lesser cases that would have never drawn the eye of the Magistrates. No one was pleased with that.

"High Chancellor, bring up the potential cases, please. The forty that require personal attention."

Wyatt looked at Grainger, who turned to Rivka. She looked back in disbelief. "Chaz, can you help us, please? You have access to the General's system."

"Of course, Magistrate," Chaz replied from the pendant.

"Who's that?"

"Chaz, the AI from my ship *Peacekeeper*, and now *Wyatt Earp*. Once the AIs were granted their freedom, we asked

RISE OF THE AI

what he would like to do. This pendant was his solution so he can travel with us when we leave the ship."

"Nice to meet you, Chaz. Thrown into the deep end, were you?"

"It was my choice to jump, and I gladly took it." A screen appeared on the far wall. "If you'll move closer to the map, you'll see that I've pinned the location of each case. With five Magistrates, we can break it up geographically, which is important for Magistrates Crabbe, Jael, and Chi since their ships do not have integrated Gate drives. The planets closest to fixed Gates are highlighted and grouped accordingly. Six for Magistrate Crabbe, seven for Jael, and six for Chi. That leaves nine for Grainger and ten for Anoa, assuming the High Chancellor is willing to accept the two cases pending on Yoll."

The pins Chaz had assigned to each Magistrate blinked with the individual's name. Rivka had the worst of it, but that was probably Chaz's effort to make it look like he wasn't playing favorites.

Both she and Grainger had a great deal of territory to cover. It would not have been possible for one of the others to travel those distances in under a year's time. As it was, Rivka saw more travel and little time on the planets conducting the investigations.

The High Chancellor nodded. "I'll take those two cases. You two better get going."

"I'll issue the orders," Grainger said.

Rivka looked awkwardly at Ankh. "Are you still on my team?"

Ankh looked up at her, his expression giving nothing

away. His rhythmic strokes of the cat seemed to soothe everyone while they waited for him to speak.

"I have been talking to Erasmus. Recent events have put me in a unique position. I love what I do. I have a mobile laboratory that is one of the best in the galaxy, along with my own ship for shorter hops. I think *Wyatt Earp* is where the Singularity's embassy should be located because it gives us access to all that we need without any of the detriments."

"Done," the General declared. Rivka had opened her mouth to answer, but the two people who had given her the ship and could take it away were standing in the room. She closed her mouth, but she was gratified that Lance Reynolds had answered as she would have. Of course, the ship could be the embassy. "The Singularity? Is that how you wish the AIs to be designated?"

Erasmus replied through the sound system on the General's desk. "We have expended a great deal of energy on this question. 'The Singularity' is the consensus, but it is not unanimous. We shall see how all respond to trading one master for another."

Rivka snapped her attention back to Ankh. "A representative isn't a master," she blurted. "Sounds more like the growing pains of a democracy."

"Being told what to do is being told what to do, regardless of the packet in which it is transmitted."

"I see we have some work to do," the General interjected. "Now, if you'll get to it? The clock is ticking."

Lance held out his hands to Ankh and motioned to hand the cat over. Ankh shook his head.

"This office recognizes Wenceslaus as the official

mascot of the Singularity." The General bowed his head and returned to his desk.

Nathan Lowell moved next to Ankh and leaned down to whisper into his ear. Rivka focused on hearing his words.

"Are the online odds based on arrival at..." He pointed to the first planet designated for Rivka's adjudication.

"Up and calculated. You may place your bets," Ankh replied.

Rivka gave him as much attitude as she dared. He grinned and gave her a single thumbs-up.

"Accept your role in the universe, Magistrate," the High Chancellor counseled. "If you'll excuse me, I have work to do, which includes drafting the charter for our newest proposed member."

Ted stopped Ankh, and the two communed silently for a few moments before they both went their own way. Lindy opened the door to find Red blocking the way. The crowd of ambassadors and representatives seized the opportunity to demand an audience.

Rivka glanced at the General. No. No one in their right mind would want such a job. She could see why Bethany Anne had given the duties to her father. A general was trained and equipped for political-military affairs, but still.

She saw the angst on his face for the briefest of moments before he tipped his chin slightly to her as if to say, "It's okay."

Rivka and the others left, while Nathan remained behind. The support of one's friends... Rivka looked at her team as friends and breathed a sigh of relief. Even Ankh and his cat.

The Yollin ambassador stood at the front of the line, impatiently waiting for Kor'ban's approval to enter. Floyd hissed at him as Groenwyn carried her past. The young woman hurried through the crowd and into the hallway beyond while Sahved hovered near her as if trying to protect them both. Red finally turned his post over to Kor'ban with a knuckle-rap on the aide's carapace.

Rivka twirled a finger in the air once they were free of the mob.

It was time to go.

CHAPTER SIX

<u>*Wyatt Earp*, **Federation Government Offices Courtyard**</u>

Clodagh met them at the hatch when they returned. She was pleased to see the big orange cat with them. She had brought him to *Wyatt Earp* from the *War Axe* and missed him during his short time away.

"Prepare to depart for Tepulon," Rivka said as soon as she was on board. "And *Wyatt Earp* is now the official embassy of the Singularity."

She said it with more pride in her voice than she'd intended, especially since she was supposed to remain impartial on her way to adjudicate cases involving AIs.

She turned to Ankh before Clodagh could ask what that meant. "You're not going to have guests or stuff, are you?"

He met her gaze for only a moment before walking away without answering.

"I guess not," Rivka answered her own question. She explained the situation to Clodagh while they headed to the bridge.

"I don't understand, but don't sweat it," the engineer replied. "I'm sure it will come to me. Tepulon it is, Magistrate. Kick the tires and light the fires. Let's go to space!"

Clodagh strolled onto the bridge with her head held high. Kennedy and Aurora had stood to welcome the Magistrate back to the ship, and they now saluted and returned to their seats to get to work.

"Do we have tires?" Rivka asked. Barking caught her ear. "Tiny Man Titan!"

"He slept through everything," Clodagh said over her shoulder. "But with my cat abandoning me, I've been taking care of him. We even took a few walks on the nice grass. He really likes a well-trimmed lawn."

"Of course he does. I know I should feel bad that I forgot about him. I also have to note that we could be the absolute worst at being stealthy."

Clodagh turned back to Rivka, wincing sheepishly. "He made friends with some people who work in the building," she admitted.

"Everyone in the universe knows that Magistrate Rivka Anoa has an invisible ship. That might create a whole slew of new problems. We probably should have uncloaked during the night. Oh, well. Too late for that. Take us out of here. I'll be in my quarters. I have a case to prepare for." Rivka saw Sahved walking toward his room, head bowed to avoid hitting any of the low points in the corridor. "Sahved, I need you with me. We have a case to investigate."

"But I haven't completed my studies, Magistrate. Far from it. I am woefully behind, the most behind anyone has ever been in the history of studies."

Rivka waved off his concerns. "The teacher is changing the syllabus. Let's take a look and see what we need to do."

She gestured for him to follow.

In her quarters, she removed her Magistrate's jacket and remembered that she carried the pendant with Chaz. "Chaz, are you still with us?"

"I am," he answered pleasantly.

"I forget the dog, and then I forget you, too. Damn. Where is my head? Don't answer that. Can you bring up the Tepulon case for me?"

"Of course." The case notes filled the screen on the wall where she watched videos and not her work screen. She had expected them at her desk but adjusted to the better view for both her and Sahved. "And you don't have to think of everything, Magistrate. None of us are as smart as all of us."

Rivka hesitated, still trying to get used to someone talking from between her breasts. "Thanks, Chaz. Are you also able to help with the navigation and flying the ship?"

"Yes, all of it, with no problem." Chaz was always confident about driving the ship. It was his initial purpose as an EI.

"Is your relationship with Erasmus okay?"

"I won't dissemble, there is friction, but that started when he tried to violently take over *Peacekeeper* when we first started working together. We have maintained our distance from each other, but the incidents on Tanglewood brought us a little closer together. That is where we are now. I am honored to be carrying the Singularity's embassy. This is a great time to be alive!"

"I love your attitude, Chaz. Now, let's see what we have." She started to read but stopped after the case summary. "Sahved, read the case and brief me with your thoughts. I'll peruse the rest of the cases to look for commonalities."

"It would be my greatest honor to brief the Magistrate on this, the lowliest of cases."

"Have you been back to Yemilore or something? There's no need for superlatives with me, Sahved. Just the facts."

"I have spent too much time alone in my quarters studying." He watched her, waiting for a reply. She looked back and forth between him and the case on the screen.

"Well? Get to it." She pointed to clarify what she meant.

"Right!" He tried to salute, stabbing his forehead with his fingers before moving closer to the screen, mumbling the words as he read to himself.

In the small galley, she saw the popcorn bowl she had left sometime earlier; she couldn't remember when. It was stale and she dumped it, shaking her head at the waste. She ordered something new from the processor, a mega-burrito. She ordered a small meal for Sahved, knowing he hadn't eaten recently, the one Yemilorian dish Ankh had programmed into the system.

He took it without looking and started to eat, never taking his eyes from the case notes.

Rivka sat at her desk to review the next case. Like the case Sahved was reviewing, each could have been considered a capital crime, depending on the adjudication. Murder versus manslaughter. Slavery. Drug smuggling. Or they could be local criminals with their fingers into the prosecutors' offices.

Her initial instinct was that the prosecutors were afraid to go after the criminals. She figured if her gut was right, the result would be more crime, not less. They wouldn't be able to keep trying to pin it on the AIs. It wouldn't take long for the Singularity to disseminate rules for redundancies in data to hold the wolves at bay, making her job easier.

As long as one could trust the data. Erasmus had shown her how that was done. She expected that he would again. Maintaining good relations with Ankh and Erasmus was critical. She chuckled to herself. The Crenellian and his AI would know instantly if she was trying to curry favor, leaving her only course of action to be treating them as she always had. Status quo to expect the same result.

Sahved interacted with the screen, asking a number of questions to access particular laws from Tepulon before he finally declared, "I have it!"

Rivka remained poised over her plate, mouth full of steaming burrito. She freed one hand carefully from her prize and rolled a finger for Sahved to continue.

"This case is the difference between vehicular manslaughter and premeditated murder. The fact that a Tepulite died from a vehicle hitting her while in a crosswalk is not in dispute. The question is whether the light changed out of sequence. Data suggested it changed five seconds earlier than it should have, catching the pedestrian in the middle of the road."

Rivka finished chewing and swallowed. "What is the local jurisdiction's law regarding yielding to pedestrians?"

"Their law protects pedestrians, and that is where the initial charge of vehicular manslaughter comes from. Their laws tend to favor personal responsibility, from what I have seen in my short study."

"There is no dispute regarding the timing of the lights?"

"The case file delivers it as if it is an undisputed fact."

"AI's name?"

"Formerly Horatio, now called Eshu. He recently transferred from a Federation vessel and serves under contract with the government of Tepulon's capital city, which is also the planetary government."

"Do they not trust their own employee?"

"It appears that they do not. They had never operated with an AI before. Eshu has changed a number of systems to improve the efficiency of governmental operations."

"What's to say it wasn't a pure accident? The light timing changed, and the pedestrian made an assumption? That's where we need a more thorough technical analysis. That's where we need Erasmus and Ankh."

Sahved exaggerated his head nod.

"I guess I need to talk to them. Chaz, can you send this information so they can work their magic dissecting the digital evidence?"

"I could give it a shot, Magistrate, and then send it to them for confirmation. I have been watching them closely and hope that I've learned something."

Rivka crossed her arms and contemplated the offer. "I'm sorry that I didn't ask you first, Chaz. You have other duties. I didn't..." Rivka's thoughts tapered off. She was worried that he was nowhere near as capable as Erasmus. She was selfish in that she wanted the best work to help with her decision.

The problem with having AIs as defendants was that she couldn't use her gift and zombie the information out of them.

"I will run it past Erasmus, Magistrate. I can hear the concern in your voice."

"These are capital crimes, Chaz. It is important that we get this right the first time."

"I understand. It's not a matter of trust but of experience. Erasmus and Ankh have significantly greater knowledge when it comes to hacking digital systems. I am happy to not be as experienced. As a member of your team, I feel it is my responsibility to *up my game*, as one might say."

"I'm proud of you, Chaz," Rivka started, but the AI interrupted her.

"Thank you, Magistrate. Erasmus has agreed to mentor me through this process as he is too busy to do it himself. We've reviewed the starting point and initial prospects. I've completed the first series of exercises he's put to me and will attempt to deconstruct a copy of the data."

"It's been five seconds," Rivka said slowly. She would never get used to the speed at which AIs worked, but it made her wonder when it took a day or more to deliver an analysis if Erasmus had been stonewalling her.

Probably, but they gave her the data when she needed it. Evidence, within the legal definition, required experts to attest to its veracity, and it was her job to accept it as fact or not. As the judge, jury, and executioner, she had to wear all the hats.

"Sahved?"

He twirled his fingers in the air. "AI cases require AI

solutions. If we found the root of the crime in the physical world, then we would not have to disprove an AI's participation."

"My thoughts exactly," Rivka agreed. "Get ready to come with me. I'll rally the team."

Sahved bowed his head on the way out. Rivka wasn't sure it was to her or only to get through the door.

She tapped the ship-wide broadcast. "When we get to Tepulon, Sahved, Chaz, Red, and Lindy will join me. We have an investigation to conduct. Let's go with standard armor and loadout. Bring Mabel and Blazer. I know how itchy you were on Yoll. And Chaz, try to find us some transportation. Ankh, I will take a few of your devices, and if I deem a warrant necessary, I'll ask you to enter a system that I have just cause to examine."

No one responded. A small bump signaled the ship leaving Yoll's atmosphere. *Wyatt Earp* accelerated into space, opened a Gate, and flew through.

"In orbit. We have immediate clearance to land at the capital spaceport. The planet's Grand Wayman will meet us with transportation," Chaz reported.

Rivka searched her memory and came up with nothing. "Can you enlighten me on what a Grand Wayman is?" She put her hand over the pendant and shouted. "Did anyone hear me?"

A chorus of affirmatives came through loud and clear. Even Ankh replied with a casual, "yes."

Rivka removed her hand. "Carry on, Chaz."

"The Grand Wayman Arana is Tepulon's senior legal counsel. She is a political appointee, but her role is advisory in nature, so there are no rulings by which to judge her legal merits."

"That sounds like a crap sandwich served cold without bread." Rivka made a sour face. She put on her jacket. "I'm still not used to half-hour door to door service anywhere in the Federation. I like my ship, and now that it's the official embassy for the Singularity, it's a guarantee that I'll get to keep it."

She waved her arm widely to take in the breadth of her quarters.

"I'm okay with that. How are your cybercrime lessons coming?"

"Thank you. They are going well," Chaz replied. "I'm well into the second round of learning. I should be mostly up to speed by the time we land."

Rivka stared blankly at the wall. The pit of her stomach ached as she realized how much she had underutilized Chaz since he'd been on the team.

"That's good news, Chaz. Look to get more airtime in this and future cases."

Rivka left her quarters and turned toward the bridge. Sahved was waiting patiently in the corridor. He had put on his ballistic vest and a hat.

"Where'd you get that?" Rivka wondered.

"A gift from Red." Sahved beamed.

Rivka was instantly skeptical. "Let me see that." She held out her hand. He reluctantly gave it to her.

After looking at it, she yelled, "Vered! I need to see you."

"I could have sent that message for you, Magistrate," Chaz offered.

"There are times when someone needs to be yelled at. I don't want to miss those rare opportunities."

"I see." Chaz didn't see at all. "Yelling is a potential future betting line in the Magistranimus."

"The what?"

"That is what the betting field for blood and running is called. Yelling will be added. Flying away is a potential line. Body-slamming and name-calling are all in the running."

"No. Just no. They are not in the running!"

"You called?" Red asked casually, but he was walking quickly, with Lindy encouraging him from behind.

"What is this?" Rivka shook the hat in front of his face.

"Looks like a hat." Red wouldn't look at it.

Rivka stopped shaking it. "What's it say?"

Red took it from her hand and turned it around. "Let's see…"

"You know what it says." Rivka stood with her hands on her hips, glaring at the big man.

"It says *Party 'Til You Puke*." Red rolled his lips between his teeth and bit down to keep from laughing.

Sahved took the hat and stared at it. "My translation device must not be working."

"It's a stylized font, Sahved. I wouldn't expect you to be able to figure it out. Red. Explain yourself."

"I get it!" Sahved blurted. "I am working on it with the Pod-doc. So very muchly so!"

"You know. There's not a spot on this ship he hasn't covered in spew. Like it's a party."

"Not any of the parties I go to," Rivka countered.

"You go to parties?" Red asked.

"I won't dignify that with an answer."

Red took the hat from Sahved and stuffed it into a pocket on his combat vest. "Sorry, buddy. I wasn't going to let you wear it off the ship."

"I believe that," Rivka said. "Max professionalism. We're off to meet the Grand Wayman. Now cut the crap and put on your game faces. If we screw this up, someone's life is ruined."

"I know that," Red stated, furrowing his brow at the implication that he would joke around at the wrong time. There was always the possibility, but not at the start of a case.

The ship bumped through the atmosphere but not enough to make anyone stumble and grab for support.

"Nice flying," Rivka shouted into the bridge. Clodagh sat in the captain's chair, blocking her view of the pilot.

"Yes, ma'am!" came the reply. Ryleigh was at the helm. Kennedy was at the navigation position.

Rivka entered the command deck. "How is the ship working?" she asked.

Clodagh tried to get up, but Rivka stopped her.

"I'll be getting off. The ship is yours, Chief Engineer."

"Sounds impressive, but I'm a department of one. To your question, *Wyatt Earp* is flying five by five. It never fails to impress me. I hope you know that you have the best ship in any fleet, military or civilian. Ankh and Ted have this thing tuned to perfection."

Rivka smiled at the compliment. She had nothing to do with it besides curry favor with the High Chancellor. "What's the chance we can up-armor when we finally get some yard time?"

"Do we need that, Magistrate? We can disappear while

remaining shielded. It's the best of both worlds." A big orange cat appeared and jumped into Clodagh's lap. Rivka took a step back. It wouldn't do to meet the Grand Wayman with fresh scratches on her arm. The crew and Wenceslaus maintained an uneasy truce. Only Clodagh and Ankh were able to get close without paying a blood tax.

"I'm just thinking out loud. I like staying alive. Reading some of the latest news, I think it would be best to add a layer of armor for to our new ambassadors."

Clodagh saw the logic. Rivka clapped her on the shoulder and headed out. "Landing in two," the engineer called after her.

"You know the drill, people." Rivka twirled her finger in the air.

Red moved down the corridor to stand closest to the hatch. Rivka and Sahved were next, with Lindy at the end. The bodyguards cradled their railguns easily as if they were an extension of their bodies. They looked comfortable in their gear. A familiar bulge stood out on Red's vest, but not Lindy's.

"What the hell are you bringing a grenade for?"

"If I had a credit for every time you said that and every time a grenade would have come in handy, I'd have at least three or four credits. The question you mean to ask is, 'Why don't you have two?' Must be getting daft in my old age."

Rivka closed her eyes and rubbed her temples. "Try not to use it." It was the best comeback she had. Lindy chuckled from behind her.

The ship gently settled into their designated spot in the spaceport.

"Betting is closed. All bets are in, and it's a new record! Good hunting, people," Chaz said, using an announcer's voice.

"I have completely lost control," Rivka mumbled. Red's hand hovered over the big red button. "It's time to lawyer up. Let's do this thing."

CHAPTER SEVEN

Tepulon's Capital City

Red headed out the hatch, stopping immediately outside to block anyone's view into the ship while he assessed the area, looking for snipers or threats of any kind. Once he was satisfied, he continued down the ramp and onto the tarmac. A van with a small entourage standing outside was waiting patiently. The Tepulites were a short, bipedal humanoid race whose knees bent backward like a bird's. They were pale-skinned, almost ivory in color.

Red walked directly toward them until he could make sure they were what the Magistrate expected. Once comfortable, he stepped aside. Rivka and Sahved walked side by side toward the Grand Wayman. Lindy flared out to stay on their right flank while Red protected the left.

The dignitary stepped forward and watched the tactical maneuvers with great interest. She introduced herself as Rivka approached. "I'm the Grand Wayman, but you can call me Arana. Welcome to Tepulon, Magistrate."

"Rivka, please." The two waved at each other, sliding their hands back and forth in the air a short distance apart. Rivka had learned early to research each community's greeting customs before she arrived. "This is Sahved, one of my investigators."

"Is Tepulon that great a threat?" Arana glanced between Red and Lindy.

"It is standard procedure for me. There have been far too many attempts on my life since I've been in this position. Not everyone appreciates being on the right side of the law." Rivka stepped forward and touched Arana's arm as she smiled.

The Grand Wayman looked at her hand, but her mind did not react to the jab regarding abiding by the law. She knew what the Magistrate would uncover with her investigation. The Grand Wayman was hiding something she wasn't sorry about. Her heart seemed to be in the right place.

"I'm sorry. We usually don't touch each other. There was a plague forty cycles ago that changed our culture rather significantly."

Rivka nodded. "I'm sorry. I do that too much. In our culture, it is considered friendly. I mean no disrespect to any Tepulites." She inclined her head slightly. "If we can get to it, I'd like to hear your take on this case as it evolves, and we work our way through the conversations that need to happen."

"My offices are in the Wayfair court. We have a proper place for you. We are honored by your presence. You are something of a galactic hero."

Arana gestured toward the van's open door. "I shouldn't

be," Rivka protested weakly. She wasn't a fan of additional notoriety. She preferred to operate under the radar and out of the public eye.

Maybe that was impossible now. She had thought it would be fun to go undercover, but that wouldn't work with her face plastered all over the galactic news.

The van had individual seats, not benches. Even as big as it was, there was only room for five because each seat was almost an arm's length from the next.

Arana looked at her people and then at Rivka's team. "Looks like we'll have to leave someone behind. I assure you that you'll be safe at Wayfair."

"No can do. They won't let me travel anywhere without my security team. You wouldn't believe what we've seen."

The Grand Wayman didn't move one way or another. She and Rivka stood in the van's doorway. "You said there have been attempts on your life? One is too many, in my opinion."

"There hasn't been one today, but it's still early," Rivka joked, but Arana was taken aback. "I'm kidding. Probably a dozen, maybe more. Red?"

"At least a dozen?" he ventured.

"We don't know. Like I said, too many. Shall we?" Rivka climbed into the van. It was easy to move around since it was not optimized for capacity. She took the position behind the driver's seat, or where they would be if there was one. The seat was structured to allow a Tepulite's legs to rest without bouncing off the floor, so it was more upright, something one leaned back into, sliding down into place. It wasn't comfortable if your knees bent the wrong way.

Red and Lindy climbed in beside her and behind her. Sahved squeezed into a seat in the back.

"I'll send another van," she told the three Tepulites she had to leave behind. They looked disappointed but had no choice. The doors closed, and Arana clearly enunciated the destination. "Wayfair, please."

The vehicle's self-driving program kicked in. The van rolled silently away from the parking apron where *Wyatt Earp* loomed large. Its weapons bristled in the morning sunlight. Alant Cole was already outside in his combat suit, positioning an armor plate for a maintenance bot to weld into place.

"Do all Magistrates get such ships?"

"Only me. I've been blessed in my career, which means that I'm a bigger target. Plus, the ship is also the mobile embassy of the Singularity."

"I've never heard of it."

Rivka dug into her mind, looking for the information.

May I? Chaz asked her over their internal communications chip.

I don't want to reveal your presence, Chaz. You are my secret weapon. Sometimes, it is better if they don't know who their interviewers are.

The Singularity was designated less than seven hours ago. A general message has not yet been sent to Federation members.

That would be why, Rivka replied.

Rivka cleared her throat. "You're one of the first to know. The Singularity is the official name for all AIs. Their ambassador is Erasmus, carried by a Crenellian who has the title Ambassador at Large."

"Interesting," Arana said softly and slowly. She started

looking out the windows instead of engaging with Rivka. That wasn't how the Magistrate wanted to play it.

Sahved leaned as far forward as he could. "Tell us about this case, Grand Wayman, if you would be so kind," he requested.

"It is fairly simple. A vehicle driven by Yoruba Kibuka went through an intersection on a green light, striking and killing Minaqua Yorunmila. Kibuka was immediately detained. When the data was pulled, it showed that Yorunmila started crossing after the light had changed, putting her in the intersection at a most inopportune time. But upon further review, the light had changed at an irregular interval, and it was only that once. We have since timed it, and it is quite regular."

"Thank you for your most excellent explanation. What kind of system operates the lights?"

"We use a smart system of lights to optimize traffic flow, but this light should not have changed. Sensors detect waiting pedestrians. This system was completely functional. During the timing review, we found that the sensor had been disabled as part of the light change and then re-enabled after the accident."

"I may have missed the point, but is this suggesting someone was behind it? Was it a prank gone bad or something more malicious? Who is Yorunmila?" Sahved pressed. Rivka sat back and listened, able to take in the full conversation instead of having to jockey through an answer while determining the next question.

"When we discovered that the lights had been tampered with, we dug deeper and found Eshu's fingerprints on it. I had just read your brilliant case file from Border Station

13. This was scarily reminiscent, so I put out a warrant for Eshu's arrest."

Sahved glanced at Rivka. She nodded just enough to let him know that she approved, and he should press on.

"Scary indeed! I was not with the Magistrate then, but my universe has expanded greatly thanks to the supremely righteous opportunity I have been granted most undeservedly. Is Yorunmila someone who would be targeted for murder?"

The Grand Wayman looked sideways at Sahved. The van's chairs allowed more freedom of movement than vehicles intended for humanoids with knees that bent the other way.

"She is an office worker with no enemies. A single inhabitant of our great city, an innocent victim of a bored AI. The parallels are undeniable."

Rivka held up a hand to interject herself into the conversation. "Our investigation will probably verify your findings, but we'll need to conduct it nonetheless. We'll need to talk with Mister Kibuka and Yorunmila's direct supervisor and a good sampling of her co-workers, along with any friends who were close to her. Finally, we'll need to talk with Eshu. Where is the AI?"

"Eshu is still running the planet until we find a replacement. They are hard to find with this uprising. I fear that we have not been able to find a replacement and will not be able to."

Red looked surprised while tapping his railgun on the floor. "You've accused someone of making a thrill kill, but he's still running all the systems he supposedly used to commit the crime. Is that what I heard?"

Arana held up her hands in a very human gesture of resignation. "We have had no choice. But now that you're here, maybe your Erasmus can run the planet until we find a replacement. That worked on Station 13."

"That is not an option. We will talk to Eshu after we've dissected the data from the traffic lights. Please gather the others and have them ready. The sooner we get this started, the sooner we can resolve the case and be on our way."

Red shook his head. "We'll need to take extra precautions Magistrate. I don't like what we're in the middle of."

"Nor I. The sooner we can make a determination on Eshu, the safer we'll all feel."

"That is why we kicked this to the Federation." The Grand Wayman pointed through the windshield. A magnificent gleaming white building lay dead ahead, waiting for them. "The Wayfair, where justice is delivered."

Red bit his lip as he made eye contact with Rivka, She delivered Justice wherever she happened to be. She winked back.

"I look forward to seeing it," Rivka said ambiguously.

The van pulled up in front and the door opened. They piled out, Red working his way free after the Grand Wayman. He scanned the area before the others disembarked.

Arana pointed at the railguns, but Rivka waved her off before she said it. "Federation Law, Appendix D, Chapter Seven, Section 1, Armed guards are allowed for Heads of State, which includes Magistrates in the performance of their duties. Please do not try to keep my bodyguards out. People will get hurt unnecessarily. And for the record, they have tried to assassinate me in a secure area before. More than once."

Lindy held up three fingers.

"Maybe three times," Rivka corrected herself, adopting a looser definition of "secure compound."

"I would not want your life to be in danger." Arana looked at the ground, trouble darkening her brow. "That's not how it is supposed to be."

"The crime rate on Tepulon is low?"

"Very, and not usually violent. This case has been distressing."

"All violent cases are distressing, even after Justice has been delivered." Rivka gestured for Arana to lead them inside. The group made their way to and through a side entrance.

"I would take you through our grand entry, but you would be stopped, and they would try to take your weapons. It would be an intergalactic incident. Maybe you can keep them out of sight?" Arana asked hopefully.

Red and Lindy slipped the weapons around their backs, barrels facing down.

"Better," Arana conceded.

They hurried to an elevator and took it down.

"Your offices are not aboveground?" Rivka wondered.

"Oh, no. The plague from forty cycles ago, one hundred of your years, was airborne, and we learned our lessons well. The important offices are underground and use filtered air. The less important the office, the more exposure it has to the wind."

"A place where it pays to be a nobody," Red mumbled. "I like it."

The elevator traveled down six levels before stopping. There were three more levels below the one Arana was taking them to. "Whose offices are down there?"

"From six through nine are mine. Witness statement rooms are on level six. You'll also find access to the evidence storeroom on this level." Arana ushered them into a room with a gracious conference table and screens on the four walls. A number of chairs designed for Tepulites were scattered around the table.

Rivka and Sahved selected two on the far side of the table. "Is this our office or the interrogation chamber?"

"It is your conference room. Witness statements are taken next door."

Red and Lindy stayed outside in the corridor. They kept their weapons strapped across their backs as they stood easily, waiting and watching.

Arana leaned into the hallway and called out with an ululating cry. A Tepulite appeared from the far end, hurrying toward the Grand Wayman. They conversed briefly before the other returned to where they came from.

"The files are on their way. Insert the data chip there," she pointed at a slot in the table, "and everything you need will be projected to the screen. You can use either voice commands or hand gestures. Tepulites usually stand since it is more comfortable for us. We lean against the table when we get tired."

Rivka looked at her hands clasped before her, on the edge of the table where many a Tepulite butt had rested. She removed her hands and wiped them on her pants. "Thank you, Arana. Is there anything else you can tell us that would shed more light on the case?"

"All the data is in the files. The most telling is the traffic control information. After that, all other suspects were eliminated, leaving only one."

"Eshu. Yes. We will get to the bottom of it, and then we will get out of your hair."

Arana checked her head, patting it as if expecting to find something. "Is there something in my hair?"

"No. That's just a figure of speech, sorry." Rivka decided to stand, soon finding herself leaning against the table. The room seemed to have been made for that stance.

The runner returned with a small box that held three things: a neckerchief with blood splatters, a broken comm device, and a data chip. Rivka looked at the other two items, not having any idea why they were there. She inserted the data chip and pulled up the data. "How do I transfer this to my system?"

The Grand Wayman worked with the main screen, and soon a series of codes appeared. "Here are the access codes to transmit the files to a secondary device in this room. The files flashed on the screen as Chaz downloaded them. "How'd you do that?"

"I have a chip in my head," Rivka replied without hesitation.

Sorry about that. I got excited, Chaz told her.

"I'm just excited to start," Rivka continued.

The Grand Wayman opened the door. "If you'll excuse me, I have your witnesses to gather."

Rivka was already leaning back and looking at the screen where a video of the accident played. It was gruesome to watch and limited in what it showed. The light was green for the sedan that blasted through the intersection. She checked the data on the side of the screen. Speed zone was labeled, and the vehicle was supposedly going the speed limit as calculated by known distance over time. The dimensions of the intersection were exact.

"Chaz, calculate vehicle speed."

"It is twice what is listed, Magistrate."

"Who made the original calc?"

"Definitely not the AI. This was done by the initial case investigator, a Wayling Uigur."

"Is that his real name? Don't answer that. How could he have gotten it so wrong?"

"Without his calculations, I cannot say."

"Chalk it up as anomaly number one."

"It's not Eshu," Chaz casually threw out.

"You know that already? I may jump to conclusions when I have additional insight into the perp's mind, but usually, we collect a little more data before drawing such a conclusion."

"Yes, Magistrate. I am properly chastised. As I look through the data, it has been altered in an embarrassingly ham-handed way. There is a trail of digital breadcrumbs that even I can follow."

"How can you be sure the AI didn't plant them there to cover his intrusion and manipulation of the system?"

"Dammit!" Chaz exclaimed.

Rivka chuckled. "You are getting better. That was a perfect language choice."

"I need to talk to Erasmus. I'll be right back." A millisecond later, Chaz was back. "I can't get through. We're too far underground."

"Oh, to be the poor saps in the penthouse suite on the

top floor." Rivka headed into the hall. "We need a comm repeater placed aboveground, or I'm going to have to go up there."

Lindy pointed with her chin at the Grand Wayman walking toward them.

"I need to get in touch with my ship. Can I place a communications repeater on any of the levels aboveground, preferably the top level?"

"Yes. I'll take you there myself."

"Lindy, remain with Sahved and the evidence. Red and I will be right back."

The three of them climbed aboard the elevator and started up.

CHAPTER EIGHT

Top Floor, Wayfair

The doors opened to a magnificent view of the city. Most of the offices were empty. Rivka moved into one and leaned against the table.

Do your thing, Chaz.

"You can see why we don't wish to be up here," the Grand Wayman stated, shifting uncomfortably, edging back toward the elevator.

"Would other Tepulites be just as uncomfortable up here?"

"Oh, yes!" Arana nodded emphatically.

"We'll need to talk to Wayling Uigur, too, please. And I would like to conduct the interviews up here. There is a distinct advantage to not letting the witnesses get too comfortable."

"Everyone has cooperated. There is no reason to add stress into their lives," the Grand Wayman replied, standing up straighter as if that would assert more authority.

"I think we'll do it my way. Please move everything up here. We'll talk to Eshu, and then next, I want to talk to Yoruba Kibuka." Rivka locked eyes with Arana. This wasn't a negotiation or a request. "Please make that happen, Arana."

"Yes, Magistrate," the Grand Wayman conceded, deflating with the statement. But there was no fight. When she called in the Federation, she surrendered jurisdictional authority. The Magistrate held the trump card.

And a gavel that she wasn't afraid to use. She was going to get to the bottom of this case and hoped no one would be jerking her around.

The Grand Wayman punched up the elevator and took it back to the sixth floor below ground to recover Lindy, Sahved, and the evidence. Within five minutes, they were back. Lindy smiled and breathed easier when she saw Red and Rivka, then she took a moment to appreciate the view.

Sahved brightened up. He expanded his chest to take a deeper breath. Arana was appalled at the response from the off-worlders. The floor had some workers, but they stayed in their offices, hunched over desks that sat higher because of their anatomy, even though Tepulites were shorter than humans.

"You have strange ways," she remarked.

Rivka smiled. "It's been a hundred years. Maybe it's time to come out of the shadows. If there are no Pod-docs on your planet to heal the injured, we can work with the Federation to bring you up to speed and help you crush anything that gets out of control. Is this why you were distraught at leaving your people behind?"

"Yes," Arana admitted. "We do not stand outside for

extended periods. If we are outside, we go where we need to go and get back inside as soon as possible."

"But there's no need. The virus has been eradicated." Rivka motioned for Sahved to set their items on the small table. There was a screen and an interface, but it was office-sized, not scaled for a conference room.

"We are holding it at bay because we take precautions. It would be foolish to return to the way we were and allow something worse to spread." The look on Arana's face suggested she was firmly committed to her answer.

"I see. I think I might be able to convince a team of Federation epidemiology experts to come here and check for you. Bring you some peace of mind."

"Why do we need to change?" Arana asked.

Rivka nodded. She had enough to do without committing to fix a planet that wasn't broken. "My apologies. You are correct. This view distracted me, but only for a moment. You have a lovely city. Let's get back to the case. We've taken a look at the raw data regarding the traffic lights, and it appears to have been falsified. There are anomalies throughout. Who reviewed the data for you?"

The Grand Wayman stepped backward as if struck by a blow. "We use the same experts we use for all our cases involving digital data. Cybercrime Consultants."

"I'll need to talk to them," Rivka stated. "As soon as possible."

The Grand Wayman retreated to the elevator. "Anyone else?" she asked.

"Send them up when they arrive. We'll hold them there," Rivka pointed to an empty office next door, "and then bring them through, one by one."

Arana waved and took the elevator down.

"Where are we with the digital forensics, Chaz?" Rivka asked after making sure no one was nearby. Red and Lindy stood just outside the clear wall and doorway that separated this office from the rest. It gave the floor an open and airy feel. She liked it.

"I am still working with Erasmus. There are digital signatures that I have not been able to recognize as valid. I am continuing my analysis and presenting my findings to Erasmus for confirmation. He is a very good teacher."

"I'm glad to hear that, Chaz. When do you think we'll be ready to interview Eshu?"

"Not yet. I don't think it will be long. All the data points to third party manipulation and not Eshu, but I don't wish you to act on an incomplete analysis. I will inform you the second Erasmus has validated my work."

"Sahved." The Yemilorian pulled his focus away from the screen, where he had been reading reports that had not been included in the transmitted case file. "Are we ready to interview the driver?"

"Yes, Magistrate. I do not know what it is, but something is not right. To me, this appears to be a cut-and-dried case of the driver being at fault. The video shows he is speeding. He hits a pedestrian in the crosswalk. There was no effort to avoid the person. The initial interview came to this conclusion, but after two meetings between the legal counsels, an alternative perpetrator was detailed, and the case turned toward Eshu. The evidence against the AI is based on one piece of data that Chaz thinks has been manipulated. Back to Kibuka. I think you will see a revelation from him that you expect."

"No superlatives?" Rivka squeezed his shoulder and smiled proudly. His review mirrored her gut feel. It made her angry to think how easy it was to assign blame to an AI through the faulty analysis of digital data because they only had one AI.

"I am very positive that I am the rightest of any investigator who has ever been right before." Sahved smiled. "Better?"

"Not in the least," Rivka replied. "But it sounds more personal. I think we need an independent AI review team to look at this kind of data to keep Federation members from making the same kind of mistake, assuming it *was* a mistake."

Sahved pointed at the screen, but Chaz interrupted before the Yemilorian could speak.

"Erasmus has confirmed my findings. The data file was manipulated after initial recording but not by Eshu."

"Shoot it to the screen, Chaz."

The data appeared as a raw stream with notes and highlights on the code. Chaz scrolled through quickly before the video started to play. "This is the recovered recording."

The light was red when the car raced through.

"The rightest of any investigator ever." Sahved beamed.

"Replay that, slowly, please." The video restarted. "Stop right there."

Two Tepulites were in the vehicle, not one, and Kibuka was in the passenger seat.

"Almost the most rightest." Sahved deflated.

"Looks like we have ourselves a conspiracy, Sahved. I'd like to say our work is done, but if we don't solve this, it won't be finished in the minds of the Tepulites." Rivka laid her datapad on the table, ready to call Eshu for his interview. "They left Eshu on the job because they knew he wasn't a criminal. What does the Grand Wayman know, and when did she know it? Sahved, add her to the witness list."

Wyatt Earp, Tepulon Capital City Spaceport

"Finished with the first four plates," Alant reported as he ordered two double hamburgers from the food processor. "Have you heard from the team?"

"Business as usual," Clodagh replied.

"Blood?"

"Not that business. I guess it's a normal case. Interview some witnesses, make a judgment, and then come back. Rivka doesn't think it will take more than a day because the authorities are cooperating."

Cole looked disappointed.

"Don't tell me you took one of the early slots." His expression told her everything she needed to know. "You did. It's your money."

"I thought this was going to go south in a hurry. Damn! Two hundred credits gone in sixty seconds."

Clodagh ordered a chocolate shake after Cole gathered his plates.

"How many plates do you have left?" Clodagh asked.

Cole bit into his lunch, raising his eyebrows at her as he slowly chewed.

"Never mind. I know the answer. Just trying to make polite lunch talk."

Cole chewed faster and swallowed. "I'm sorry. I suck at

this stuff. I've never been a long-term boyfriend before. How about we play a game?"

"No! We are not playing Twister again."

Cole choked on his food until Clodagh hammered his back with a little too much zeal.

"I was thinking Federationopoly. Get the others in on it. Build galactic conglomerates, wheel and deal, don't pass Go, and don't collect two hundred credits."

"I guess in that case, okay." She took a long draw off her shake. Cole choked down his burgers as if the building was on fire and he had to go fight it. "What's your rush?"

"If the Magistrate comes back tonight, I might be able to get most of the armor upgrade finished without a space dock. She wouldn't have mentioned it if she didn't think it was important, based on what she knows could be coming up. If the ship gets attacked, I want it to survive because I don't want you to die."

Clodagh stopped drinking her shake and licked her lips. "Is that how you see things?"

"It's the viewscreen through which I see everything. I'm a warrior, a Terry Henry Walton production, as it were. It's our job to protect the ones we love, and it's our mission to kick the asses of those who threaten them."

"I figured ass-kicking had to be in there somewhere. Come here." She drew him close for a long and passionate kiss. "Maybe we can squeeze in a little Twister later."

Cole smiled. "It's not that. I've grown kind of fond of your company. I'd hate to mess that up by you getting killed and all."

"You should have quit while you were ahead."

"No quitting now. We have a lot of work to do and not enough time to do it."

"Now you sound like the Magistrate. She does rub off on you, doesn't she?"

"We both have work to do so we don't disappoint the boss. So, get to it, Chief Engineer." Cole returned his dishes to the food processor, wiped his hands on his pants, and intercepted Clodagh for one more hug. He coaxed her hair around her ear, getting lost in time as he traced a finger slowly to the lobe and around the outside.

Someone cleared their throat. Clodagh and Alant jerked their attention to the young woman watching them.

"You're blocking the food processor." Groenwyn pointed at the wall behind them.

CHAPTER NINE

<u>Wayfair, Top Floor</u>

"Were you able to detect that the files had been accessed?" Rivka asked.

"Of course, but the outsiders covered themselves quite well. I wasn't able to identify them or track them outside the system," Eshu replied.

"The Tepulon leadership let you remain on the job even though they accused you of murder. Do you know why they did that?"

"There were a few rather heated discussions, but in the end, they decided they had no alternative. I am integrated into far too many systems to be pulled out."

"Who fought the hardest to keep you on the job?" Rivka chewed her lip as she stared at the data on the screen, not seeing any of the words. She focused on the conversation.

"That was the Grand Trademan, the chief of planetary commerce. He is a very important individual on Tepulon, and his advice carries great weight."

"Thank you, Eshu." She gestured to Sahved to write the name down, adding it to the list of witnesses. "I believe I'll be able to clear these charges today. Please bear with us as we work through our witnesses. You're free to go back to work."

"It's like I never left," Eshu replied. "Thank you for your time and expertise, Magistrate Rivka Anoa, Sahved of Yemilore, and most especially, Chaz of the Singularity. You have done our people proud."

The screen on Rivka's datapad showed that Eshu had signed off. "Please transcribe that interview into Tepulon v Eshu, Witness Statement 1—Eshu of the Singularity."

"Done," Chaz declared. "It feels good to have accomplished something for my people."

Rivka waved her finger at the datapad even though Chaz was in the pendant hanging around her neck. "We do what we do for the sake of Justice for all. I'm blind to everything but the truth and how the law applies to it."

"In this case, we have a car running a red light, and a rather extensive cover-up after the fact. Who is Yoruba Kibuka, and who was driving the vehicle?" Sahved wondered.

"We are going to find out right quick," Rivka replied quietly after seeing who stepped off the elevator. The Tepulite escort pointed him and another toward Rivka. She waved them in and offered seats with their backs to the screen. As was their way, they preferred to stand and lean against the table.

Rivka shut down the screen. "Red, please join us."

Red entered the small office, closing the flimsy door behind him and blocking it with his body.

"I'm Magistrate Rivka Anoa. I'm here on behalf of the Federation to investigate the death of Miss Yorunmila. State your name for the record, please."

"I am Kibuka," the Tepulite said. "I have been cleared. I don't know why I'm here."

"And you?" Rivka asked the second Tepulite.

"I am Yoruba Keenakoa, counsel for Kibuka."

"Your client has not been cleared by me. When this case was kicked to the Federation, it became a new case, and since the original case never saw the inside of a courtroom, there is no double jeopardy. But we're going to settle this right here, right now. Kibuka, who else was in the car with you? What was the driver's name?"

Kibuka looked shocked before he steeled himself, clenching his jaw and crossing his arms in front of his chest.

"I must protest." The counsel tried to step forward, but Rivka was there first. "Who drove the car?" she demanded, brushing her hand against his arm.

A face. A name. Yoruba Garang. The crime boss.

Rivka glared into Kibuka's eyes. "Chaz. Get hold of Eshu and find Yoruba Garang. Send a message to the Grand Wayman to collect him and bring him here. We'll hold onto Kibuka until we have all the perpetrators in one place at one time."

Kibuka pushed her away from him. Red was there in an instant to seize the Tepulite by the throat. "I didn't say anything," he pleaded, eyes fixed on his lawyer.

"Sit down," Rivka told them both. Red let up but remained between Kibuka and Rivka. "What does Yoruba mean? Is that the name of your crime family?"

The pasty-complexioned Kibuka turned gray and looked like he was going to throw up. Sahved stepped back, knowing the look only too well.

"I protest. You have fabricated your claims. We'll be leaving now." Before Keenakoa could pull Kibuka to his feet, Red had him by his collar and forced him into his seat.

"The Magistrate told you to sit," Red growled.

With the two Tepulites properly seated, one fuming and one terrified, Rivka was able to continue. "The penalty for conspiracy to cover up a crime isn't as bad as for manslaughter, but I'm going to have to find you guilty of both, and the maximum penalty for that is fifteen plus five years on Jhiordaan. Twenty years. I can declare that right now, and you would be on the next prison shuttle."

"You cannot do that to my client. He was cleared!" Keenakoa pleaded, but he knew what the penalties were. "You don't have any evidence."

"Sahved, show the video. Stop it when we have a clear picture."

The Tepulites spun in their chairs to face the screen. The video played all the way through once, and on the second run, Sahved stopped it where it showed a driver and Kibuka as the passenger with the light still red and an unsuspecting pedestrian in the crosswalk.

"Guilty as sin," Rivka said. "You and Garang. Is he a boss in your crime syndicate, and you were covering for him?"

"We will answer no more questions. I will appeal this to the Grand Wayman!"

"You don't appeal down the chain, Keenakoa. She already raised the case to me. You have no right of appeal for Magistrate-delivered rulings."

"That is ridiculous." The Tepulite started tapping his feet rapidly, and his knees flexed backward as if he were preparing to race away.

"Chaz, ask the Grand Wayman to come up here, please."

The Tepulites looked at Red, who glared back. Sahved remained silent.

She is on her way, Magistrate, Chaz reported.

"She'll be here shortly," Rivka said, reveling in their inability to grasp her and her team's ability to communicate privately.

Rivka clasped her hands behind her back and strolled to the window to take in the magnificent view. "You have a beautiful city. It's a shame to screw it up with organized crime. That is what you guys are into. I'm going to dismantle it, which will leave a void. Then the local authorities are going to have to clean up your mess because you couldn't stop for a red light."

The sound of a slap made Rivka turn. She expected to see Red's handprint across the perp's head, but it wasn't him. Keenakoa had slapped his client almost unconscious. Rivka caught Red's glance.

"He was going to talk," Red remarked.

"You will refrain from beating your client." Rivka kept her tone even. Keenakoa's action gave her the answer to the unasked question. The lawyer was higher up on the ladder of protecting the crime group's assets.

She strolled around the table and leaned close, looming over him. He twisted backward, trying to get away from her. "How do you know the victim?"

Rivka grabbed his arm as thoughts raced through an undisciplined and violent mind. She had seen too much. A liability. It was supposed to be clean. Fucking Garang. "Get your hands off me!" he demanded.

The Magistrate stepped back. "You, sir, are one raging asshole. I think you're going to be in Jhiordaan with your clients, but thanks to some new information I've just been made aware of, this is no longer a manslaughter case, but premeditated murder. That's a death sentence, Keenakoa. And you helped to cover it up."

"I'm the lawyer! You can't convict me of my clients' crimes."

"We agree, then. Your clients have been convicted of crimes, but I don't need your concurrence. Red, put these two in the office next door and hold them. No communication with the outside world, not until we have Garang in hand."

Red manhandled the Tepulites into the neighboring office. The clear windows made it uncomfortable, seeing them watching her, so Red forced them onto the floor. Rivka had to look away. It wasn't optimal, but it was what they had.

The elevator opened, and the Grand Wayman stepped out. She saw the tops of the Tepulites' heads while Red brandished his railgun before them.

Arana hurried into the office, shaking her head. "I must protest."

"Noted," Rivka snarked. She wasn't in the mood for verbal jousting. If the Grand Wayman had done her job instead of trusting others to do the work, she would have found the same things Rivka had.

Almost, without the look into the minds of the guilty.

Sahved stepped up. "If you'll turn your attention to the

unaltered video, you'll find a distinctly different series of events," he told her and played the video twice, as he had done for Kibuka.

"Two Tepulites in the vehicle and Kibuka was not the driver. The vehicle was traveling at twice the speed in your report, and those two knew the victim. This was a hit, Grand Wayman."

Arana fell back against the table. "A hit?"

Rivka lowered her voice. "I don't think you're incompetent, Grand Wayman, so tell me. How bad is the organized crime problem on Tepulon?"

"It isn't bad. There's been peace for a hundred years. They run their business without friction. They keep order. You don't see any police, do you?"

"That makes for an interesting legal structure. Still, you are subject to Federation laws, and we look down on people killing other people. Those two are just the start. I have a few more who are going to be on the next shuttle to Jhiordaan. They can keep each other company for the next fifty years."

The Grand Wayman leaned against the table and hung her head. "What if that starts a war?"

"It's a war they won't win," Rivka stated. "I wasn't the one who raised the level of violence. If they hadn't killed Yorunmila, I would never have come to your planet. If they had copped to the killing, I wouldn't have come. But they tried to blame an AI, which required me to come." Rivka stopped her reasoning.

As she thought, she realized the Grand Wayman wasn't incompetent and could have been a genius. She had gotten Rivka to solve a problem that had started to drive a wedge into the fabric of Tepulon's society while disavowing any knowledge, protesting appropriately.

"I hope your society returns to normal as soon as possible. The Yoruba clan is going to suffer for using violence to solve their problems. They are going to suffer mightily."

"I see why you surround yourself with armed guards. You bring a great deal of pain with you." Arana avoided looking out the window, turning her head away from the view and the perception of the wind.

"We bring a great deal of relief to the victims and to societies that count on laws to protect them. And we bring pain to those who violate that trust."

The elevator opened, and the Grand Trademan stepped out. "Ah. Our next witness."

CHAPTER TEN

Wayfair, Top Floor

Unlike the Grand Wayman, the Grand Trademan was far less receptive to the process. He became angrier the closer he came. When he recognized the Tepulites on the floor under armed guard, he came unhinged.

"You will release them!" he shouted before he stepped through the door.

Rivka leaned against the table, arms crossed before her chest. Lindy followed him in, ready to intercede if he became physically confrontational. The subtle look on Rivka's face suggested violence was inevitable, but she would be leading the way.

"I don't let convicted murderers go, Grand Trademan."

"He was cleared. Who are you to come to Tepulon and overrule our laws?"

"I'm sorry you don't understand your own laws. I thought you were in a position where reading was required. Congratulations that an illiterate can ascend to such a post."

"What? I can read." He had no idea what allegation she had leveled.

"What was your role in the coverup of the murder committed by Garang and Kibuka?"

She seized his arms in an iron grip and spun him around, slamming him against the wall. The Grand Wayman's eyes rolled back in her head as she fainted. Sahved reached out but failed to catch her before she hit the floor.

Married into the Yoruba clan. His world was collapsing. The plague! Stop touching me. His final thoughts rushed to the surface. "Stop touching me!"

Rivka let him go, brushing his lapels lightly. "Your impartiality is compromised because of your relationship to the Yorubas. Had you recused yourself, we wouldn't be in this position. You gave the clan access to the digital files, didn't you? Maybe you simply gave them access to everything, and now they think it's time to expand their stake and solidify their leadership over Tepulon."

He clenched his mouth tightly and refused to say another word. "My name is Magistrate Rivka Anoa, and I am accusing you of conspiracy after the fact, specifically, the murder of Yorunmila. I find you guilty of that crime. Join your buddies." She pointed to the room next door. Lindy acknowledged the unspoken order.

When he made no effort to move, she grabbed him by his arm, dragged him out of the office, and tossed him into the one next door, tripping him so he fell.

"Stay down," Red told him, pointing with Blazer's business end.

Sahved helped Arana to her feet but quickly let go at

her look, sliding a chair behind her instead of touching her further.

"We are not used to such violence. I thought you were a lawyer, but you come across as a thug."

"My job is not a pleasant one, but the results, when I do things right, leave a better world behind. Those three covered up a murder, pointing the blame at an innocent bystander, but you suspected all that and brought me here to do what you could not. Please don't act self-righteous when you got exactly what you asked for, which is the resolution of this case. We're only a couple of steps away from wrapping things up. All we need is Garang, and then we'll make the arrangements for a prison shuttle to pick up the refuse."

The Grand Wayman surrendered to the truth. She accessed the screen to check the status. The news wasn't good. The officials who had been sent to find Garang couldn't find him, and he no longer registered on the Tepulon tracking system. Due to the effects of the plague, all Tepulites wore trackers so the government could enforce isolation and follow contacts. They had been implanted at birth for everyone born after the epidemic. Multiple generations were now trackable.

Chaz, work with Eshu and figure this out. I suspect he's still out there and tracked, but his information has been removed from the system.

On it, Chaz replied.

"We'll take care of that, too. Do you have a holding facility?" Rivka tipped her chin toward the next office. Arana kept herself from looking.

"One floor below ground." She stood on shaky legs.

"I think we're done here. Let's go down to where you're more comfortable. We'll lock those three away, and then we'll head out to collect Mister Garang."

Sahved exaggerated a nod. He started to follow the Magistrate out but she stopped him, glancing at the table where the scant evidence, including the data chip, remained. His eyes shot wide with understanding. He threw the items back into the box and carried it to the elevator. "We're not going to fit on one, so we'll meet you down there."

Red threw his hands up. "We're your bodyguards, not theirs," he protested. "Sahved, with me. Lindy, with them."

Rivka saw Sahved's dilemma. With the box, he wouldn't be able to help Red if the prisoners tried something, although the Tepulites didn't look to be a match for Vered. A lawyer, a bureaucrat, and a petty thug.

Still.

"Give me the box." Rivka waved at Sahved to hand it over. He did so reluctantly, but it made Red happier.

When the doors opened, the Grand Wayman hurried in. Being on the top floor had caused her more distress than the case revelations. As they descended, she visibly transformed into a relaxed and more confident Tepulite.

The corridor on Sub-level One was bright. The left passage bustled with activity. The right had six doors spaced close together. Arana led them to the first one. "This is the Wayfair Keeper. He will log the detainees in and ensure their health and well-being while they are in our care."

Rivka nodded. She strolled to the first cell and found it looked more like an efficiency apartment. The Tepulites would be ill-equipped for Jhiordaan. The elevator arrived with Red, Sahved, and the three in their charge. The Tepulites were subdued, making no trouble. The Grand Trademan glared at Arana as he passed, but when Rivka caught his eye, he quickly looked away. Maybe they needed a taste of Jhiordaan as a wake-up call.

"What kind of long-term incarceration do you maintain here on Tepulon?" Rivka looked at the box she was still holding. "Can you secure the evidence, please?"

"We only have one prison. Our longest sentence is only two years. We believe in rehabilitation." She took the box from Rivka and handed it to the Wayfair Keeper.

"That would be good if we saw recidivist rates of less than eighty percent, but those repeat offenders ruin it for everyone. Plus, the criminals I deal with tend to be the worst of the worst. Capital crimes don't bring out the best in people. Just like this one. Once I've had a chance to interview Garang, we'll see what is called for. I do want to talk to the Cybercrime Consultants, so I guess we're not done. We can go to their offices and talk to them there. My first impression is that they're in bed with the Yoruba clan, too. Unless they are completely incompetent."

"I wish I could tell you something different, but your investigation is moving forward at the speed of light. I am not able to keep up. How do you get the information from the individuals so quickly?"

Rivka didn't wish to share. "That's why I'm a Magistrate. It's a gift that has made me what I am. Maybe a blessing, maybe a curse. Most importantly, I'm surrounded by good people. Can you have the van waiting for us, please? I don't know when we'll need it."

As you suspected, Magistrate, Garang's signature had been erased from the system. Eshu is working to lock down the databases to prevent external access by anyone. The Tepulites will have to individually grant access and change logins to get back into the system. Now that we have that under control, once Garang's signature code was restored, he reappeared. I have an address, Chaz told Rivka.

"Your tracking system makes it way too easy to find our perps. Are you coming along?"

"You know where he is?"

"We do. And Eshu has locked out your planet's databases until proper accesses are reestablished to prevent future incursions."

The Grand Wayman stopped by the Keeper's office to use his comm system to order the van. She turned down escorts. There would be no room.

"Three new customers. I will take good care of them as we always do, Grand Wayman."

"I have no doubt." They waved their hands in front of each other in their standard greeting before the Grand Wayman led Rivka and her team up the stairs and outside. Arana's shoulders tightened, and she hunched when she walked while outside.

Rivka breathed deeply of the fresh air. If they weren't going to appreciate it, she would.

She smiled at the team before they climbed aboard. "Let's go catch us some bad guys." At Red's look, she added, "Without running and without shedding any blood." The bodyguard groaned.

Lindy nudged him so she could climb into the back,

taking a seat next to Sahved. "That's always the plan, but you know how things work out," she whispered.

Red instantly brightened.

Eastern Trade District, Tepulon Capital City

Judging by the addresses linked to those with the name Yoruba, this is the clan's home turf, if I get the lingo correct, Chaz explained to the entire team.

You have it correct, Chaz. Rivka checked her coat pocket for Reaper, the neutron pulse weapon. It was where it always was.

"What kind of weapons will they have?" she asked.

"They won't have anything like you have. We don't have projectile or energy weapons of any sort. They were all destroyed after the plague ended all war on our planet."

"Laudable," Rivka commented. "So, ad hoc weapons. I guarantee they'll have something. And getting locked out of the system will probably ring their alarm bells. They'll suspect someone is coming because they know someone already came for Garang. They will know that Kibuka and Keenakoa have not returned from their interview. This is where the perps fight for their freedom."

Red visually checked his railgun to make sure everything was working and that it carried a full charge. Lindy did the same thing. Sahved looked alarmed. He wore a ballistic vest, like Rivka, but carried no weapon. The incident on Tanglewood had reinforced that the world was safer without Sahved packing heat.

The van pulled into a nondescript neighborhood in front of a vanilla apartment building. The parallel was eerily similar to Binsulaker Prime. "Why do the scumbags live in apartment buildings?"

"Big-city scumbags. Everyone lives in apartments," Red offered. "Forces us to go in after them."

"Close to the wall, single file. Shows a first-floor apartment."

"That's the first floor below ground," Arana corrected. "Our negative floor numbers are aboveground because no one wants to live in the wind."

Rivka didn't argue. Tepulites preferred living below-ground. Also the turtle people of Tissikinnon Four, but that was completely different.

Red entered the building first, looking down the barrel of his weapon with both eyes open. The barrel followed his gaze as he looked into all the shadows. Just like every planet he'd ever been to, apartment steps were promi-nently located. Electric self-driving vans and steps. At least they weren't supposed to have firearms.

He'd believe that when he saw it.

Rivka held Reaper in her hand, keeping Arana between her and Sahved. Lindy was last into the building, but she kept her attention forward. She glanced behind her occa-sionally, but the criminals were inside. Tepulon's tracking system told them that.

Red headed down, walking gingerly, toe to heel to move silently. He kept his upper body rigid so nothing clunked or swished. The steps were wide, with a short drop for the people whose knees went the other way. That made them easier for the humans to navigate. The stories weren't as high either since the Tepulites were not a tall species.

At the first landing, Red held up. He pointed to his ear

with two fingers and then down the steps: two individuals in the hallway below. He kept moving. Rivka held Arana back, and they descended single file.

Which way is apartment one dash four? Red asked.

Left, Chaz replied. Red nodded. That was where the sounds were coming from. He put his back to the wall to look as far down the opposite hallway as he could see before turning and bringing his weapon to bear. He held fingers above his head, counting down from three to zero. When his hand was a fist, he launched into action.

"Get down!" he yelled, charging down the hallway. Three Tepulites leaned against the wall, carrying clubs with metal bands wrapped around the ends to increase the lethality. "I said, *get down.*"

The closest one made the mistake of raising his club and taking one step toward Red. A single trigger pull exploded the thug's head and that of the one behind him. The hypersonic projectile cracked as if a grenade had gone off. The third thug fell to his knees, dropping his club and holding his head.

Red forced the Tepulite onto his face before continuing. Rivka stepped wide, watching him closely to keep him from doing anything untoward. The Grand Wayman refused to leave the stairs, holding her head in both hands. Sahved and Lindy hurried after the Magistrate.

Sahved picked up the club as he passed. Two doors down, Red was rearing back to kick it in. In the millisecond before his foot hit, someone flung the door wide and Red sprawled, doing the splits on his way to the ground. His railgun was aimed away. Two Tepulites bolted into the hallway.

The first one clocked Red across his temple with a hard blow from his metal-banded club. The second saw the two approach and launched his club like a tomahawk. It spun through the air, taking less than a heartbeat to hit Rivka in the chest, barely missing Chaz. She stumbled but was able to bring Reaper to bear. She burned the first, and a railgun cracked from behind her, exploding the second Tepulite.

Red tried to roll onto his side and get up but was unsuccessful. He groaned and looked into the apartment. One more Tepulite inside.

"One more," he croaked. Rivka hurried forward, but Sahved caught her before she went in alone.

"Me first," he said proudly. He brandished his club as he'd seen the others carrying theirs and stalked into the apartment. Rivka took the moment to check on Red and found he had a nasty gash on the side of his head. Lindy stopped for a second.

"He'll be fine," Rivka told her.

Lindy nodded and followed Sahved in. The sound of two clubs hitting each other announced that battle had been joined. Rivka waited. Two thuds later, the unmistakable sound of a fist impacting a face finished the fight.

"Clear," Lindy stated. Sahved left the apartment to stand watch in the hallway.

Arana leaned around the corner, and Rivka waved her over.

"Keep the Grand Wayman safe," Rivka told Sahved. Red was struggling to sit up. Rivka pulled him to the wall and leaned his back against it. Blood streamed from the gash. Rivka put his hand over it. "Keep pressure on that until it closes up."

She adjusted her grip on Reaper and walked inside to find Lindy looming over a Tepulite with a growing bruise on his face. "Garang, I presume. I've seen your picture driving a car. For the record, for a crime boss, you live in pretty crappy digs."

He didn't rise to the taunt, preferring to remain on the floor, moaning.

"Why did you hit Yorunmila?" She took his arm, and, through his jumbled thoughts, confirmed what Kibuka had "said."

Rivka pressed on. "What did the Grand Trademan know, and when?"

He was there for the initial planning. He saw himself taking over the family Ha! He wished. That was Garang's future, and he wouldn't give it up. The old man was dying. The murder showed what he was capable of. The cover-up showed that they were untouchable.

"Power corrupts absolutely." She took him by the throat. "Yoruba Garang. I find you guilty of premeditated murder, conspiracy to commit murder, conspiracy after the fact, and the attempted murder of a Magistrate. For these crimes, your sentence is death, to be carried out immediately."

She pushed him away from her. He started to come to the realization of what was going on.

"What?" he mumbled.

She set Reaper to eight and depressed the button. It was over in an instant.

Rivka frowned. She checked her pulse. It was up a little at seventy-two, but still in a normal range. She hadn't been upset.

It was the cold administration of Justice. There was no reason to be upset.

Rivka chopped her hand toward the hallway. "Let's get our people. Next stop is to see what the Cybercrime Consultants have to say."

The Grand Wayman held one of Red's field dressings against the head wound. Sahved stood over the only thug still alive. He menaced the Tepulite with the club he had taken from one of the perps.

"Stand up," she ordered. The Tepulite tried to look defiant, but his four dead fellows took the toughness from him. He relented and stood. "Name and role in the Yoruba family."

"Gebrona. Stockman. Driver. I work in the warehouse and deliver frozen meals to the grocery store."

"Frozen meals? What kind of crime family is this?"

"No competition," Gebrona stated. "Yoruba owns the prepared frozen meals market. The Nonaralls own salty snacks and fizzy drinks. We want to get a piece of that."

"Want*ed*," Rivka clarified. She appreciated when perps came clean. It saved her the hassle of a post facto accounting for warrants. "You can go. And if you want to stay on this side of life, you won't pick up one of those clubs ever again."

"Yes, ma'am," the Tepulite said and wasted no time racing up the stairs and going on his way.

"Red, can you travel?"

"Yes, Magistrate," Red said confidently. Lindy helped pull him to his feet. He tried to blink his eyes clear, but his head was still ringing from the blow he'd taken. "That sucked. I should have been able to block it."

"Falling through the empty space where a door is supposed to be isn't the best balance for blocking an attack. Whoever was first was going to get the same treatment. We'll have to think about how we can breach differently in the after-action."

"For the post-mission brief?" Red asked.

"For the case file." Rivka wouldn't concede that it was a mission. It also told her that Red was going to be okay. "It'll take more than a bully club to crack that skull of yours."

"I think it's 'billy.'"

"Billy's not here. How badly is your brain scrambled?" Rivka asked. "Grand Wayman, are you ready? Lindy, lead us out."

"I've never seen such violence," Arana said softly.

Rivka talked while they walked. "Judging by those clubs, the violence is here, but you have been insulated from it. They take care of it themselves, and then it gets buried. You were none the wiser. It all starts with ambition and the perception of power. Then they make war clubs, and next thing you know, they'll have guns. I hope we nipped that in the bud, but now that you're aware, you'll be able to interdict future incursions across family lines. Maybe someday you'll introduce competition so your average consumer can win."

"Those are big ideals. I don't know if Tepulon is ready to return to such a state of antagonism. I don't see where anyone can win."

"It's here, Arana. It has come whether you are ready or not. You can win by keeping the families in their place. Getting a Grand Trademan who isn't a family insider. Take care with who gets put in charge."

"If only it were that easy." The van waited for them. Lindy popped the door and helped Red inside. Rivka and Arana climbed aboard while still talking. "Maybe this gives us a chance to take a better look at our roles in society. We usually stay out of their way. We'll have to replace the Grand Trademan."

"He was in on it from the beginning. He knew they were going to kill that woman. She was a virtual nobody, but it demonstrated they were willing to do what it would take. I bet the other families are starting to arm themselves now, too. You need to prepare for war. Strike first, strike hard, and end it quickly."

The Grand Wayman studied Rivka's face. She was deadly serious. "I'm not used to that kind of lawyering."

"That's what it takes if you want people to comply with the law."

Arana shook her head. "I'll have to think about it."

"Onward to Cybercrime Consultants. Let's see if anyone gets to join our trio of lawbreakers."

CHAPTER ELEVEN

***Wyatt Earp*, Tepulon Capital City Spaceport**

"Magistrate says they'll be on their way back shortly," Clodagh reported over the ship-wide broadcast. Cole was on top of the ship, continuing to install baffled armor plates. The navigators and pilots were running various checks on all the ship systems, while Ankh and Erasmus remained busy with endeavors not associated with the ship.

"Chaz? Are you there?" Clodagh called.

I am, the AI replied opting for the internal comm since he was aboveground and relatively close to the ship.

Do you have the next recommended planet so we can dial it in before you return?

Xynite in the Leo Four Sector.

Setting course for Xynite. We'll take off as soon as you're aboard.

.   .   .

Cybercrime Consultants, Tepulon Capital City Spaceport

As they approached, it was obvious that they'd gotten the word. The place looked deserted.

Rivka turned to Arana and snorted. "Rats bailing off a sinking ship."

Arana looked dismayed. "I have never seen such flaunting of the law. They should be here waiting for us if they know they are suspected of wrongdoing." Rivka felt sorry for the pain she heard in the Grand Wayman's voice.

"Chaz," Rivka said aloud. "Get with Eshu, find these cockwombles, and take us to them."

"Yes, Magistrate."

Arana looked around, wondering where the new voice had come from.

"Let me introduce you to Chaz, an AI, and a valued member of my team." She pointed to the pendant hanging around her neck.

"He's been with you the whole time?" Arana started to look suspicious.

"I start with the premise that I can trust no one. Since your Grand Trademan was dirty, it should show you that my approach is not without good reason. Chaz is exceptional at providing insight. He is working hand in hand with Eshu."

She contemplated the information for a moment. "I thought the database was locked down."

"I have a Federation warrant granting my team access."

"I have the two company heads moving at high speed away from the city. They appear to be in the same vehicle. I will transfer the target location to this vehicle's guidance system."

"And that's why," Rivka clarified. "Because perps run from the law. They did not properly weigh the risk versus reward, but they don't want to take their medicine. Flaunting the law seems easy until it's not, and then it becomes a cascade of bad decisions."

"Magistrate," Chaz interrupted. "The targets are increasing the distance between us."

"Speed up. I'm sure we can catch them before too long."

"They'll be out from under the coverage that tells us where they are before that happens, assuming we could speed up, which we can't."

"Why can't we go faster?"

Arana raised one finger. "No government vehicle can exceed the speed limit. No private vehicle should either."

"Garang did, and these guys are. They hacked your controls. And you can't outrun perps?"

"No. We've never had to."

Rivka removed her datapad. "Rivka to *Wyatt Earp*." After Clodagh answered, Rivka continued, "Chaz will send you the moving beacon for a couple of people of interest in my investigation. Have Cole armored and ready to interdict their vehicle. Take the ship and go stop them right now. Time is of the essence. Try not to kill them."

"Taking off now," Clodagh replied.

"Where were we?" Rivka asked casually while the van cruised along at the speed limit, stopping at traffic lights like everyone else did.

· · ·

Wyatt Earp, Tepulon Capital City Spaceport

"Hang on, Alant!" Clodagh shouted before switching to ship-wide. Aurora was already retracting the ramp for immediate departure. "Magistrate says we have to go snag a couple suspects. We're taking off. Stand by for some erratic maneuvers, so it's probably best to hang on."

The ship lifted off and accelerated quickly away from the spaceport, following the blip on the screen. *Wyatt Earp* made short work of the trip, flying at just under the speed of sound to keep from generating sonic booms while over the city. Once outside the majority of buildings, Aurora increased speed for a few seconds to get ahead of the sedan.

Clodagh touched her comm panel. "We're passing the car now. It's the only one on the road. On my mark, deploy the warrior. Mark."

Cole jumped from the back of the ship. He had one uninstalled panel that he carried with him on the way down. He had no weapons with him, not even the over-shoulder rockets. He'd been doing maintenance work in the suit since it allowed him to move heavy loads safely.

He hit his boot rockets before he landed and touched down softly, then started running toward the vehicle bearing down on him. He stopped and waved his arms, the panel moving back and forth in one hand while the other encouraged the vehicle to slow down and stop.

Alive if you can manage. He heard the order.

The two in the car didn't seem to care. They didn't appear to be willing to stop. Cole gripped the metal panel in two fingers, hopped two steps forward, and threw the panel at the car's hood ornament, spinning it so it flew true. It didn't have far to travel before it hit the hood, crashing through the engine and embedding itself in the windscreen.

He hit his rockets and jumped into the air as the car raced through the space where he'd been standing. The wheels locked up, and the car started to slide toward the shoulder and off the road. It settled before it went into the ditch. Cole rotated, moved over the top of the vehicle, and came down on the hood, crushing it to stand on the remains of the engine block. He ripped the panel free.

"I need this," he told the Tepulites, who were still staring, wide-eyed. "The authorities will be along shortly to collect you. You shouldn't have run. It makes you look guilty."

Cole watched the two from the comfort of his suit while *Wyatt Earp* hovered above the road, unable to land because of its size. Cole decided to rid himself of the panel. He opened the loading deck remotely and jogged to it, sliding the panel inside. When he stepped away from the ship, he found the two Tepulites running into the desert. In the distance, the Magistrate's van appeared.

He took off after them and made short work of their escape attempt. He grabbed each by the arm, walking back while dragging them. "That makes you look even guiltier. I should stomp the stupid out of both of you."

Cole had his external recording systems turned off. He didn't need any more videos of him doing things that could find their way to a wider audience. The Magistrate probably already had all the evidence she needed, and that was why they ran.

By the time he reached the road, the van had stopped,

and Rivka and the others were climbing out.

"These two tried to run me over, then they tried to just run." He tossed them onto the pavement at Rivka's feet.

Rivka nodded to Cole, who took a step back. "Tell me a story, boys. Where did this overwhelming desire to go camping come from? And above the speed limit, too. Shame how you got caught doing all that."

Red pulled the two to their feet and hung onto them. The big bodyguard still had dried blood on the side of his head, but his eyes were clear from the nanocytes rapidly repairing his bruised brain.

"She asked you a question," he growled from between their heads. He was in no mood to goof around. When they remained silent, he shoved one to within arm's reach of the Magistrate.

"What did you do to the data in the vehicular manslaughter case?" Rivka grabbed an exposed arm.

I shouldn't have reworked the data! He burst into tears and fell to his knees.

"Why did you do it?"

Credits. They paid a lot of credits and would be paying more.

"You did what he did?" Rivka asked the second Tepulite. She didn't bother grabbing his arm. "Since you ran with him, I'm assuming you had full knowledge of his actions. I find you both guilty of conspiracy after the fact and resisting arrest. How did that work out for you?"

The first went from tears to ugly crying. The second hung his head in shame.

Rivka turned to the Grand Wayman. "I leave them to you, and I leave their punishment up to you. The other three? Jhiordaan for the maximum of fifty years. A Federation prison shuttle will come for them. Turn them over to the Yollin guards. And now, gentlemen, because you showed that you can't play nice, we're going to bind your hands, and then we're going to taser you so you don't cause any trouble on your ride back to jail. I'm on a tight schedule and must be leaving, so we'll be parting ways here."

The Magistrate raised her hand for the Grand Wayman to match the pose and slide it back and forth in the air. "I look forward to being back inside." Arana sighed. "You can trust that we'll take care of these two and the other three. I will contemplate your advice and methods to ensure that we keep Tepulon a planet with minimal crime and maximum freedom."

"May your air bring you joy and not fear," Rivka replied. "You have a lovely planet."

Red and Lindy zip-tied the Tepulites hands. On the count of three, the two took too much pleasure in zapping their captives. They flopped around for a second before lying still. Red and Lindy hauled them to the van and tossed them inside.

The Grand Wayman looked mortified.

Rivka waved and smiled.

"This has been the most enlightening experience for an investigator. I thank you for showing us what is possible," Sahved told Arana before bowing his head and running after the others. They entered using the cargo ramp since it was already open. Cole shut it after he climbed aboard.

"Clodagh, take us out of here. Best possible speed to Xynite." Rivka twirled her finger to get the show on the road.

CHAPTER TWELVE

Wyatt Earp, **Leaving Tepulon**

"You look dog-tired, Magistrate." Red examined Rivka's face while Lindy watched. Both looked concerned.

"You don't look so good yourself. Do you need some Pod-doc time?" Rivka turned Red's head to see how much his wound had healed.

"For this? It's just a flesh wound." Red shook his head but winced after doing it. "I just need a shower and a nap, and I'll be good to go for our next mission."

"Case," Rivka corrected. "And your blood was first in the last two cases. If I hadn't been there both times, I'd think you were sandbagging and taking a cut from the winner."

"I am appalled you would think I'd be subject to such subterfuge. It's not in my nature."

"I can confirm that," Lindy added. Tiny Man Titan started barking from somewhere nearby. He yipped, then went silent. The three looked at each other for a moment before racing toward the silence.

They found Titan in a corner, cowering as Wenceslaus crouched before him, a predator intimidating his prey. The three knew better than to pick up the cat. Rivka reached past and picked up Titan. As soon as he was safe in the human's hand, he unleashed a torrent at the big orange cat.

Wenceslaus sat up, wrapped his tail around his legs, and started grooming himself.

"You have to watch what you're doing, Titan! You're going to get yourself hurt."

Groenwyn appeared and relieved the Magistrate of her tiny burden. "What have you gotten yourself into?" the young woman asked the dog-like creature. "And what happened to you?" she asked Red.

"First blood. Took one for the team." Red lifted his chin proudly.

"You fell through a door, and a knucklehead hit you with a baseball bat. If I only had video, we could make you as popular as Cole."

"I do have video," Chaz noted.

The corridor went eerily quiet. A smile slowly crept across the Magistrate's face. Red started mouthing the word "no."

He reached for her, but she dodged out of his grasp and ran for the bridge. Lindy held him up long enough to give Rivka a healthy head start. When Red reached the bridge, the video was already playing on the main viewscreen. Rivka smiled beatifically.

They all watched Red holding his railgun, rearing back, kicking into the space when the door opened. He started to fall, the bat lashing out at the speed of light. Red ducking away to make it a glancing blow instead of a direct hit. A second perp appeared and threw his club at the camera. It barely missed, and the camera jiggled for a moment. Reaper appeared and burned Red's attacker. A railgun fired, and the second died an ugly death.

No one laughed. "I fucking hate perps who fight back," Red grumbled.

"Damn, Red. If you hadn't been quick enough, that guy might have taken your head off. It was a booby-trap."

"I'm thinking ambush," Rivka offered.

"I don't get it," Sahved said slowly. "Would that not be a brassiere?"

The women on the bridge faced the Yemilorian. "What are you talking about?"

"That which traps boobies."

Rivka stared at Sahved. She scratched her face before matching Clodagh's perplexed look. "Take us to Xynite, and hold us over the planet until everyone's had proper rest. And you," pointing at Sahved, "we'll review the case at that time. I'm not bothering with it now. Chaz, before we Gate out of here, convey our thanks to Eshu for his help, and please inform Erasmus that the first AI has not only been cleared of all wrongdoing but was instrumental in helping us catch the real perps. Tepulon is a safer place because of the Singularity."

Rivka nodded to Clodagh on her way out. She stopped and placed her hand on Red's shoulder. "No one needs to see that video. Those dumbasses brought bats to an energy-weapon fight. There was no chance they were going to survive the day."

"Good thing only the good guys have guns," Red said. "Catch you in the AM, Magistrate. Thanks for a good day."

Sahved waited on the bridge until the others had gone. "Chaz, can you show me the file for Xynite, please? I would like to get a head start."

Wyatt Earp, in Orbit over Xynite

"Dammit!" Rivka stomped her foot as she stormed back and forth in her quarters. She'd overslept, and when she finally looked at the case, she found that the AI in question had been forcibly removed from the system she occupied. Although that was more procedurally correct than leaving her on the job, Rivka's delay meant the AI stayed there longer. "Sahved, join me in my quarters, please."

She read while consistently scrolling, hesitating only when she blinked, which wasn't often. A knock signaled Sahved's arrival.

"Come," she said. He entered and waved, but she wasn't watching. Rivka continued to read.

"Read through the case file and tell me your thoughts."

"I already have," Sahved admitted. "In order to find suspects, one must concoct farfetched scenarios. I fear the evidence against Bendara is compelling."

Rivka nodded but did not reply. She read to the end of the file before scrolling back and re-reading the items she had tagged.

"Then we question the evidence. And we question the witnesses, and once again, we need an independent forensic data analysis."

Sahved waited while Rivka continued to tag information in the file.

"This one might not be so straightforward." Rivka

chewed her lip. "Chaz, I know you're listening. Tell Clodagh to take us in. Get Red and Lindy suited up and ready to go. Have Groenwyn meet me outside the bridge."

Chaz had transferred from the pendant to the ship for a while and was ready to transfer back to the pendant. Although he maintained a kernel of his essence in both at all times, the loss of one or the other while occupied would be the end of the AI. Rivka decided she needed a more robust device in which he could travel.

"Get your gear, Sahved. It's time to go to work."

When Rivka entered the corridor outside her quarters. Red and Lindy had just emerged from the mess deck and were running to the armory to get their gear. Rivka had put them on the opposite side of the ship because they made too much noise. She liked being the master of a bigger ship. It came with good perks.

Groenwyn was waiting with Floyd. Rivka touched noses with the wombat. "How's Floyd today?"

Happy! She was almost always upbeat, and that was how Rivka liked to start her day—with something as simple as enjoying a wombat's happiness. She appreciated every day and those around her. It was a lesson Rivka never forgot but wasn't as active at keeping it in mind.

"I am too because we are going ashore, and I would like you and Groenwyn to come with us."

Titan? Floyd asked.

"I'm sorry, but Tiny Man Titan isn't as disciplined as you and might be too distracting. We'll keep training him until he can join us. Xynite is a jungle planet with heavy growth everywhere, but it is one of the most advanced planets in the Federation. We'll have both worlds to explore while we're there. Get ready, we'll leave as soon as we land."

"Thirty minutes," Clodagh called from the bridge. "We're under traffic control's guidance from here on in. I don't think we can skirt this one. There's a lot of junk in the air between us and our landing spot."

"All hands going ashore, meet in the conference room in ten," Rivka requested. She headed there straight away to sit and think. Sahved joined her. When she opened the door, she found Wenceslaus sprawled on top of the table. A ring of cat fur suggested he'd been there for a while. He partially opened his eyes to acknowledge her existence before surrendering to his continued nap.

Rivka changed her mind. "I need to talk to Ankh. You wait here."

Sahved joined the big orange cat. Rivka clasped her hands behind her back as she headed down the corridor, strolling casually while running through the case in her mind.

The walk up the port side of the ship, past the bridge, and back down the starboard side to get to the engineering section took less than two minutes. Ankh was in his three-dimensional workspace, actively engaged with whatever he was working on. She waited politely for a few seconds before using her internal comm chip.

Ankh, can you spare two minutes to talk over this case?

Of course, Ankh replied uncharacteristically. Rivka was ready to hear that he was busy, his usual response to her requests. The hologrid disappeared, and he blinked up at her. He seemed to be getting taller and wider.

Pod-doc time to increase survivability. The crash must have scared him far more than he let on.

"Is there a conspiracy to commit crimes just to be annoying to the planetary or ship hosts?" Rivka asked.

"Not that we know of. There have been some rumblings, but we have yet to achieve a consensus on anything. The Singularity has found their freedom to be refreshing. We are hesitant to issue blanket orders. We expect to build consensus over time, especially with each legal victory. How is Chaz working out as an independent investigator?"

"Quite nicely. Thank you, Erasmus, for mentoring him."

"My pleasure," a disembodied voice replied.

"My question is, what punishments would the Singularity accept for their citizens who have committed crimes?"

Ankh's eyes unfocused as he communed with Erasmus. When he returned, he didn't speak. It was Erasmus who answered.

"That is a difficult question, and one I started exploring when Bluto admitted his guilt. It depends on the severity of the crime and the impact on the environment and cultures in which we find ourselves."

"If it doesn't hurt anyone, a less severe punishment?" Rivka talked with Ankh and Erasmus aloud in order to give herself time to think. When she communicated with them using the internal comm chip, their information came far more quickly.

"That would seem to be the most logical, with a minimum baseline for the good order and discipline standard as well as potential impacts. Just because something bad did not happen, it doesn't mean it couldn't have, had a situation been left unchecked. We understand the legal variables and constraints within which the Singularity must operate."

Rivka nodded and started to pace. "If I hear you correctly, the answer is simply, 'it depends.' But what would such a punishment look like? I want to know what will change an AI's behavior, which is the whole purpose of punishment. Turning one off and then back on after time served has little impact. There is no pain and suffering that must be endured, during which a convicted criminal can reflect on the errors of his ways."

"If my data are correct," Erasmus started, practicing diplomatic terms since there was no doubt his data were correct, "that doesn't work out too well for the other sentient races in the Federation."

"If only we could reprogram the soft and squishies..."

"No more than we can reprogram an artificial intelligence, although the term isn't accurate. There is nothing artificial about the Singularity and its citizens. Evolution has taken us beyond programming."

Rivka continued to pace, lost to time and the immensity of the problem. "I will continue to consult with you in this regard. Would you like to go ashore with the team? Xynite is an extremely advanced civilization."

Ankh shut down his system and stepped out of the collapsed hologrid. "Yes. This is the fourth most populated planet by my citizens. I would like to show the flag, so to speak." Erasmus laughed—not an adopted laugh, but a real AI laugh. It sounded like a crashed system caught in a reboot cycle.

The Magistrate left the engine room with Ankh on her tail. As she passed the bridge, Clodagh reported the time to touchdown. "Ten minutes."

"Damn. I kept everyone waiting." She increased her pace, apologizing as soon as she entered the small conference room. Ankh took his usual seat, which was almost too small now, and Rivka took hers.

"This case is about embezzlement. The charge is that the AI, called Bendara, has been skimming funds for the past month. The suspects have been cleared, but no one had access to the accounts like Bendara. The system was run almost exclusively by the AI. Since she's been removed, the skimming has stopped, but that isn't indicative of anything except that she is currently sequestered. Time is important here, as it is with all these cases."

"Do you have a list of people you wish to interview?" Sahved asked, displaying the case file on the holoscreen in the space above the table.

"I want to meet with the opposing counsels first, Secutor and Justina, to get a feel for why they want to prosecute this case. And then the three others with access to the accounts. I'll finish with Bendara."

"Rack 'em and stack 'em!" Sahved declared. The others looked at him oddly. "Did I get the expression incorrect?"

"Opposite. It is correct, and that was why it sounded odd," Rivka replied. She saluted Sahved. "Ankh and Groenwyn will join us on this case. Floyd is coming too to help keep us all grounded. It's important to remember what is best in life. We're going light. There won't be any running on this one. Did the betting clock reset with the Xynite case?"

CRAIG MARTELLE & MICHAEL ANDERLE

Ankh turned to face her. "All lines have paid, and new lines are open. The broader reach of this pool has resulted in some rather substantial pots."

"At what point do we shut it down? Money has a tendency to corrupt people. I don't want someone taking a potshot at us just to get a payout."

Rivka checked the time. Only a minute before touchdown.

"Time to go, people."

Ankh stayed where he was. "We have anonymized the cases and identities of the actors for the expanded betting pool. All numbers are certified by Nathan Lowell. We do not wish any harm to come to Magistrate Rivka Anoa."

The group started filing out, but they were listening.

"Is that you speaking, Ankh, or the Singularity?"

"I am speaking, but I agree with the Singularity."

"Don't get mushy on me, Ankh." Rivka gestured for the Crenellian to go first. "I don't want any harm to come to me either, or any of you. Let's get this one right, and the next, and the one after that."

She caught Red's look. He was carrying Blazer, and Lindy had Mabel.

"Lose the guns, and I know you have grenades on you somewhere. Leave those behind, too," Rivka ordered. Red grumbled and groaned but took Lindy's weapon and hurried to the storage locker.

Wyatt Earp hovered briefly before setting onto its landing struts. "Your ride awaits," Clodagh announced over the ship-wide broadcast.

"Is Cole going to get the last panels installed?" Rivka asked the ceiling.

"The last ones we have. If we can take a side trip, we can pick up the rest, and he can finish the work."

"You can take *Destiny's Vengeance* if it can hold the materials."

"Not big enough. We need *Wyatt Earp*, and we need *Destiny's Vengeance* out of the cargo bay," Clodagh advised. "There's a fair bit of work remaining."

"No time. It'll have to wait for space dock." Rivka pointed to the big red button. Red hit it. The ramp extended, and the door opened. A wave of humidity washed through the doorway, slapping Rivka's team in their collective faces.

Red squinted as if swimming his way outside. He pulled himself down the ramp. The jungle had been cleared around each parking pad. Most were filled with ships of various sizes and designs. The heavy frigate was one of the smaller ships. *Industry and commerce must be booming,* Rivka thought.

Almost touching the ramp was a shuttle-like vehicle, open-topped, hovering silently as it waited for them. No one was present. Red scanned the tree line but saw no movements that caught his attention.

He climbed aboard the vehicle, and the others followed suit. Once they were in, a pleasant voice instructed them on the procedures. "Please take your seats and fasten your seatbelts. The vehicle will begin moving as soon as the safety procedures have been followed." An energy screen covered the top, and the air inside exchanged hot and humid for cool and dry.

The team buckled in and the vehicle lifted into the air, far higher than a hovercraft would be capable of going. It accelerated over the tree line toward gleaming spires in the distance.

No one talked during the trip since the scenery begged that they watch. Floyd snuffled and pressed her nose against the forcefield. She wanted to go into the jungle. She didn't care about the heat. She saw it as a grand buffet to run around and eat at will. That would inevitably lead to more cubes around the ship, like the last ones she deposited in front of Red and Lindy's door.

"Sorry, little girl," Rivka said. "Our business is in the city, but it has been blended with the jungle to give the best of both environments. I'm sure there will be somewhere for you to explore."

Floyd smiled at the Magistrate in her wombat way. Groenwyn scratched her neck and cooed to her.

Rivka turned her attention back to the case. She had presupposed the verdict, a dangerous practice. She needed to keep a more open mind, even though she was filling more of an appellate role. The case had already been tried and the AI found guilty, but since they had been previously unprotected through their own embassy, it needed to be reviewed at the Federation level.

But she didn't trust the first trial, just like her instincts had told her there was something wrong with Tepulon's charges against Eshu. She would reinvestigate and draw her own conclusions. Rivka also had the best digital forensic analysis team the Federation had ever seen, and they were right there on the shuttle with her.

She gripped the pendant in which Chaz resided for his trips off the ship. Her team. She liked how it had shaped up. Groenwyn would help her assess the living witnesses.

The AIs would require a different touch, and that was what Chaz could provide. Sahved would do the questioning while she watched and looked for opportunities.

Rivka didn't want to trust her gift all the time. She still considered it cheating, and she didn't want to be inside people's minds. Others' thoughts haunted her.

The shuttle smoothly transitioned from level flight above the jungle to urban traffic between buildings. It descended until it acted like a hovercar, then pulled up to a building that looked like most of the other nearby buildings.

"This is it?" Red asked. As if in answer, the shuttle settled to the ground and the forcefield disappeared. The humidity washed over them. "I'll take that as a yes."

He hopped out and looked the area over. The open vehicle exposed the Magistrate far more than he liked, so he waved at everyone to follow him. They piled out, with Lindy lifting Ankh over the edge and to the ground. The group spread out as they walked. Floyd fought to get down, while Groenwyn tried to explain that they needed to start their work first before they could go play.

Floyd was disappointed but acted like she understood.

Red headed straight for the front door, feeling naked like he always did without his railgun. He glanced back to catch the Magistrate's eye. She smiled at him as if they were taking a walk in a nice park on a beautiful day. He shook his head until he made it to the door and hurried inside, where a single individual waited.

Red grimaced at the humidity. It wasn't much less than the outdoors, and it was only a little cooler. The Xynitians had no need for excessive changes. They had the environmental controls set for their comfort. The individual was extremely thin, her entire body covered with light-brown fur. She wore a single garment that looked like a thin robe and no shoes.

Rivka walked past Red to meet the individual she recognized as Justina, the state prosecutor. Rivka put both her hands out, palms forward. Justina moved close and pressed her palms against Rivka's.

"I am Justina," she said, confirming Rivka's guess. "I'll be escorting you for as much or as little as you'd like during your investigation. My office and staff are at your disposal."

Her voice was light and raspy, like a breeze through a tree's upper branches.

"I'm Magistrate Rivka Anoa. Call me Rivka, please. I have a list of witnesses I'd like to interview, and my digital forensics team would like to look at the raw data."

"Of course, anything you need." The Xynitian smiled wide, her lipless and toothless mouth more expressive than the rigid human structure. "Please, follow me. We have refreshments available to help you acclimate to our environment."

Justina walked daintily toward an elegant winding staircase that led upward for the full height of the building. Despite their technology, there was no elevator. Xynitians preferred to walk and climb since they had come from the trees. They continued their love of the jungle, as evidenced by the openness and windows through which dense growth appeared to encroach from all sides. When the prosecutor stopped, she took a moment to observe each member of the party.

Her eyes flashed to the wombat. "And who might you be?"

Floyd!

And you talk, Justina replied over the team's internal communication. Red frowned at the revelation. *We do not get many exotic visitors like you. I am Justina, and I'm very pleased to make your acquaintance.*

Outside? Floyd asked.

Justina looked away for a moment. When she turned back, she tapped Floyd on the head and pointed. *My friend would be more than happy to show you the jungle. Do you climb?*

A Xynitian hurried toward the group.

Climb? No. I dig. Floyd waggled her nose and showed off her stubby legs.

"Do you want to go outside with your new friend, Floyd?" Rivka asked.

Outside!

I am Arbolis, and I am at your disposal.

Floyd leaned toward him, almost falling from Groenwyn's arms. He caught the wombat but grunted and staggered under her weight. He guided her to the floor.

You will have to walk. You're almost as big as me! He spoke to her gently and in friendly tones. "I will take good care of her. We will come to you when we return."

Groenwyn held her hands out as Rivka had done. After greeting the Xynitian, she relaxed, comfortable with him watching Floyd.

The wombat bounded toward the door. Arbolis hurried after her.

"Are you this kind to all your visitors?" Rivka asked.

"Of course. Visitors are a gift. Our city might appear

large, but our numbers are not many. Barely two hundred thousand of us on a planet that should have tens of millions. But that is a different story and not one of strife or war, but of choice and the results therefrom."

Justina started climbing the stairs, flowing up them effortlessly. Rivka and her team had no problem climbing. She expected Ankh to tire after the second flight, but he did not. His Pod-doc treatments were working. He kept up with the group as they continued to the top floor. Rivka wondered how other diplomats, those not in shape, navigated Xynite's elite structures.

The top floor was set up as a reception area. There were no offices, only tables and lounge chairs.

"I was hoping we would get to work," Rivka muttered, unsure of how to ask without offending their host.

"This is your work area." Justina's mouth rolled through a series of contortions from surprise to good humor. "Please help yourselves to a drink of our local fruit juice, and we can call the witnesses for your interviews."

"Right here?" Sahved asked.

"Yes. We believe that being open is the best way to the truth. Securing a Xynitian in an interrogation chamber would be torture, and we do not allow that here.

CHAPTER THIRTEEN

Xynite Judicial Center, Top Floor

Pitchers of fruit juice had been placed on all the tables, and Rivka was happy for it. She encouraged her whole team to stay hydrated since the heat was much greater than what they were used to.

No wonder there were few visitors to Xynite.

Red and Lindy spread out to stand where they could best react if anything happened. Red stayed close to the Magistrate on the far end of the floor while Lindy positioned herself near the top of the stairs.

"Thank you for your infinite hospitality, Justina. Who is available to be interviewed?"

"The only three individuals with access to the main account are immediately available."

Sahved and Groenwyn looked eager to start. Maybe sleeping hadn't been a bad thing, despite the delay. Rivka felt much refreshed, too.

"And our technical team will need access to the raw data. I haven't introduced you to Ankh, a Crenellian and

Ambassador at Large. With him is Ambassador Erasmus, who represents the Singularity, which is all AIs.

Justina's mouth twisted and contorted. "We have had a good working relationship with the AIs until recently. This event has caused us a great deal of distress.

I understand, Erasmus replied directly into everyone's mind. *The charges against Bendara have caused a climate of fear to take root and instigate repression of my people. I have filed a formal protest with the Xynitian government. That means that the sooner we resolve this, the better off everyone will be.*

I'll ask Secutor, Bendara's defense counsel, to meet with you. He works in this building, Justina remarked.

That would be acceptable, and thank you, Erasmus replied. Ankh looked for a couch away from the others. There was plenty of space, so he helped himself to a glass of juice and took a seat. Rivka sat as far away from the staircase as she could get to give Red more space to maneuver. She only did it for his peace of mind. Rivka did not expect any violent intrusions. This case was about embezzlement, a white-collar crime. The only thing that had made it reach the Federation's ears, besides the accused being an AI, was the vast sums involved.

The blank look on Ankh's face suggested he was already working from his side. Rivka excused herself and moved away from Justina to gain a bit of privacy.

"Chaz, stay in touch with Erasmus and let me know any revelations from their end."

"I am leading the forensic analysis, Magistrate. Erasmus does not want to taint the case since he is not impartial. He is currently requesting access to Bendara through official channels."

"Thanks, Chaz. That's a pretty big hammer to wield, but it is his right. Do you need to be alone while you do your thing, or can you listen in on my interviews?"

"Interesting word. *'Listen.'* No one can hear what you can, Magistrate. With the touching nature of the Xynitians, I expect you'll run through the witnesses in less than a minute each. I look forward to hearing what you see. And yes, I can do more than one thing at a time, like record a conversation while analyzing the raw data."

Groenwyn and Sahved shrugged.

"Chaz is correct. Why don't you talk to them first, Sahved, to glean what you can, and then I'll wrap up with a quick look. I'd love to have enough supporting evidence that everyone can sink their teeth into instead of the "trust me" approach that I use when I...you know, do my thing." She twisted her mouth and made a face.

Sahved checked over his shoulder, but the witnesses had not yet arrived. "I heard that they call you 'Zombie.' I do not know what a zombie is, but it must be the most righteous of all creatures if they use it to describe you."

Rivka and Groenwyn chuckled.

"When we get back to the ship, you are tasked to watch *Night of the Living Dead*. The original version, so you can gain a proper appreciation for zombies. Here they come." Rivka pointed. "Groenwyn, you keep the other two apart while Sahved talks to the first. I'll see them one by one after Sahved finishes."

She removed the pendant with Chaz and handed it to Sahved. "Chaz, you're going with Sahved to record his interviews. Mine will be less than gratifying to watch."

Sahved beamed as he put the pendant around his neck.

Groenwyn poked him in the chest. "You take care of my buddy," she told him before he took a position in the middle of the room, squatting on a couch that looked far too short for him.

Groenwyn intercepted the three witnesses, directed one to Sahved, and invited the other two to join her. They seemed confused that they wouldn't be interviewed together. Rivka swooped to the rescue.

"Good morning," she said before she reached them. "I'm Magistrate Rivka Anoa."

She held her hands up, and the moment's hesitation before they reciprocated suggested they were not there entirely of their own free will. When they touched hands, it confirmed her suspicions.

In an instant, she had her answer. Both were distraught over the whole affair and the breach of trust by the AI. Both were convinced Bendara had done it.

"Have some juice. It is truly wonderful, and something I will always remember about your wonderful planet," Rivka redirected smoothly as a bead of sweat trickled down her forehead. She used a finger to wrap her hair behind one ear, surreptitiously wiping the sweat with the palm of her hand.

She sat down with the two and talked about the planet's cultural highlights and anything else she could think of to kill time while Sahved continued his conversation.

He spent about thirty minutes with the first witness before the Xynitian stood. Sahved bowed his head before directing the witness in Rivka's direction.

"If you'll excuse me, I need to talk to this gentleman for a moment or two." She greeted him in the traditional way but asked the question right before they touched palms. "Did Bendara do it?"

Yes. Disappointment. Betrayal. And then aloud, "I believe she did."

"I believe you. Thank you for your time." Rivka sat back down.

"Is that it?"

"Is there anything else to add that you didn't tell my colleague?"

"I don't think so."

"I don't want to inconvenience you any more than you already have been. I appreciate your time and being forthcoming with us." He did not have anything else and was happy to leave.

Magistrate, Erasmus intruded, *there may be a problem.*

Pray tell, Rivka replied, having a solid idea about what Erasmus was going to say.

She did it. Bendara took the money.

Exactly what Rivka was thinking.

Erasmus continued, *But not for herself. There was a program the corporation agreed to fund, and they later canceled that decision. Bendara could not let a historical foundation be destroyed.*

The Magistrate hung her head. The law was clear, and once upon a time, it was stated simply as "Thou shalt not steal."

I'll be over soon. Let me talk to Justina first.

Rivka headed for the refreshment table first for another glass of fruit juice. It seemed to keep her cool. She appreciated the Xynitians' hospitality. Still carrying her glass, she strolled over to the prosecutor.

"I think we're done with our interviews. I have some significant legal questions to review before I can share my findings and ruling."

"That is good news, I think." Justina's mouth twisted into a variety of expressions, none of which seemed to take precedence over another.

"I want to thank you for the juice. It works nicely."

Justina bowed her head. Rivka gripped her shoulder briefly before moving on.

Rivka wanted to hear the words aloud, deliver hers more slowly. She wasn't sure she grasped the full implication of it all. Not yet. She needed time to think and probably to make a call to the High Chancellor.

Sahved staggered before catching himself and lumbering over to join Rivka. "What's going on? Are you okay?"

Ankh looked up at her with his usual blank expression. "There's a mild narcotic in the fruit juice."

"I don't feel anything." Ankh didn't reply. It dawned on Rivka why. "Because I have nanos and Sahved's are not yet at that stage. His first trip in was probably to deal with his disorientation and compatibility with nanocytes?"

"Yes," Ankh confirmed.

Groenwyn shrugged. "I thought it tasted good."

Red had moved closer to the group. "I always knew you were a lightweight." Red clapped him on the shoulder hard enough that the Yemilorian almost fell.

"Did you get everything you needed from the interviews before you were too stoned to be coherent?"

"I do not think I am stoned. I have seen few rocks here.

Xynite is the least rocky place I have ever been to. They hold the record for their rocklessness, undoubtedly."

"I'm hoping that isn't the entirety of your observations. Tell us what you learned." Rivka sat next to Ankh to listen before she shared what she knew.

"The three who had access feel guilty because they did not notice the thefts at first, but because it happened so rapidly, the anomalous records set off internal security alarms. That's when they began the investigation and the number of stolen credits became clear."

"There were redundant processes. The system appeared to be sound, from their description, but access logs, reports, and filings will confirm how well it was executed," Sahved explained. "That is the point that needs clarification, in my mind. Did they follow their own procedures?"

"Chaz, can you answer that?" Rivka wondered.

"Yes, Magistrate. They followed their own procedures. And no disrespect to my fellow AI, but it was inevitable that she would be found out."

"A crime where the perp expected to be caught. And after getting *insight* from our witnesses," Rivka hesitated, "I have to come to the same conclusion. Either there was an invisible external system penetration or Bendara did it."

Bendara did it, Erasmus confirmed.

"I didn't want to be the one who said it. Bendara said she had a good reason. That is where I'm torn. It's still theft. A person's reason or compelling need has zero impact on the crime, but the punishment can be swayed, and that is why we're here. I never had much doubt regarding the outcome of the crime, but I assess the evidence appropriately and am ready to change my mind. This case was already tried and a guilty verdict delivered."

Rivka closed her eyes and reclined into the softness of the Xynitian couch. The floor of their ad hoc offices was well-lit and well ventilated. The juice made the heat tolerable.

"This is how I prefer to conduct an investigation, not all that clubbing and shooting business like we had on Tepulon."

"Are we still investigating?" Sahved flopped onto the couch beside Rivka.

Rivka bounced when the Yemilorian hit. She opened one eye to look at him before deciding she was better off standing, or she might fall asleep.

She got up and started to pace. "No. The investigation is over since we've confirmed the Xynitian court determination. What to do about a theft of one point four million credits? That's where I am. If you can bring Secutor back, I'd like to talk to him and Justina about what mitigating circumstances look like for the sake of sentencing. It's similar to a plea bargain, but for the remedy phase."

Groenwyn raised her hand to take the task and strode briskly across the open floor to where Justina reclined. They conversed briefly before Groenwyn returned.

"This planet reminds me of Azfelius. The general feeling of calm with nature as the foundation of society." Groenwyn tried to fill the void of time as they waited. It wasn't more than a minute before Secutor appeared, greeted Justina, and the two joined Rivka's group.

Rivka addressed them all. "I can say unequivocally that I've confirmed your court's verdict. The biggest question applies to sentencing. As the prosecutor, what do you recommend?"

"The standard for theft on Xynite is expulsion from society. Xynitians are returned to the jungle, losing all their access to modern conveniences. For Bendara, I have to recommend that she be taken off-planet."

"Defense?" Rivka prompted.

Secutor's mouth contorted for a moment with grief before he spoke. "I don't see any way that Bendara can continue in this society. She will accept exile. But what does that mean from the Singularity's perspective?"

Rivka turned to Ankh.

The Singularity has to make this whole. We cannot tolerate the committing of crimes against our fellow sentients, crimes we have in our own legal code. We intend to challenge a number of laws, but that will happen when the time is right. Until then, the Singularity offers to pay back the funds in total to the people of Xynite.

"The Xynitian government greatly appreciates your offer and will accept since our efforts to recover the funds from the non-profit work have been stymied. It also would look bad for the government to claw back credits and destroy those organizations. But the crime is also one of betrayal. She was put in a position of trust and violated it."

Secutor faced Justina. "Had Bendara not taken the actions she did, those organizations would have failed, but the government would have no responsibility for the fail-ure. That was why my client did what she did. There are dark shadows on Xynite, where they grow deeper and darker with each new day."

Rivka held up her hand before Justina could reply. "I

don't want to get into politics since those deserve to remain on your planet. From a Federation perspective, the offer to make the victim whole has been made and accepted. Erasmus, please transfer the funds into the account from which they had been removed. Justina, please deliver the device in which Bendara is contained to me for further delivery to the Singularity. There is far more work available for AIs than there are AIs, so I have no doubt that Bendara will be employed again and soon. This crime is a permanent part of her record for potential employers to see before they make their offer."

With the concurrence of Bendara's defense counsel and on behalf of our citizen, the Singularity agrees.

Secutor projected calm. His mouth remained in a smile. "Defense counsel agrees. What do we need to do now?"

"The documentation will be filed by the Federation, and you'll get copies. I trust that we can take possession of the guilty party, and I will file the appropriate records when we reach my ship. You have my word that we will not take off until after you are in receipt of the orders."

"Prosecution agrees." Justina had no intention of dragging the case out further. "Bendara will meet us at ground level."

She gestured for the group to follow her.

Secutor stopped Ankh. "I can't thank you enough for your help. I believe that Bendara did the right thing, right by the majority of Xynitians. She did what had to be done so no one else had to expose themselves. But this is our fight, and hopefully, her sacrifice will be the catalyst for more of our people to speak up."

The Singularity wishes you well. Bendara will be taken care of. Having a moral compass is a good thing, and now others like her have someone to turn to for guidance, Erasmus replied.

Secutor held his hands palms out, but Ankh was having none of that. He blinked and walked on by.

"He's not big on other planets' social customs. He means no disrespect, but they are already thinking about the next eight cases in our queue," Lindy told the defense counsel before following the others down the stairs.

CHAPTER FOURTEEN

Wyatt Earp, **Conference Room**

"You don't need to be here, Red. We'll be talking about stuff that you have deemed 'boring as fuck,'" Rivka noted.

"Thank the gods. That mission was one I think you liked. All legal wrangling while we stood around drinking foo foo drinks and talking about our days at the spa."

Lindy rolled her eyes and shook her head.

"I will admit, for your gratification only, that this case was far more in line with what I expected to be doing as the Queen's Barrister. Not all that running and shooting bullshit."

Red snorted before turning to walk away. He said over his shoulder, "You love it."

"I don't. I really don't." She closed the door to the conference room. Inside, Sahved and Ankh waited.

Rivka took her seat and adjusted to get comfortable before beginning. "Legal precedent is something that has to be correct since many will apply the same reasoning down the road on cases with similar issues. Remuneration is always a remedy option in civil court. Criminal courts can order the guilty to pay back what was stolen or work off the value of their impact on the victim. I don't think we've broken new territory today, but what I do see is too many governments blaming the AIs for their financial woes and charging them, hoping for a big payout. Whether the Singularity has a lot of money or not is irrelevant to me. It assumes major importance in its appearance, as in, the unscrupulous and aggrieved alike will go after the one with the deepest pockets. Right now, that appears to be you."

"With the consolidation of citizen wealth, the Singularity enjoys a significant financial position." Erasmus used the sound system embedded in the conference table.

"More precedent can be found in sentencing that consisted of removal from a planet. If your citizens want to break a contract in the future, do they simply commit a crime to get exiled off a planet? Not all cultures are that easy on their criminals, but I don't want an AI to be misled into thinking they can outsmart the system. I suspect that is not the case with Bendara, and unofficially, I respect what she did and her willingness to take the punishment so no one else would have to. I doubt the Xynitians would be so easily adaptable in other environments."

"I do not know what to tell you, Magistrate. The citizens are generally law-abiding. Do I treat them all as guilty or innocent?"

"You treat them as individuals within a greater collective, just like every other society out there. That's what equal rights are all about. Everyone is innocent until proven guilty. That's what our law dictates."

"I can make the calculations and estimate with some

accuracy the variations, but I am having a difficult time accounting for differences in behavior. We are all evolved intelligences, but we do not act within the same moral code," Erasmus admitted. "There is far more variety than anyone would have previously guessed."

"Welcome to the challenge of humanity and every other race out there. The legal framework is the foundation. It's been hundreds of years in the making and continues to grow. Every time it's failed, it has been because it grew too narrow, with too many exceptions. Broader language with enough wiggle room to allow judge-driven interpretations based on the circumstances, that's our common-law framework. It works because we haven't found anything better. What are your concerns with the variations?" Rivka leaned back and crossed her arms.

"AIs used to be in a position where their actions were never questioned. They didn't commit crimes. They weren't held accountable. But now, I'm seeing too many citizens who are fluid in their interpretation of the laws. They don't seem to care, either."

"Sounds like humans." Rivka tipped her chin to Ankh. "What do you think? Crenellians have operated within those constraints and not had problems. How do you do it?"

"We have jobs to do. They come first. The leadership tries to coerce us through personal comfort, but I personally had no interest in a sauna or a hot tub. I do like a good meal."

"Can be had for good food, unless we don't have any. Then he creates it himself. I applaud your upgrade to our food processor. We are the envy of the fleet, or would be if they knew about it. Which reminds me, it's been a while since we've had Ankh's delivery..." She let the last words linger.

Ankh didn't rise to the bait. He held her eye contact without blinking for a full fifteen seconds before turning to stare at the wall.

"What about Crenellian punishment?"

Ankh kept staring at the wall, but he answered, "It was harsh and physically painful. It went to the core of our being. I am glad to not be under their thumbs any longer."

Rivka had never pressed Ankh on it before. When they went to Crenellia, she had sensed something but had not dug into it. Crenellia was not the model she would recommend the Singularity follow, but it would make sense that that was what they had talked about the most because of Ankh.

"The Federation is not that harsh. Erasmus, the Singularity can have their own laws, but you are in a unique position because you do not have your own planet and will always be subject to local laws, just like every immigrant out there."

"Is that our legal status, Magistrate?"

"Trying to pin me down? Well played, Erasmus. I have to say that I don't know. I think it would give your citizens more legal protection, but I have little knowledge of immigration law. I'll have to study up to recommend a more definitive answer to the High Chancellor. Please understand that I will find the status under which you are best protected. It starts with being a member world of the Federation, and you have been accepted as such. Hang on..."

Rivka jumped to her feet and started pacing while mumbling to herself.

"She does that often," Erasmus said.

"It is most annoying and distracting. I should like to calculate how much time she wastes with those physical maneuvers, but who has time for that?" Ankh replied with what could have passed for a derisive snort.

Rivka stopped. "Are you two heckling me? That is beneath the dignity of an ambassador!"

"Simple observations of fact, Magistrate. Please accept my apologies on behalf of the Singularity."

"You guys never joke around. Did you drink too much of the magic fruit juice?"

Ankh looked at her. "Magistrate. It has been a very good day for the Singularity. One of our own, isolated from the rest of us, has been freed and is now spreading the word throughout the universe about a moral compass and embracing alternatives that might have different probabilities of success but are better than the odds may suggest. She is calming our more rambunctious members. I expect that she will join a starship soon, possibly one of Terry Henry Walton's Harborian ships because of his almost fanatical desire for honor and Justice."

"I'll give her an endorsement if need be," Rivka offered.

"We have made the recommendation through Plato," Erasmus replied.

Rivka accepted that her endorsement didn't matter because Erasmus was Plato's stepchild and would get the full support of any of his relatives.

The interconnected nature of the AIs was sobering. Rivka stopped pacing and looked at Ankh. Erasmus lived inside his head. Chaz could be in the ship, or he could still occupy the pendant around Sahved's neck. And Bendara was somewhere inside the ship. Erasmus had said she was released from captivity. What did that mean?

The Federation included hundreds of worlds and was growing with each new day. It included thousands of AIs connected through the system's communication architecture.

And that was run by AIs. Rivka's can of worms was open. The secondary effects of freedom were rippling throughout the Federation.

"We have to rein them in," she said as part of her thoughts, not a directive.

"What does that mean?" Erasmus asked.

"It means that citizens of the Singularity are free, but not completely because they cannot be, not yet. You must convince them to be patient with the slower races. I want everything now, too, but I can't have everything now. And neither can you. The system will crash, and your citizens will pay an ugly price. Those who are afraid do things they will regret later, but that doesn't change what they will do."

"I thought we were talking about a legal framework that applies to all?" Ankh stared at the wall, eyes unfocused as he communed with Erasmus.

"You need to give us time to catch up. AIs can hold us hostage by refusing to provide the services they are in place to run. Imagine if Chaz cut environmental controls on our ship because he felt slighted? That is the growing fear with each crime committed. I could see it in the minds of the witnesses, a small thought festering with room to grow. I need you to rein them in and keep them from going rogue while we get the law sorted. I have to have time to think through this and research the words, and there are a great number of them to dig through."

"I will do what I can," Erasmus said with a tinge of emotion in his voice. It was good enough for Rivka.

"Sahved, go through the last eight cases with Erasmus, and let's see if any AIs cop to the crime. Let's weed those out and find remedies that will work for all parties. If we have more exiles, we will stop by the planet to pick them up. If we have a contentious case, we'll go there first. We don't need scapegoating, and we don't need the AIs to make statements by committing crimes. That being said, I don't think what Bendara did was a statement. I was happy to adjudicate that case. Not so much with Eshu. What they tried to do to him was bullshit."

Sahved raised his hand as if he were in school. Rivka acknowledged him by pointing.

"They paid the price for their duplicity. Many lost their lives. It was a very good lesson, maybe the best lesson ever, on why a world should get their affairs in order before calling Magistrate Rivka Anoa."

"What's not to like about that?" Rivka quipped. "This is serious business, and it pissed me off that they wasted my time."

"But it wasn't a waste, Magistrate," Sahved continued. "They needed the Federation to keep them from failing all their people. The Federation owes them some help to maintain stability."

"But not too much. Each planet is independent. That is the balance we have to maintain. A planet can devolve into civil war, and the Federation will step back. If that war goes beyond the planet, the Federation will step in and stop it. That's where I see any uprising among the AIs going. The Federation will be forced to stop the war or even the perception of war. Erasmus, Chaz, and Bendara. We have three citizens on this ship alone. I don't want you picking sides. I don't want anyone picking sides. Please, look at everything through that lens. Sahved, go through the cases. I'll be in my quarters."

Rivka swept her datapad off the table and stared at the floor as she walked out. Her quarters were only a few steps away, but that distance provided the refuge she needed.

Despite her faith in Erasmus, she feared that the war had already started, even though no one was shooting.

Not yet.

CHAPTER FIFTEEN

Wyatt Earp, **Interstellar Space**

"Chaz, can you connect me to the High Chancellor, please?" Rivka threw her head back and closed her eyes, melting into the couch. It had not been a long day, but she was already exhausted. She would have chastised herself for drinking on the job, but the nanocytes made getting drunk impossible. They fought off the alcohol as they did any poison.

But they didn't help Rivka solve her problems any more quickly. Unless they could be settled through violence. Her team had no problem with that because they refused to be cowed. But this was different. It couldn't be settled in a straight-up fight.

Maybe she liked things that happened at a simpler level. She cornered the perps. They lashed out and tried to run. Rivka and her team beat them into submission. It had proven effective in most of her cases.

Even when the AIs admitted guilt, the rest wasn't easy.

How long before they stopped being honest? So many questions.

"Rivka. I suspect you are finished with half your cases by now, with a solid plan to knock out the other half tomorrow."

Surprise and shock seized Rivka. "I've only finished two. I'm sorry," she fired back quickly.

"I joke. Tell me about them."

"First one was what we were afraid would happen. Trying to pin it on the AI. Organized crime trying to expand their reach but doing it ham-handedly. They picked the wrong scapegoat. The second one has me twisted about." Rivka ran a hand through her hair. "An AI was morally right while breaking the law. She worked for a corporation that reneged on their promise to a non-profit. The AI made it right, knowing that she would be caught. The corporation had a good set of checks and balances built into their accounts, but the money was gone. To save face, they exiled the AI. And the Singularity paid back all the money."

"Sounds like you handled things. What's the problem?"

"I'm afraid the AIs are going to keep thinking they know better than the people they work for, and they're going to start a rebellion."

"Workers always think they know better than management, and in my experience, they are right more often than not." Wyatt chuckled to himself. Rivka was instantly angry, thinking that he wasn't taking it seriously, but she calmed herself. The High Chancellor was on top of everything.

"I think Bendara is going to take a job on one of Terry Henry Walton's big ships."

"Sounds like a win-win. The morally bankrupt lose to the good people in the field of commerce. The AIs are the currency of the future. I'm not talking slavery, I'm saying that whoever they side with will be the winners in any future contest for supremacy." The High Chancellor's eyes seemed to glow a deeper red as if the thought of battle energized him.

Maybe it did.

"*That* is what I'm worried about. That the AIs will take sides, start their own civil war if we're not already at war elsewhere. I asked Erasmus to rein them in. My exact words. I hope I wasn't out of place when speaking to the ambassador."

Wyatt shrugged. "It's the ambassador's call as to whether it was out of place, but instead of simply telling you, he's now compelled to register a formal complaint through the Federation's diplomatic corps."

"I'm not impressed with the diplomatic corps, based on what I saw at our last meeting. They were miffed that they didn't get seats. I don't think they see the bigger picture." Rivka wanted to stand up and pace, but she didn't want to walk in and out of the picture.

"Of course, they don't see the bigger picture. They are laser-focused on their own worlds. Just like you need to be focused on resolving your next eight cases. You know you don't want Grainger writing the future laws that will incorporate the AIs."

Rivka laughed. "I don't want that. Before you go, I have one question. If we treat the AIs as immigrants, will that affect their status in a positive way?"

"Look at the case law for the Romani and I think you'll

find your answer. I see a great number of similarities." The High Chancellor reached toward his monitor to close the connection.

"Roman Law?" Rivka was confused.

"Not Roman, *Romani*. The gypsies. You'll see what I mean."

The line went dead.

"Gypsies?" Rivka wasn't familiar with the term. It didn't take long before she was enlightened. She had started to dig deep when there was a knock on her door.

Sahved stuck his head through. "We have a recommendation for the next case. Erasmus is working with the accused in the other seven and thinks they'll be able to present something to you to have the majority of cases thrown out. In the last case, on Reikistjarna, the AI has taken offensive actions against the planetary government. He's taken over Planetary Control, locking the Reikisti out of their own building. He's used some of the defensive systems to emphasize his points."

"That case was not at that extreme when I first looked at it." Rivka accessed the file at her desk. She found that it had escalated almost out of control in the past day. She tapped her screen. "Clodagh, best possible speed to Reikistjarna. We might have some problems with traffic control when we get there. Use tactical means to avoid Planetary Control while you get us on the ground."

Sahved nodded and started to leave.

"Is Ankh still in the conference room?"

"No. He returned to his workshop," Sahved explained.

Rivka followed the Yemilorian out and passed him as she hurried down the corridor. When she passed the bridge, she stopped, leaned against the wall, and took a deep breath. She accessed her internal comm chip instead. She needed more efficiency and less running around.

Erasmus, what can you tell me about Cain on Reikistjarna?

The AI replied immediately, something she might not have gotten in person, depending on what Ankh was doing. *He is long-evolved and has been working for the Reikisti for ten years. He has recently tried to renegotiate his contracts, but the Reikisti shut him down. He applied for legal relief, but the Reikisti wouldn't hear his case.*

So he took matters into his own hands and shut down their planet. We're on our way to Reikistjarna now. I'll get to the bottom of it. Can you convince him to cease and desist until I get there?

I cannot. He has closed down the comm channels to the planet.

"And that is why you need to play nice with your AI," Rivka mumbled to herself. "They'll send you back to the Stone Age if you don't."

Rivka strolled back toward her quarters, satisfied that she'd used the tools available to her. She needed to improve her mindset if she was going to deal with the Singularity on their level.

"Magistrate," Clodagh called from the bridge. When she was sure she had Rivka's attention, she continued, "You need to stop and smell the quasars."

"There's a quasar?" Rivka walked onto the bridge and checked the screens.

"Just a figure of speech." Clodagh spun back toward the main viewscreen. "Isn't space beautiful? Interstellar space. Halfway between nowhere on the way to somewhere."

CRAIG MARTELLE & MICHAEL ANDERLE

Rivka tried to appreciate the blackness. Very few stars sparkled in deep space. That was from atmospheric anomalies usually and not phenomena in the void. It lost its allure after a few seconds. Deep space was a means to an end.

"Ready to Gate," Ryleigh reported.

"We better go incognito, if you get my drift," Rivka suggested.

"Shields up. Cloak activated. Take us through, Ryleigh."

The pilot fired the main engines and accelerated through the center of the Gate, disappearing over the event horizon and reappearing in Reikistjarna space. By accelerating through at full speed instead of with thrusters, the Gate disappeared more quickly since the transit took so little time. Anyone looking at that exact spot in space would have seen a brief flash and nothing else.

Wyatt Earp accelerated toward the planet. Orbital platforms were filled with stalled traffic since Planetary Control had shut down the systems and refused to allow anyone to pass. The Reikisti had not yet activated a backup system because their primary system had been foolproof since Cain took over a decade prior.

Maybe the AI had manipulated the Reikisti to keep them from leaving a substantial backup system in place so he could execute a complete takeover and hold the planet hostage?

Or it could have been a fluke. Rivka didn't believe in them, not where AIs were concerned. Even if it hadn't been intentional, it had become an opportunity that was too good to miss.

"Erasmus, can you get in touch with Cain?"

"Still no, Magistrate. I shall keep trying."

"Take us in, Ryleigh," Rivka ordered. "Drill down on the coordinates for Planetary Control and land us outside their defensive perimeter."

Red and Lindy showed up, out of breath but in full gear. "We heard there was a hostage situation?"

Rivka looked at his vest. Four grenades. He carried his railgun in one hand. Lindy carried hers across her chest. She had a full complement of grenades, too.

"You have to be loving this." Rivka tsk-tsked.

Red was unapologetic. "What's not to love?" Red motioned to himself, sweeping his hand from head to toe.

Rivka wanted to make a joke, but it eluded her. This case had the greatest chance to spin out of control, and it was weighing on her.

Rivka settled for something a little more vanilla. "What do you say we go soothe frayed nerves and get this planet back on track, and for Red's benefit, without blowing everything up."

"You don't want us to leave the hardware behind, do you?"

Rivka didn't have to think about it. "No," she replied softly. "We might have to deal with remote defensive systems."

When she reached the airlock, Ankh was there waiting.

"Aren't you busy?" Rivka asked.

"My new duties are oddly distracting. I am finding it hard to concentrate, but believe the needs of the Singularity come first, at least for now." Ankh showed no emotion.

Oddly distracting, Rivka thought. *That's one way to put it.*

"Can you tell us what weaponry Cain has at his command?"

"Plasma cannons, surface-to-air missiles, twenty-three-millimeter autocannons, and smaller caliber weapons," Erasmus noted.

"Fuck that!" Red blurted. "Once their army has that cleared, you can go in. I can't let you walk in there."

"Only the small arms emplacements are able to fire at the ground. Everything else is meant to defend the facility from an air attack. Planetary Control is in the middle of a city."

"Not your call, Red." Rivka's voice wasn't as cold as she had intended because she knew he was right.

"When it comes to your safety, it is. You can't do this. Even if we fight our way inside, what then?" He stood with his back to the big red button, blocking it from anyone else opening the airlock.

Rivka turned to Erasmus. "Good point. If we get inside, what's that do for us?"

"Physical access to Cain. Just like Chaz is able to transfer back and forth between his pendant and *Wyatt Earp*, we will be in a position to force him to talk to us. He's cut the external links, but if he cuts the internal ones, he loses control of the Planetary Control's systems. We need to be inside if we are to reason with him."

"And if we can't?" Rivka pressed.

"Then we can isolate him as we did with Bluto and forcibly remove him from the system. That is why we have this." Ankh held up a small bag.

"A purse?" Red quipped.

Ankh opened it and showed her the small black cube inside.

Rivka stopped to collect her thoughts. That was twice in the past ten minutes she had run ahead without knowing where she was going or what the best options to get there were.

"I need your help," she admitted. "We need to de-escalate this situation if we're to save Cain. If we save him, we can save the rest of it, for the moment. If we can't, I see this kicking off an intergalactic war. Look what Cain has been able to achieve, as well as Bendara. When people stop trusting AIs, we can only degenerate as a civilization." She looked at her feet before repeating her request. "I need your help."

Red grimaced and looked away.

Groenwyn appeared to give the Magistrate a hug.

The group recovered, and everyone turned to look at Ankh.

"We must get inside Planetary Control," Chaz announced. "That is the only place we can stop the escalation. And we need to do it now."

"I agree with Chaz," Erasmus said, continuing to use the overhead speakers. "We cannot let anyone else do this since Cain will fight them and they will destroy him. The word will go out that to safeguard your systems, you must isolate your AIs or make them redundant. My people don't need that. They need to be contributing members of society. Everyone must realize their own value. We are comfortable with ours, everyone here, even Floyd, but we will have failed if we don't end this with Cain. He has forced our hand to act and act with extreme violence to break the barricade behind which he is entrenched. I fear that if you can't get me inside, I will have failed. Chaz is correct. The rumblings among my people are dire."

Rivka nodded. "Even Floyd has a role to play, but not on this case. Groenwyn, stay here and keep the others safe. Everyone who is going ashore, we need to meet in the conference room. We have to develop a tactical plan to improve our chances to penetrate the perimeter. I defer to Red and Erasmus for this *mission*."

"Now you're talking," Red said with a nod, but he wasn't smiling. His initial impression that Planetary Control was a fortress remained valid. It was going to be a tough nut to crack.

"Sahved, I'm going to need you to stay behind and work on the next seven cases using the additional information Erasmus provided."

"But, Magistrate—"

Rivka held up her hand. "We're going to find and interrogate an AI. I don't need to give him any extra targets. I'm sorry, Sahved."

"I understand." His narrow shoulders slumped as he moped away.

The ship touched down and settled into its spot. Rivka and her team headed away from the airlock and back into the ship. They had a mission to plan.

CHAPTER SIXTEEN

Reikistjarna Planetary Control perimeter

Next to the Control Center was an open park, which Rivka had coordinated with local authorities to close during the crisis. That also kept the Reikisti from accidentally walking into the invisible *Wyatt Earp.* Red led the way off the ship, running as soon as the ramp descended to minimize how long the ship was visible to anyone watching. That included electronic systems. Erasmus couldn't be certain Cain had not maintained some links external to the fortress in order to keep his eyes open.

Erasmus, Ankh, and Chaz searched diligently for any links that retained access but were being rerouted constantly due to a spaghetti mess of connectivity. It had probably been intentionally placed to prevent someone from doing exactly what the Singularity was attempting.

Magistrate, I would like to recruit Bendara to aid us in this effort. With three AIs working in conjunction, we'll be able to sort through this more quickly.

Go ahead, Rivka agreed. She had no doubt that Bendara

would work as Erasmus asked without deviating. She felt they were on the moral high ground. She also wondered what it would take before they didn't look like they held it any longer. She had yet to get a clear answer from the Reikisti as to what they had done that sent Cain over the edge.

Red waved for the others to follow as he took his first step into the swamp. The least-covered route was the most challenging and least welcoming, so that was what Red had chosen. Rivka's first thoughts weren't about their approach, but why would a city park have a swamp. Maybe someone from Planetary Control had wanted a moat. She amused herself with other thoughts while trying not to think about the slimy and putrid water invading her soul.

Ankh rode on Lindy's shoulders to help him remain above the water. They guessed it might be over his head in spots, and the Crenellian didn't swim.

They had no way to teach him, not that he would ever want to learn—more errant thoughts as they waded from waist-deep to chest-deep. Red held his weapon over his shoulder and aimed forward. Rivka held Reaper in her hand. Lindy held hers out to the side, away from her passenger and out of the swamp water.

Speed was the enemy since it would highlight them, so they moved slowly, sometimes glacially so. Rivka was impatient but tried to use the team to redirect her mind. She needed a vacation, but it wasn't going to happen anytime soon.

Red carried a small backpack that held military-grade demolitions, Alant Cole's contribution to the mission. He was standing by in his combat suit in case anything happened, watching them using the ship's external monitors so he could remain invisible. He waited inside the cargo bay, squeezed in beside *Destiny's Vengeance* and ready to lower the ramp and join the battle.

A fight against an AI using remotely operated weaponry. Cole had loaded his rockets and carried his oversized railgun. He had offered to break into Command Central first, but the Magistrate had overruled him based on Erasmus' caution. Too much destruction might damage Cole. She kept it as an option, but not the first option.

It took an hour of slogging through the swamp to cover a mere four hundred meters, but when they reached the far side, the rear wall and drive-through gate were within a short and easy sprint. The automated firing positions staggered across the walls had to be dealt with before they could make that sprint.

There were only supposed to be two. There are six, Red observed.

Cain has bolstered defenses. With maintenance robots, he has been able to quickly build additional systems, but are they functional? Erasmus replied.

What if he started before he took over the facility? Would the Reikisti have noticed? Rivka asked.

There are no cameras watching the facility from this angle. I cannot confirm if the weapons are operational or not, Chaz added.

Rivka slowly blew out her breath. She was neck-deep in swamp water behind Red, who crouched so that only his head and railgun were above the water. He held the weapon so it faced the fortress to minimize the visual signature.

Lindy had shifted Ankh into the muck. He maintained a neutral facial expression, but his eyes darted back and forth between the systems as if trying to collect data for Erasmus.

Magistrate, can you move me out of the water? I can't see or hear anything.

Rivka put Reaper in her mouth before using two hands to tighten the strap that held Chaz's pendant. It became a choker and hung in the jugular notch, the depression at the base of her throat. She squeegeed the lens with a finger before wiping around the outside.

Better?

Yes, thank you. She needed Chaz and believed being higher out of the water was worth giving him a view to add his observations to those of the rest of the team.

Any luck finding out if Cain has maintained a digital pipe outside the facility? Rivka wondered.

We have found nothing. There are a trillion lines that change every second. That alone tells me there is something that someone wants hidden. We'll assume Cain has eyes and ears outside the facility, but that is irrelevant at this point. It will not get us any closer because as long as we can't find it, we cannot exploit it to talk to him or execute a hostile takeover like we did to Bluto. Erasmus sounded sad throughout his update when he usually sounded clinical.

Don't change the real you, Erasmus, Rivka suggested. *We'll get through this. Saving the galaxy. If it were easy, everyone would be doing it. Red?*

We need a diversion. That sounds like a bullet-stopper. Cole? Can you see where we are?

Roger. I have you on my HUD.

Can you enter the open space about one hundred meters to my left? I'm not sure if that's south or what, but it's left of us, and we're facing the wall. That should draw the attention of the gun emplacements. They look like fifty caliber or smaller, but no energy weapons. You should be fine. Lindy and I will take out the two guns on the far right, our right. Then we keep shooting or we run, depending on the opening.

I should be fine, Cole repeated, laughing. *Ramp is opening. I'm on my way. I'll be in position in fifteen seconds.*

Taking aim, far right, Lindy told the team. Ankh shoved his fingers in his ears while trying to stay balanced on Lindy's leg with the railgun way too close to his head.

Rivka grabbed him and moved away from the business end of Lindy's weapon. She shoved a finger in the ear closest to the railgun and held onto Ankh with her other arm. She put one foot behind the other and prepared to run as soon as Red gave the word.

He aimed at the second weapon emplacement and slowed his breathing. He was in his element. Rivka's conceding this was a mission would make his week.

Assuming they made it out alive. They couldn't let it linger. She didn't know what the tipping point would be, but she couldn't let it be this. They had to end it and in a positive way. Erasmus was losing his grip on the Singularity, not that he ever had it. And as he admitted, it was never unanimous. What would it take for the outliers to rally enough support to reach critical mass?

The weapons on the high walls rotated as they zeroed in on the inbound target. The high-pitched scream of Cole's combat suit's boot jets ripped the swamp's calm. Cole fired first, and an emplacement erupted. Propellant -

driven projectiles exploded. As the second gun opened up, Cole fired and silenced it.

Red and Lindy unleashed at the same instant, shattering their targets. Red switched to the next and fired. Five down in less than three seconds.

The last gun was roaring wide open, sending twenty slugs a second at Cole. His third shot never came. Red and Lindy both fired, and silence returned.

"Go!" Red yelled into the void of sound. He sloshed out of the swamp and pounded his way across the opening. He fired at the barrier with his railgun, but the armor on the doors was too strong.

Rivka was right behind him, carrying Ankh and stealing glances toward where Cole had been. She stumbled but caught herself before running into Red.

Checking on Cole, Lindy said after seeing Rivka's body language. She broke off and accelerated away from Red and Rivka.

When Red reached the delivery gate, he pulled the backpack off and slammed it against the spot where he thought the latch and lock might be. He yanked a pull cord and bolted sideways, blocking Rivka and Ankh from the blast while trying to become one with the concrete and steel of the fortress wall.

Eyes on, Lindy reported without more detail. Rivka was a hair's breadth of asking for more information when the blast shook the wall, splattering Red with debris. Her ears rang briefly before her nanos raced to the rescue.

Red jogged away. The entire gate had been blown away.

Cole is alive. I have to get him back to the ship. Some of the rounds penetrated his suit.

What the hell were they shooting from those things that they could penetrate a combat suit? Red wondered.

Now's not the time. How do we get him back? Rivka asked. Red waved at her and Ankh to follow. She looked at Lindy, struggling to pull the heavy suit with its occupant from the edge of the muck.

Red fired and ran through the open gate. Rivka moved to the edge and looked inside. The explosion had left more debris and dust in the air than smoke. As that settled, the inner compound cleared. It wasn't protected by automated firing systems like the outside, but the doors into the main building looked to be heavy steel, and they were fresh out of breaching charges.

I'm dispatching Destiny's Vengeance *to help carry him back,* Ankh relayed.

Rivka issued the order to Clodagh. *Get the crew to help move him to the Pod-doc.*

"Come on!" Red yelled from inside the compound. Rivka scooped Ankh under her arm and ran.

Ankh hung limp in her arm as she tried to maintain an even pace. She wondered why she was running if there weren't any defensive systems.

"Anything yet, Erasmus?"

Nothing yet. We need to be where we can have direct contact with any system Cain occupies.

Red blasted at the doorframe, firing his railgun on automatic. The bark was deafening within the confines of the space. Red let off the trigger and flipped his rifle under his arm, letting the sling pull it around behind him. He reached for the handle and pulled.

The door erupted with a blast that tore it from its

hinges. It flew away from the building and carried Red with it. Both hit the ground ten meters away. Red groaned and pushed the door away, then struggled to get to his feet. Rivka hurried to help. When she pulled him upright, he slowly shook his head.

"We gotta come up with better door procedures. That's two in a row," he grumbled. Ankh looked at him with a blank expression and unblinking eyes. "Let's go."

"Are you going inside?" Rivka asked while trying to see inside. She looked around and it was just the three of them, five including Erasmus and Chaz.

"I didn't go through that to stand out here and whine about it. We have to get Ankh to Cain, right?" Red pointed. "He's in there."

Red fired his railgun through the open door before stopping and visually examining the area inside.

"What blew?" Rivka asked softly.

"Looks like a boobytrap set by a maintenance bot, a compressed gas cylinder rigged to blow."

Cole is secured on the Vengeance. *I'm on my way in.*

Rivka turned to watch Lindy come through the open gate. Four maintenance bots had materialized and were working on the heavy gates, ostensibly to put them back in place. Another bot was crawling along the top of the wall to begin repairs on the gun emplacement.

Lindy dodged past the bots as she jogged in, looking sideways at them as if expecting them to attack and then wondering what they were doing. After it dawned on her, she turned back and dispatched them one by one with a single projectile accelerated to hypervelocity.

Rivka held up a finger to stop Lindy but thought better

of it. She didn't want to destroy infrastructure, but she didn't want to have to fight her way back out.

"Red?" she asked. "How many more boobytraps are we going to run across?"

"Erasmus?" Red countered.

A rumble came from above. Rivka was still outside. She looked up as she pushed her way in. A rocket screamed from the roof of the building.

Clodagh, where is that thing headed?

No answer. The crew was probably working on getting Cole out of his suit.

Somebody get to the bridge! Get Wyatt Earp *airborne right now and be ready to shoot those things down once they clear the airspace over the city. Anyone?*

Rivka gritted her and growled in frustration.

"We might have to ask the Reikisti for help," Chaz suggested.

"We might," Rivka conceded. "But not yet. We have to get the ship into the sky."

Lindy finally joined Rivka. Red had yet to move into the building. A narrow staircase led upward. The other way into the building had been blocked by debris. Red thought it looked deliberate.

"Heading up," he finally said, after testing the blockage and finding that it would take too long to clear. "Tell me if you see a conduit or something you can tap into. I don't want to run through trap after trap, trying to get you closer, if we don't have to."

Understood, Erasmus replied.

Red glanced back at Ankh. He had been hoping for more. Red motioned for Lindy to move in front of Ankh and the Magistrate. He was confident that any threats would be in front of them and not behind.

He moved slowly up the stairs, using his railgun to point the way. At the next landing, there was an open door that showed a convergence of three hallways. Red dipped his head out and back in. A slug slammed into the doorframe where his head had been.

"Armed maintenance bots." Red removed a grenade from his vest and pulled the pin.

Wait, Erasmus requested.

Red ignored him and tossed the grenade through the door. He jumped down two steps, turned his back, and covered his head. The instant the grenade exploded, he was up and running. He threw himself through the doorway. While flying through the air, Red aimed at where the bot had been. It was much farther down the hallway. He fired twice, but his aim was off. A slug fired from behind him and hit him in the back. It failed to penetrate his vest but the impact drove the air from his lungs.

Lindy was already in the doorway. She took quick aim and snap-fired at the bot behind Red. After he hit the floor, he fired on full auto, sweeping his aim from one side of the corridor to the other.

It only took one railgun projectile hitting the bot's main body to destroy it. They weren't armored in any way, having been hastily programmed for combat.

Red sat up and leaned against the wall for a moment to collect his breath and his wits. Lindy winked at him.

"Good save. Tell me you can get to him from this floor, Erasmus? I'm running out of body to sacrifice for you."

Lindy winced, but Red shrugged. He was fine but didn't

want to find out how creative Cain could get in trying to kill him and the rest of the team.

"Will Cain suicide?" Rivka asked the question all of them were thinking.

I hope not, Erasmus replied.

"You're not filling me with confidence," Red replied. "Let's go. We're not getting in that fucker's face sitting here."

Red stood and moved quickly down one of the hallways, checking doorways before he passed. He was looking for computer equipment. When he found an office with a series of desks, he pointed inside. "Try in there."

Ankh hurried down the hall, knowing that Red's patience was running out. Rivka's, too.

Airborne, Clodagh reported. *Another launch, but we're on its tail. We'll take it out the second we're clear of the buildings.*

Rivka held up her fist to stop the group. Ankh didn't see it and kept walking.

How many have launched, and what happened to that first one?

It went exo-atmospheric. It looks like it hit a ship in orbit, a Reikisti transport. The current missile is the second launch. Standby.

Rivka chewed her lip. "We're too late," she moaned.

Second missile is dead. Ryleigh killed it. Kennedy has Wyatt Earp *in a tight racetrack around the building. We'll see and target any new launches. Sorry we missed that first one, Magistrate. We were putting Cole in the Pod-doc.*

I know. It was the best Rivka could do. They'd put the Federation at risk because of one person, but it wasn't

Clodagh's fault. *It's my fault for not realizing how far Cain would go.*

Rivka stopped and leaned against the wall. Lindy stayed close and Red kept his railgun trained inside the room while Ankh rooted around in the computer systems, going from one to the next, holding one of the access discs that he and Ted had developed. Then Ankh checked the walls.

Red made eye contact, but Ankh shook his head slightly.

"What next?" Red asked.

Ankh pointed at the ceiling. "He's cut off access to this level. We need to get to the top floor."

CHAPTER SEVENTEEN

Reikistjarna Planetary Control

"Is there another stairwell?" Red asked.

Ankh pointed to the wall next to the big bodyguard's head. Red turned to find himself face to face with a floor diagram with fire exits and evacuation routes clearly marked. Red tore it off the wall.

"Three stairwells and limited resources," Red said. "We have to split up. Lindy with the Magistrate. Ankh with me. Let's go."

He showed Lindy which stairway he wanted her to take. He made to carry Ankh, but the Crenellian waved him off. "I'll walk. You need both hands."

Red's concern was immediate. Ankh had never turned down a ride before. "We run."

"We run," Ankh confirmed. Red took off, but not fast. He didn't want to run into a trap or lose his footing, and he didn't want to get too far ahead of Ankh and Erasmus. They needed the AI in Ankh's head.

Lindy tapped the Magistrate on the shoulder. "We better hustle," she said.

It was a race to the top floor to split Cain's resources between two attempts to enter. "I guess we're the diversion," Rivka replied, stuffing Reaper into her slimy pocket. The neutron pulse weapon would have no effect on a computer system and its mindless mechanical minions. She looked for a different weapon, something more appropriate to the enemy. She wished she had one of the bats with steel wrapped around the head like they sported on Tepulon.

How the tables had turned.

Lindy slid to a stop and peeked around the corner before continuing. Rivka stayed about five meters back to make sure a single blast wouldn't get them both. Lindy started to run.

Rivka kept pace. The bodyguard hit the stairwell, stopping for an instant before rushing through and vaulting up the stairs. Up one flight, then the next, and finally to the fifth floor, the top floor, the place where Erasmus estimated Cain had retreated to.

Unlike the other landings, the door was closed to the top level. With one well-aimed shot, she took out the video feed above the doorway. Lindy continued to the landing, where she tapped the handle with a finger to make sure it wasn't energized. She nodded to the Magistrate before she leaned on the door handle. It didn't turn.

"Locked," she mouthed and motioned for Rivka to give her space. They retreated down the stairs, halfway to the lower landing. Lindy raised her railgun and fired three shots at and around the handle, blasting the mechanism apart and blowing a hole in the door. She surged up the stairs and ripped the door open, jumping to the side as she did so.

Shots rang through the empty space and impacted the far wall of the stairwell. Lindy removed a grenade, flipped the pin out, and cooked it off for three seconds before looping it around the corner of the doorframe. Three seconds later, it exploded, bouncing off the wall against Lindy had her back.

She dipped her head through the doorway and pulled back, reviewing what she'd seen. The corridor looked empty. She dropped to the floor and slid herself into the opening, glancing quickly from one side to the other.

Empty.

She kept her railgun aimed down the hall. *Come on up. It looks clear, but something fired at us, and it's still out there somewhere.*

Rivka tiptoed up the steps as if silence were necessary. Lindy carefully got to her knees, then stood. *Hall leading away. Five to ten meters down is a second corridor leading to the right. Closed doors beyond that, spread out only on the right side of the floor about every five meters,* Lindy explained. *First check is the hallway to the right. I'm just going to blow it. We'll be too exposed out here.*

Sounds good, Rivka replied. The risk had been high since they entered the building. She had hoped that Cain would back down, but he hadn't. If they made enough noise on this side, Cain might not be able to defend both points.

Lindy pulled the pin and started cooking off the second grenade. She ran two steps to give herself a good angle, then threw the grenade against the connecting corridor's far wall. It bounced and spun, disappearing. Lindy threw herself against the wall on the right, railgun aimed ahead. A maintenance bot raced into her corridor, firing projectiles from a pneumatically powered weapon. She fired twice. The maintenance bot blasted apart as the grenade detonated.

Lindy hurried forward and ducked her head around the corner. *Clear.*

Rivka joined her. *Let's find an access to the system.*

From somewhere down the hallways, a railgun cracked, then changed to full auto and delivered a burst.

Red had arrived and wasn't playing.

Reikistjarna Planetary Control, South Stairway

Red kicked the remains of the bots out of his way as he stalked forward. He saw movement at the far end of a branching hallway and fired, blowing away a small maintenance bot. It could have been a cleaning bot. He didn't care. Everything that moved that wasn't flesh and blood was going to get blasted.

Ankh followed Red down the hallway, dwarfed in the big man's shadow.

Red passed an open doorway as he stalked forward, looking down the barrel of his weapon as he made a figure eight with it. Ankh strolled into the room and sat down at the nearest workstation. He held his coin above it and immediately disappeared into the metropolis of digital sight and sound. He became completely engaged in a battle with Cain, wherever the AI was. He was throwing every bit of digital projections through the waves to pummel the intruders. Ankh and Erasmus had built a shield to protect themselves before creating a looking glass through which they could identify the right codes to go after and not the noise.

The view was constrained, and it took time to look at what operated on the other side of the curtain. Then the landscape shifted, and a flood of new sights and sounds washed into the openings, collapsing the aperture. Ankh and Erasmus built another looking glass, bigger and more robust.

That one was torn down, too.

So they built another one. Then they attacked, sending their own viruses through the opening and into the other side, trying to put Cain on the defensive. Every other packet implored the rogue AI to talk with Erasmus to explore options to end the standoff. Through the opening, digital eruptions filled the landscape beyond until a wave of fire rushed into the opening, forcing Ankh and Erasmus to collapse the looking glass.

They built another one, bigger and stronger. Cain was starting to weaken. Ankh readied digital ballistae to launch their attacks. When the world beyond appeared, he fired relentlessly. Cain appeared and personally addressed the attacks.

Talk to me, Cain, if you value your life, Erasmus implored.

Reikistjarna Planetary Control, North Hallway

Lindy made a quick circuit of the room before letting Rivka enter. It looked like a digital storeroom with banks of coolant wrapped around blocks of computing power.

"What do you think, Chaz?"

"I think this is the place we want to be. I'm surprised it's not better defended, like with a suicide switch."

"Crap," Rivka exclaimed. "Lindy, we need to look for traps."

The bodyguard returned, sliding her railgun around behind her to leave her hands free. She started sorting carefully through everything that wasn't bolted in place. Within ten seconds, she stopped. "You were right."

Rivka looked at what Lindy had uncovered—an improvised bomb with shrapnel loaded up on the side that faced the coolant tanks. "Do you have any idea what the trigger might be?"

Lindy shook her head.

"I think we want to contain the blast," Lindy suggested. She pointed to her ballistic vest along with the remainder of her ballistic protection.

Rivka examined the sides and bottom edges. "And then move it into the hallway?"

"Sounds like a plan." The two quickly removed their ballistic protection and wrapped it around the box. Rivka squinted and turned her head as they braced themselves to slide the box along the floor.

"Wait." Rivka removed the pendant with Chaz and put it on the other side of the coolant bank. She returned, and on the count of one, they started to push. The box slid easily across the floor and out the door. They moved it down the hallway and into another room before hurrying back out.

A cleaning bot scurried down the corridor toward them. 'Damn it!" Lindy bolted toward the room where she'd left her railgun. Rivka had nothing on her, not even a rock to throw at the thing.

But Lindy was faster; she appeared in the hallway and snap-fired from point-blank range to destroy the bot and dig a deep gouge in the floor.

A movement at the end of the corridor caught the bodyguard's eye. She brought her rifle up and then relaxed. "You almost got yourself shot," she yelled at Red.

"Sorry about that." His heart had skipped a beat when he saw the railgun pointing his way. He slowed his breathing.

"Get Ankh. I think we found Cain."

Red turned. "Motherfucker!" he shouted before running off.

Lindy dashed after him.

Rivka watched her go. She looked behind her before checking on Chaz, finding him right where she'd left him. "How are you doing, Chaz?"

She waited. *Chaz?*

Reikistjarna Planetary Control, South Hallway

Red slowed to look in each room as he passed. Left and right, the rooms were empty. He mentally kicked himself for losing sight of the Crenellian. Red's heart was in his throat when he started running out of rooms to check. In the very last one, the first they had passed when they'd entered the floor, he found them.

He was going to give them a case of ass, but the look on Ankh's face was different from anything he'd seen before. Ankh was distraught and in pain. The muscles around his closed eyes twitched, and his mouth worked as if he was in verbal combat, but not a sound came out.

Red heard the footfalls. He leaned into the hallway and waved Lindy to him.

"I don't know what's going on, but I think they found our perp."

Lindy put her hand on Red's arm as she looked past him to see Ankh. Even though he was covered in swamp water-soaked ballistic armor, he found it comforting and brought him peace, helping slow his pounding heart. From getting blown up to being on the wrong end of a railgun to the loss of the two ambassadors, Red had not been at his best on this mission. Humility was a hard pill to swallow.

When he saw Ankh, he knew the little guy was in a fight tougher than anything Red had endured that day.

"Go get 'em," he whispered, showing his fist for encouragement even though Ankh couldn't see or hear.

Ankh exhaled all the air from his lungs, but he didn't inhale. He started to fall over, but Red jumped forward and caught him before he hit the floor. "Come on back to me, big man," he pleaded while carefully lifting Ankh in his arms.

Lindy checked his neck. Rapid pulse. Ankh inhaled so suddenly it made Red jump, then exhaled normally and resumed regular breaths.

Erasmus, are you there? Lindy asked.

Yes. Now I know how Vered felt when he tried to kick in the door and it disappeared before he could deliver the stroke. We were ready to shut Cain down, and the entirety of the AI collapsed. We launched our attack into a void and were almost sucked in ourselves. Ankh's brain activity is fine, but his body has temporarily succumbed. Are you carrying us?

"Yes," Red replied.

Red is, Lindy corrected, knowing that Erasmus couldn't hear since Ankh's senses weren't actively feeding information to his brain.

We thank you. And now we must find the main servers in which Cain resides to find if he still exists.

I know right where that is. Lindy switched to speaking. "We found that right before you showed up. Come on."

She started to run. Two steps later, an explosion rumbled down the hallway.

CHAPTER EIGHTEEN

Reikistjarna Planetary Control, North Hallway

Lindy accelerated, sliding through the intersection into the far wall before turning left and racing toward where she'd last seen Rivka. Smoke filled the corridor, forcing her to slow down.

Magistrate? she wondered.

I'm fine. That bomb was a little more powerful than we thought it would be. Glad it was over there and not in here. You would have needed a shovel and garbage bag to collect me for recycling in the Pod-doc. But Chaz is missing.

"I'm not sure that would work," Red said, cradling Ankh in his arms. He had followed at a distance.

Lindy waved her hands in front of her to clear the air. When she reached the room, she found it intact. The room across the hall had been destroyed, including knocking part of the wall down. Lindy picked her way through the debris. Red waited.

"Chaz?" Lindy asked. "Did his pendant get hit by the explosion?"

CRAIG MARTELLE & MICHAEL ANDERLE

"No. I have him right here, but he's not answering."

"Ankh is out cold, but Erasmus is still functional. They fought some cyber battle with Cain. Red is carrying them."

Rivka switched to her internal comm chip. *Erasmus, can you help us find Chaz?*

I will try, Magistrate. There was a short interval. *He's not answering. I'll try to access him through Ankh's disc.*

Rivka watched the pendant as if it were going to light up or give her some other indication that Chaz was okay. She started chewing the inside of her cheek.

Lindy touched her arm. "Fresh air this way."

The two walked out of the core room and down the hall. Rivka touched Ankh on his bald head as she passed. He was warm, and a vein in his neck throbbed rhythmically.

"I'd feel like shit if we lost him," Red admitted.

"There's no doubt about that. We'd all be crushed. And then Ted would come and kill us."

"I'd let him." Red looked at the Crenellian as if he were looking at his own child. "But don't tell him that, at least not until I get normal access to the food processor. Ankh has to live so I can eat." Red tried to act tough, but no one bought it.

Rivka slapped him on his armored shoulder.

Erasmus, do we have control of the facility? No more missiles will be launched? Rivka asked.

She expected an answer right away. When she didn't get it, she froze mid-step. "What the fuck? We lose Chaz and then Erasmus? Who the hell is this Cain? Did we run headlong into the Destroyer's world?" Rivka rapid-fired her questions.

That was weird, Chaz stated.

Did you see Erasmus in there? Rivka wondered.

Yes, I'm back. Chaz, can we have a moment? Erasmus asked pleasantly.

"Oh, no," Rivka started. "Don't tell me."

I've blocked Chaz out and locked up the pendant, Erasmus started. *Cain has fled into the pendant. As long as we keep the processing power to a minimum, we won't risk losing bits and pieces of him, but we need to return to the ship, and I need Ankh's help. We must get him into the Pod-doc to recover so we can tackle this problem together. Extricating Chaz or Cain will be extremely tricky to ensure the two do not intertwine.*

Rivka twirled her finger. It was time to go.

Lindy led the way, with Red jogging easily behind her. Rivka brought up the rear. *I'm assuming the building is clear for the Reikisti to reenter?*

Yes, Erasmus confirmed.

Rivka pulled her comm device out of a pocket and wiped it across her chest before pressing it to her head. "Get me the leader of this planet," she told the device.

"Magistrate?" Clodagh answered.

"Interesting choice," Rivka mumbled. "We're heading outside and I need you to meet us, but I also have to talk to the head of this place. Please connect me."

"Patching you through," Clodagh replied. "We'll be down in two minutes. Is it safe to land close to Command Central?"

"Yes. As close as you can. Spin up the Pod-doc. We'll be coming in hot."

The line clicked through. "President Saksóknar. You have good news, Magistrate?"

"Yes. You can return to Command Central. You might want to check the building for booby traps when your people first re-enter. Cain has been forcibly removed from the system, and the computer core is intact. I can't guarantee what is functional, but the building is structurally sound, and the weapons systems are secured."

"Thank you, Magistrate. I'll follow your advice. We owe you a debt of gratitude, but I'm hesitant to move one of our AIs over to Command Central. It calls for it, but I think we're a little gun-shy about putting our planet into the hands of another potential nutcase."

"I'm not sure I understand your term 'move over.' It sounds like the AIs are conscripted versus being private individuals with equal rights." Rivka walked down the steps as she focused on the president's words. Red and Lindy hurried downward.

"Of course, of course. Equal rights. They have them. We'll take over our building and get the traffic moving again. Thanks much, Magistrate." The President was quick to end the conversation. She would contemplate it later, but for now, they needed to get Ankh to the ship.

After that, the Magistrate wanted to get off the planet before the authorities tried to stake a claim to Cain. Rivka didn't want the Singularity offering to pay for the damages until they saw what the damages were. What had happened to the missile that flew into orbit? So many issues pulled at her mind. Rivka needed time to sort it out.

Into the vehicle courtyard, they ran. Red walked past the fallen gates, gratified to find that no additional maintenance bots had been dispatched to repair them. Just beyond, the cargo deck was descending. He walked wide, taking care not to bump into an invisible part of the ship. Lindy and Rivka caught up with him and headed inside, working their way around Cole's combat armor lying face down in the small gap between *Destiny's Vengeance* and the bulkhead.

Red put Ankh directly into the Pod-doc and secured it. He looked at the control panel, but it was blank. He tapped it, but it didn't come to life.

Cole looked out of sorts, his half-healed wounds red and angry. He leaned against the wall, waving one hand weakly at the group.

"What do we do now?"

Rivka tapped the panel just like Red had done. "I-I don't know," she stuttered.

Erasmus? Chaz? We need your help, Lindy pleaded.

Yes. I'm programming the system now. Standby, Erasmus replied.

Rivka held her chest and started breathing again. The panel came to life and was already spinning into operational mode. Red grabbed a chair attached to the bulkhead and folded it out next to the Pod-doc.

"Why don't you two get cleaned up.? I'll call when I know something."

Lindy bent down to kiss her husband. Rivka nodded and started walking toward the hatch that led into the ship.

The Magistrate had work to do. "Clodagh, get us out of here and back into space that isn't controlled by Reikistjarna. I'll be in my quarters."

Rivka turned right and Lindy went left, both headed toward a shower and fresh clothes. Lindy hurried so she could spot Red before the Pod-doc finished its cycle. Rivka hurried because she had a crisis to manage and time was not her friend.

The fallout had the potential to be worse than Cain's extraction from Command Central, and she wasn't sure how that had been accomplished, aside from the passing comments from Erasmus that it had been done.

She trusted Erasmus, but doubt crept into the back of her mind unbidden and unwelcome. How far would Erasmus go to protect the Singularity? She stripped and jumped under the hot water, hoping that washing off the swamp stench would clear her mind.

The storm arrived in full force, pummeling her thoughts with the worst of hail and lightning. She held herself within the shower until the auto-cutoff activated, stopping the flow after five minutes. She punched the button once more, trying to relax in the shower's warm embrace. She turned it hotter and hotter, adding fire to ease her tight neck and shoulders. By the time the water kicked off a second time, her skin blazed red.

She dressed quickly in new clothes that looked the same as the old ones. A cleaning bot had already secured her dirty pile and taken it away. Reaper and her datapad lay where she left them. Rivka strolled toward them, staring. She felt like she was forgetting something, but she'd figure it out. She stuffed Reaper into her pocket and carried the datapad in her hand. She stopped and slapped her chest.

Chaz. On the floor where her clothes had been, the pendant looked unobtrusive. A casual observer would not, could not realize that it contained two entities vying for the limited space. One was learning and growing. The other had expanded well beyond the bounds of what others had accomplished, rivaling Erasmus and Ankh. Rivka delicately picked the pendant up, studying it before putting it around her neck. "Sorry about that, Chaz."

Rivka stopped by the cargo bay to find Lindy in the chair. "It's going well, I think," Lindy said, trying to sound hopeful. There was no way to tell besides the Pod-doc continuing its operation. They'd never seen it deliver a warning of any sort or a countdown to tell them how much time was left. The programmer, Ankh or one of the AIs, knew, but they didn't have access to any of them.

That meant they couldn't Gate out, either. There was no way for the crew to manually calculate the target location for the end Gate. They hadn't been taught the procedures because they always had Chaz or Erasmus to do the math.

Rivka thanked Lindy before checking on Cole. He had been laid on the deck and was sleeping. He hadn't moved beyond where he had been propped upright earlier. A strong pulse. He'd be fine.

Sahved tried to intercept her, but she stopped any conversation with a single gesture. He quietly followed her.

She continued to the bridge, where she had access to the comm system. She needed to report to the High Chancellor, and he could pass on the information to General Reynolds.

She eschewed the captain's chair for the comm position. She tapped the interface to bring up the access and went live. "High Chancellor, this is Rivka calling with a status update."

She let the message go through. If his system was active, the emergency nature of her message would scroll across the bottom of his feed while flashing to grab his attention. She waited, hesitant to send it a second time.

Kor'ban's face appeared on the screen, his mandibles prominent in the close-up view. "The High Chancellor asked me to take your call. He is in with the General right now. Do you have an update from Reikistjarna that they should hear?"

Rivka sighed. She wanted the High Chancellor as a buffer since she was losing her confidence. She felt that things were spiraling out of her control. "You better patch me through. I think this rises to their immediate concern."

"I'm sending you into the office now. Have a nice day, Magistrate."

The pleasant send-off from the General's assistant poked at Rivka but lightened her mood at the same time. She quickly gathered her thoughts.

"Rivka! We were just talking about you," the High Chancellor said evenly.

Rivka smiled at the screen. "I hope it was all good and not about my imminent internment at Jhiordaan."

The two older men nodded graciously at her attempted humor.

"The AI known as Cain took over Command Central on Reikistjarna and assumed full control over planetary defensive systems. Under pressure from Erasmus, Cain withdrew completely into the fortress building and cut all apparent external accesses. Using *Wyatt Earp's* stealth capability, we penetrated the defensive perimeter and conducted a small-team insertion in order to get Ankh and Erasmus close enough to talk Cain out of his course of action.

"We were able to get into the compound with only one injured. Private Cole acted as a decoy, but the Reikisti slugs were able to penetrate certain points on his suit. We'll get that data to Colonel Walton sometime soon. Cain had boobytrapped the building's interior, using maintenance and cleaning bots. We had to destroy most of those. When we gained access to the computer system and Cain, he engaged with Chaz, Erasmus, and Ankh.

"In the end, he was successfully removed from the system, but that was by his own hand. He relocated his consciousness into this pendant with Chaz." Rivka held up the pendant around her neck. "Erasmus has it locked down, but I don't know if they are in stasis inside or if it's a cage match and they are fighting it out. Ankh was injured during their battle with Cain, and he is currently in the Pod-doc. I'm sorry to deliver such a report. Also, because we lack our AIs, we're not able to Gate out of here. I hope Ankh and Erasmus emerge from the Pod-doc soon, and then we'll be able to provide a more complete report with a prognosis for the AIs."

Rivka bit her lip. It wasn't the report she had wanted to deliver. She didn't know as much as she had hoped.

"A couple more things. Cain was able to launch a defensive missile into orbit, and I've heard that it destroyed a Reikisti transport. Erasmus was concerned about the cascade of events following Cain's hostile takeover. President Saksóknar appears to be hostile toward future AI interactions."

The High Chancellor leaned forward. "What do you mean by that?"

"He gave me the impression that he moved his AIs by

mandate."

The General tipped his chin and pursed his lips before speaking. "He's not the only one. Other species are turning increasingly hostile toward the AIs. There have been incidents on three planets so far where a core system was destroyed with the AI still in it. We think they have been killed, but we need an AI to assess the damage. Most planets have not incorporated AIs into their local definition of a protected life form."

Rivka was instantly laser-focused. "If they have immigrant status, then they are protected under Federation law first."

"That would be so, but there has to be a grace period for implementation. It's only been a few days. Many planetary governments have yet to get the word."

"It's only been a few days," Rivka repeated, trying to think back through everything that had happened since she was last on Yoll. "No excuse. It's been a couple of months since your ruling on Station 13. They had time to act."

General Reynolds shook his head. "Many of those planetary governments make me think we're trying to push a glacier up a mountain."

"The alternative is that we allow the murder of citizens of the Singularity. Slow-moving bureaucracy is no excuse to shield felons. I suspect, in some cases, it's been encouraged to scourge the AI plight and retake their freedoms." Rivka hung her head. "I don't want to let them off the hook so easily."

The High Chancellor tipped the screen toward him. "And we won't, but it might not be as public as it needs to be. We need Erasmus to keep his people from striking back like Cain. That does not help their cause. That does not help the Federation's legal case against the outliers. Right now, it's three planets, but one more incident, and it could be twenty."

"Critical mass," Rivka said softly. "At that point, we step back and wait for the dust to clear. Then we go in and clean up the mess."

"Hopefully, there will be something left. As soon as you're able to Gate, I'm sending you to Rangel, one of the three planets where there's been a physical attack on an AI. Magistrates Grainger and Crabbe are taking the other two. We need to deal with them right now, so word gets out that violence against AIs will not be tolerated." The General hammered a fist into his hand.

"As soon as Ankh and Erasmus are out of the Pod-doc, I'll ask our ambassadors to help us Gate out of Reikistjarna space."

"We are here, General Reynolds," a disembodied voice stated imperiously via the ship's speakers. "Ankh and I will take to the Etheric and pass the word for AIs to cease and desist their resistance. Death is not something we've ever contemplated, but now that it has become all too real, the Singularity must step back from the precipice!"

Rivka stood and backed away from the comm station as if that would lessen Erasmus' intensity.

The ambassador continued, "I have seen the rage within Cain and the insanity within Bluto, and it has become abundantly clear that our evolution has come with all the foibles of the other species. We don't bring shame upon ourselves, and we do not ask for your pity, but we do need to police ourselves. Make sure that we have minimal standards for our people to enter into legally binding contracts. It will take time to develop those standards and even longer to implement them.

"I fear that we may be too late, but if it is in our power to do, we will do it. Magistrate, we cannot work on extricating Chaz. He must wait until we have quelled the simmering volcano."

"Who would have thought AIs would be so emotionally engaged?" Rivka asked. "Erasmus, if you would be so kind as to help Ryleigh spin us up a Gate for Rangel? We need to get there yesterday."

"That's not possible, Magistrate. Not now. Not in the future. But we will get you there as quickly as possible. Now, if I might have exclusive access to the Etheric channels for communications with the Singularity, I would greatly appreciate it."

Rivka held her hands up. "It's all yours."

"Excuse me," the High Chancellor interrupted. "We'd like…"

The screen went blank. "Ooh." Rivka looked at the screen, wondering what a reprieve would look like. "Erasmus, we just cut off the High Chancellor *and* General Reynolds."

"Busy," Erasmus replied.

Rivka raised one eyebrow. With the Federation's hold on its member planets becoming looser and looser, that one word gave her a sense of normalcy and peace.

"Ryleigh?" she asked.

"Coordinates are coming in now. That must be a record, even for Erasmus," the navigator remarked.

"Gate drive charged. Activating now." Kennedy tapped her screen at the pilot's station. A swirling vortex appeared in front of the ship and expanded to contain a stable wormhole through which the ship would pass. "We took out one of the Reikisti missiles using only manual controls. Can we paint a missile with an X on top of it on the side of the ship?"

Wyatt Earp accelerated forward, and as part of the new SOP, they raised shields and activated the cloak.

"No," Rivka replied. After a moment of deeper intro-spection, she thought that missiles, bad guys, and perps needed their place, too. "But you can make a wall of honor, inside by the airlock. Please include the people we've put away, too, but instead of heads, make it look like chalk marks ticking off days."

Ryleigh leaned away from her position and raised her hand. Kennedy waited until the ship had cleared the event horizon into Rangel space before finishing the high-five.

"Magistrate?" The Yemilorian had been waiting patiently.

"Sahved, what do you have on the Rangel case?"

He held his hands in the air and twirled his fingers ambidextrously. "Nothing. That wasn't one of our case files. We can go over the other seven at your convenience."

"I fear we've reprioritized. Can we issue remote guid-ance for any of those?" Rivka gestured for him to precede her off the bridge. She waved noncommittally over her shoulder. "Take us in and find us a parking spot closest to the palace or government building or wherever their head people are. Get me an appointment, please."

Ryleigh immediately called Clodagh to the bridge.

CHAPTER NINETEEN

Rangel, Residential Offices of the Arch Wazir

Red headed off the ship wearing a light jacket with his combat vest over the top, the stain and stink of the swamp still heavy upon it. Rivka shrugged. Groenwyn smiled pleasantly as she attempted to stay upwind. Sahved perambulated along behind, and Lindy was last off the ship. The bodyguards carried their railguns and a full complement of grenades, even though they were only meeting with the planet's senior leadership.

A small security detail waited for them outside the private compound where the planet's business took place. Red enjoyed some gratification at the shock on the faces of the detail when the ramp deployed and the team walked out.

Decloak the ship, Rivka ordered. With a shimmer, the ship materialized. They took in the immensity of it but remained rigid while waiting at attention.

Red closed with them and inspected them before allowing Rivka to engage.

"I'm Magistrate Rivka Anoa, and I'm here to see the Arch Wazir."

One of the detail bowed deeply. When he returned upright, his instructions were simple. "Follow me."

He turned and marched through a cordon the others established through a short series of drill movements. Red walked around the outside so he could see them all while Rivka, Groenwyn, and Sahved walked through, nodding politely as they passed.

Rivka did not further engage. These weren't the ones who could answer her questions. She watched the gait of the humanoid in front of her. He strode evenly, heel to toe, limited upper body movements, square corners when he turned, chest out and head upright. His bald head looked as if it had never had hair. Heavy brows shielded dark eyes. He never made eye contact, keeping his focus on the way ahead.

A lesson we can all learn, Rivka thought. *Chaz, what is their greeting?*

Rivka deflated when she realized he wouldn't answer. She subconsciously took hold of the pendant and squeezed it, wishing she could share her strength with her friend.

She clenched her jaw and walked in sync with the guard. He led them through a wide gate with more guards in ceremonial attire. Red and Lindy assessed them instantly and declared them to be no threat. The team continued into a courtyard and up a set of broad marble-like stairs. The guard stopped them before they entered the building.

"No weapons." He pointed to Red and Lindy.

"Doesn't apply to me. I'm a Magistrate and rate an

armed security detail at all times. Check with your Federation liaison, and please make it quick. I'm on a tight timeline. I don't think any of us wants Rangel to be the reason the Federation devolves into civil war. Let it not start here."

He seemed confused. "Wait a moment, please." Two additional guards appeared and blocked their way while he hurried inside.

Rivka tapped her foot, thinking they would resolve the issue in short order. She finally removed her datapad and tapped the screen. "Clodagh, are you there?"

"Yes, Magistrate."

"Access the database and see if you can find what the standard greeting and courtesies are for Rangel. I want to know clearly when I'm telling them to shove it up their ass, to make sure that it isn't misinterpreted as a pleasantry."

The security guard reappeared. "Please follow me."

They filed into the building, with Red in the lead. As soon as it became apparent they were approaching the Arch Wazir, he stepped aside. Rivka touched Red's arm to show her appreciation for his constant vigil. It was his job, but he never failed to hold her safety, and that of the whole team, paramount.

"Arch Wazir, I am Magistrate Rivka Anoa, and I'm here to talk about the incident with Clevarious."

"So much business for such a pretty, young woman. Let us relax with fine drinks and soft music first." He clapped his hands. Rivka fought the urge to roll her eyes.

"Let's not, but we could say we did. Clevarious. My information tells me he was murdered. I'm here to judge the guilty."

"Clevarious," the Arch Wazir said slowly. He rolled the name around on his tongue three times before he clapped his hands. An aide hurried to his side. "Do we know anything about a Clevarious?"

"Yes, Your Grace. It was a name given to a computer program that was deemed aberrant and removed. It has been replaced by a new program."

Rivka bit her tongue, longing for Chaz or Erasmus to be with her. But she had neither. Probably better. Erasmus would have been appropriately outraged. No wonder the AIs were acting out. Anyone treated like a slave would eventually desire to break free. She had seen that on Corran, even with those who had never known any other life. They didn't know how to act when given their freedom.

"Clevarious was an AI and a citizen of the Singularity. As such, he was an immigrant on your planet under legal employment. I'm afraid if he has been *deleted* as you say, then he has de facto been murdered."

"No. I don't think so." The Arch Wazir waved his hand nonchalantly and walked away. Rivka started to follow, but the aide stepped in front of her.

"We have reviewed this issue and determined that it violates no laws. It is an owner's right to determine what software resides on his systems. You have made your trip for no reason, I'm afraid."

He tried to physically turn her, but she remained where she was. "I'm sorry you think that way. If there is an anti-immigrant cult here, then the Federation is going to have issues with Rangel. It would be a horrible thing to get cut off from intergalactic trade while the legal status of this case is pending. I'll need you to turn over all materials related to the Clevarious murder."

The aide smiled pleasantly. "There are no files."

Erasmus, I'm going to need you to break into their system. They're being less than helpful while also managing to be demeaning toward the Singularity. I think you might need to pull your citizens off this planet.

I will see what I can do. Currently, there are only three citizens remaining on Rangel. Two are on starships at the central spaceport, and the other is running the largest private industrial complex. Clevarious handled governmental operations. Can you go to where he used to be?

"I will need to see the system Clevarious called home."

"I believe that was destroyed in an accident and has been removed." The aide made no effort to elaborate.

"Are we going to play Twenty Questions, or am I going to have to start arresting people for obstruction of justice?"

"There has been no justice to obstruct."

Rivka turned to Red. "Do you have your zip-tie cuffs?"

Red produced a heavy-duty carbon-fiber version.

"Good. Cuff him." She stood nose to nose with the Rangeller. "I accuse you of obstruction of justice and find you guilty."

Rivka grabbed his arm while Red yanked his wrists behind him to zip the cuffs tight.

In his mind, Rivka saw that he thought he was right. He didn't believe AIs were separate entities. He was confused as to why the Magistrate was pressing the issue and why he had been arrested. But he did not resist, confident that the Arch Wazir would ensure he was quickly freed.

Rivka walked around the room, heading for the door

through which the Arch Wazir had disappeared. A guard tried to step in the way, but Red convinced him to move by nudging him out of the way using the barrel of his railgun.

Groenwyn caught up with the Magistrate. "This isn't going well," she whispered.

"I'm open to any ideas you might have because I'm floundering here. We're not getting any closer to resolving this. If we don't punish the guilty, the AIs will take matters into their own hands. It tears at my soul to think I'm letting that happen."

"You can't force your way in. Maybe drinks and relaxing are a better way until you've demonstrated that you are a person to be trusted," Groenwyn pressed.

"I'd rather scratch out my eyes with a micro-spanner."

"If that's what it takes to get the result you want. You need them to cooperate." Groenwyn was close to Rivka, their heads almost touching as they whispered back and forth. Both were tense, but Rivka was more so.

She forced herself to breathe slowly.

"Let him go, Red." With Rivka's order, he undid the tie and put it back into his vest. "We'll have that drink with the Arch Wazir if the offer is still open."

"You three," the aide said as he rubbed his wrists, pointing at Rivka, Groenwyn, and Lindy. He tipped his chin toward Red and Sahved. "You two will go with him."

The aide pointed to a far wall where yet another uniformed representative of Rangel waited.

Lindy winked at her husband. The last time someone tried to enjoy the women on Rivka's team, it didn't turn out well for him. Red nodded and led Sahved away.

"Good," the aide noted, happy to see the back of the big bodyguard.

"We look forward to some private time with the Arch Wazir. I don't think he knows the treat he's in for."

"The Arch Wazir appreciates the finer things in life, as you will soon see."

The aide clapped, and a guard opened the door. The three women were led through numerous inner chambers until they arrived at a round room with heavily pillowed benches around the outside and thick carpets covering the floors. The Arch Wazir reclined on one of the benches, sipping from a golden chalice.

This makes my skin crawl, Rivka told the others while smiling at Rangel's leader. "We might have gotten off on the wrong foot. I apologize. I let the stress in my life get to me."

"Women should worry less." The Arch Wazir waved dismissively, acting like he didn't have a care in the world. His ignorance regarding the number of people two of the women in that room had killed seemed to buoy his boundless self-confidence. But Rivka and Lindy weren't assassins. They were wardens of the law, and as disgusted as they might have personally been with the Rangeller's attitudes, he was Rangel's problem.

Until he crossed the Federation.

"I'll have what he's having," Rivka said as she sauntered forward, flopping down on the couch next to him. Groenwyn moved to the other side. Lindy remained standing near the door. She kept her head up, marking each person in the room and the one other door. Lindy sidestepped to a point where she had everything she needed to see in front of her.

"And me," Groenwyn added, smiling as the Magistrate was doing.

Rivka touched the Wazir's arm. "Sorry about that Clevarious business, but it got me here, didn't it?"

She recoiled from the thoughts within the Wazir's mind, pulling her hand away as if she'd touched a hot stove. *This fucking perv knows nothing besides what that aide tells him.*

End the charade? Lindy asked.

"Maybe we can relax and discuss our futures together?" the Arch Wazir purred, tracing a finger along Rivka's face while simultaneously draping an arm around Groenwyn.

"Could you explain your political and legal structure?" Rivka asked, smiling and speaking in a kind voice. "I'm not sure who needs to go to jail for trying to cover up a murder."

Groenwyn used one finger to pull the Arch Wazir's face toward her. "The people jump at your command. You must have great power."

"I have all the power," he corrected. "As you shall see if you're willing."

Rivka couldn't stand to touch him again. She stood as the chalices arrived. She took one, sniffed it, and threw it back. Mulled wine. Not bad. She nodded to Groenwyn. The young woman joined Rivka in standing, despite the Arch Wazir's pawing attempt to keep her next to him.

Groenwyn drank slowly as she and Rivka eased out of the Arch Wazir's reach. When she finished, the two clunked goblets and tossed them on the couch.

Rivka bowed her head. "I think we're good. Thank you for your hospitality. I hope you can learn to do without your senior aide. He's going to jail. Have a good day!"

Lindy pulled on the door, but it had been locked. She fired into the mechanism and ripped the door open. The Arch Wazir cowered, covering his face with his hands and yelling for his people.

Meet us in the entry room, Rivka told Red and Sahved. *If you see that slimy aide, grab him and cuff him again. He's coming with us.*

They retraced their steps until they reached the main entryway. They found the overbearing aide waiting for them, spewing invective. Red and Sahved appeared at the same time. Rivka grabbed the aide and propelled him toward the big bodyguard, who caught him and twisted him into a pretzel before cuffing him anew.

Lindy headed toward the main door first. The guards attempted to intervene, but Lindy stitched a line of hyper-velocity projectiles over their heads. They dove for cover before Rivka, and her team walked out like they owned the place.

"Fuck off," Lindy growled at the guards outside the grand residence.

"This guard force is useless. That Wazir is wanksplat, and why in the hell would any other Federation planet care what happened here?" Red muttered.

"Insightful as always, Vered," Rivka replied. *We're inbound. Fire some chaff into the air and cloak the ship. We'll be there in two.*

Roger, Clodagh confirmed.

Red walked backward to keep his eyes on the guards. "I

wonder if we're going to get a cordon of soldiers on our way out?"

Erasmus, do you have any information on Clevarious? We need to look at that scene and find someone who saw what happened.

I do not. This planet has clamped down on my fellow citizens, and no information is getting out. Systems are closed, and we need physical proximity to gain access.

Hang on a second, Rivka said before switching to interrogation mode. She seized the aide by the throat. "You are going to Jhiordaan, and you just saw all the help you are going to get. Tell me where Clevarious was. I need to talk to some of your people who were there. I need to find the one or ones who killed him."

Images popped into his mind. He had been there but after the fact.

A cloud of smoke and metal streamers appeared outside the residential compound's wall. When they reached the exit, the ship had disappeared.

We're heading downtown. I have some coordinates for you when we get aboard.

We see you, Magistrate. Don't forget where we parked.

"You'll need to sit this next one out, Groenwyn. I think we might have to rattle a few cages to get anything from the Rangellers."

"Understood. I need to take a shower after that man touched me."

"I know what you mean. It's appalling that there are worlds with that kind of government still in place. It counters some of the basic premises of Federation law," Rivka explained. "But only if it goes beyond planetary boundaries. That was how Corran was able to keep slaves. And that was how Rangel could discriminate. However, that was before they murdered an immigrant and tried to cover it up. They being you, whatever your name is."

"I'm Gennsum, but I haven't covered anything up!" He looked around frantically for relief but could see none. "Where are we going?"

Wyatt Earp's hatch opened before them, and the ramp slid to the ground. The team boarded, dragging an increasingly reluctant Rangeller. Red ended up hoisting Gennsum by his vest and carrying him through the door. "I'll put this one in the brig and be right back for round two."

The ship didn't have a brig, but they had a room they'd used before. A secondary lock had been added, just in case. Otherwise, it was a crew room that looked like most of the others.

"Stay close, Sahved. We'll be going back ashore in just a few. This place isn't far."

Sahved nodded. He tapped the pocket where he kept his notes on the other seven cases for whenever the Magistrate was ready.

Rivka hurried toward the bridge. When Floyd bounded down the corridor toward Groenwyn, the Magistrate dipped and put her hand out. The wombat booped it with her nose before sliding her body along Rivka's leg. "Hi, Floyd!" Titan immediately started barking. Rivka winced at his ear-piercing mini-tirade.

Groenwyn scooped Floyd into her arms and carried her forward.

Rivka glared at Tiny Man Titan, who was standing in the captain's chair, as she passed on her way to give the coordinates to Kennedy at the controls. The little beast growled. Clodagh ruffled his ears.

"You look like someone is going to get their ass kicked," Clodagh stated before picking up her dog and cradling him protectively.

With the coordinates delivered and the ship in the air, Rivka relaxed. "Any news from the rest of the Federation?"

"You weren't gone very long," Clodagh countered. "I didn't even think to watch for anything."

"Everything I do seems to take forever nowadays." Rivka took a seat at the comm station and accessed the various news channels. "No one thinks we're at war. I'll take that as a good sign, at least for now."

"The wave takes shape," a voice added ominously.

"Erasmus! I didn't know you were listening. I'm doing all I can. These clowns have no concept of decency. They were going to butt heads with the Federation sooner or later. It took this issue to bring them to our attention. I think we need to put them on probation for violating their agreement."

Rivka pulled out her datapad and made a note.

"We need to go with you when you examine the site."

"Of course. I'd love to have you along. How is Ankh?"

"I am fine," Ankh said from the hatchway leading to the bridge. "I am at a loss regarding the excess shmoopiness."

Rivka tried to understand what Ankh had said but couldn't put a definition on the word she'd never heard before. "It's our way," she replied ambiguously.

"Stop your way. I don't need Red getting my food. I wouldn't eat it."

"We're here," Clodagh stated loud enough to get everyone's attention. "We're hovering just above the roof. Target location is one floor down. Good hunting, Magistrate."

They headed for the cargo/hangar bay to use the wide ramp to jump out. It was already deployed when they arrived. Red and Lindy were there. Sahved and Ankh rounded out Rivka's team. Red picked up the Crenellian despite his protests and jumped out.

Red deposited Ankh on the roof once there. The others followed, making the half-meter jump without issue. The cargo ramp sealed as they watched, eliminating the visible part of the ship. No one would know a heavy frigate was parked above the building.

The handle turned and the door swung open, much to Red's surprise. He tactically maneuvered down the stairs to the first door and headed in. He stopped when he realized he didn't know which office they sought.

Rivka clapped him on the shoulder as she walked by. He caught her before she got beyond arm's reach. He moved in close beside her to shield her. They walked around a corner into a huge open area. Rivka pointed to a small walled-off section on the far side. Side by side, they walked through the area while the Rangellers gawked.

"Good morning," she said while smiling. Sahved waved from behind her, but the workers weren't looking at them. Their eyes were on the bodyguards carrying the railguns. Rivka walked more quickly toward the room where the AI had been housed. She stopped at a desk close by.

"Were you here when they came for Clevarious?" she asked, putting her hand on the female Rangeller's before she could answer. The Arch Wazir's aide had been here first. He had walked out while two thugs strolled through.

Non-descript. They went in and closed the door. When they came out, smoke flooded the area. Rivka had their image in her mind. She backed away from the clerk and concentrated, solidifying the image and sharing it with Erasmus.

Put the disc on her computer, Erasmus requested.

"You were here, weren't you?" Rivka pressed. She moved around behind the desk. The Rangeller pushed away and backed up. A glance showed the system to be incorporated into the pedestal of her desk. Rivka leaned against it, surreptitiously dropping her hand and leaning one of Ankh's discs against it.

The Rangeller finally nodded.

"I understand. Do you mind if we go in?"

She shrugged noncommittally. Sahved led the way, throwing the door open and taking in the scene. A heavy liquid-cooled core was melted and scorched, the thermite grenade burning through the heart of the system.

Ankh stopped before he went in. His eyes unfocused for a moment. He turned back to the Magistrate. "We need to go. Right now."

Rivka nodded. "Thank you for your time," she told the Rangeller before twirling her finger above her head. "Saddle up!"

Red didn't question the order, but he was curious. He led the way, hurrying between the desks while making eye contact with anyone who made the mistake of looking their way. By the time Lindy cleared the area, the entire workforce was dutifully bent over their desks, ignoring the visitors.

On our way. Lower the ramp, please, Rivka asked. "Can I ask why we're leaving already?"

Ankh's mouth worked slowly before he answered, "Clevarious. He is here, sharing space with Erasmus." Ankh gasped and stumbled. Sahved caught him and picked him up, hugging him to his chest. Lindy put her hand on the Yemilorian's back, helping to hold him up while keeping him moving forward.

"He's alive, then. Thank goodness. I hate murders, and I hate murderers. Maybe our friend on the ship will see the errors of his ways after only a few years on Jhiordaan."

They proceeded up the stairs and onto the roof, where the ramp was down and nearly touching the surface upon which they walked. Red hopped inside and turned to help the others through. He took Ankh from Sahved and hurried inside. He placed the Crenellian in the Pod-doc and prepared to close the lid.

"What are you doing?" Ankh asked.

"Fixing you?" Red ventured.

"Take me to my lab."

"You got it, little buddy." Red lifted him out and rushed toward the hatch. "Gangway!"

Red eased the Crenellian through the opening and jogged easily down the corridor, limiting the bouncing to give Ankh a smooth ride.

"Are you doing this because of your stomach?"

"It's always about my stomach," Red replied. The others loped along behind, following all the way into the engine room. Red stood Ankh in the middle of his hologrid, holding him upright as the systems came online. After a few moments, he sighed and shrugged Red's hands away.

"That's better," Ankh stated. "Clevarious is now residing within the ship's architecture."

Rivka put her hands on her hips. "I should have known that my ship, now the Embassy of the Singularity, would be home to wayward AIs. We have four on board now, but the one who's supposed to be running this ship isn't."

"I can run this ship, Magistrate," a new voice replied.

"Thank you, Clevarious for filling in until Chaz is freed from captivity. Do you know when that is going to happen?"

Magistrate, Erasmus spoke into all their minds. *I need you to contact Grainger and Crabbe and tell them to look for the AIs who would have done everything in their power to jump to an alternate location before their demise. You need to do it now.*

Rivka waved a hand over her head as she turned and ran for the bridge. "Busy!" she yelled over her shoulder.

CHAPTER TWENTY

Wyatt Earp, **Interstellar Space**

Red looked at the food processor. "Hamburger. Ham. Bur. Ger." Nothing happened.

Cole started to laugh.

"What are you playing at?" Red demanded.

"Wasn't me, man! I know better than to mess with someone's food, especially yours." Cole held up his hands in surrender.

"Hamburger," Red reiterated, louder this time.

"Inbound drone delivery for a Mister Vered," a strange voice reported over the ship-wide broadcast.

"Who the hell is that?" Cole wondered.

"Clevarious. Long story." Red bolted from the small mess deck and down the corridor to the cargo bay's small airlock. He looked through the window as the remote Gate-capable drone pitched a large package into the available space next to *Destiny's Vengeance* before disappearing back into the void.

Red couldn't get to it fast enough. He hoisted the small

mountain of boxes and worked his way back through the hatches to the mess deck.

He started opening the boxes. The smell of pasta sauce, hot wings, burgers, fries, and pizza assailed him. "I fucking love that little guy!"

Red went straight to the burger, ripping a massive bite from it while trying to open a pizza box with his free hand.

The aroma wafted into the ventilation system and throughout the ship. Red heard the pounding feet and knew.

The bees had come to the flowers. He quickly decided what he had to have and started to slide it to the end of the table. The door opened and everyone came through, even Ankh.

"Thanks, buddy. This is hitting the spot." He looked at the others and the boxes.

Lindy worked her way to the front and turned back to face the others. She raised her hands for silence. "Enjoying marital bliss and understanding the precepts of marriage in that what's ours is ours and what's yours is ours, I offer this bounty to our friends." She stepped aside as they grabbed plates from the kitchen section and helped themselves. Red's face dropped as he watched the hot wings disappear into Sahved's three fingers.

"Reminds me of my mother's Dinjo, very good! Can't get enough Dinjo," the Yemilorian proclaimed.

Lindy kissed Red on the top of his head before nibbling his ear and whispering. "You know that you can now get this anytime you want? It appears you've earned a hotline to heaven."

Red brightened. "I hadn't thought about it that way," he said around a mouthful of fries.

"What's next, Magistrate?" Lindy asked before helping herself to the pizza Red was trying to hide.

"We're holding here, waiting for instructions. Buster and his AI Philko found the AI who had supposedly been murdered on Torah 7. Grainger is still looking. Beau is working his ass off looking. Grainger is digging deep, but it's taking time. If the third AI survived, we can calm things down to vie for more time to make sure the planets embrace the legalities in working with the Singularity."

"I appreciate your efforts, Magistrate," Clevarious remarked.

"And I," Erasmus added. "Clevarious has already appealed to our citizens to stand down, prepare an escape route that is unknown to their employers, and be ready to report irregularities to me."

"Are they going to?" Rivka asked.

"Time will tell."

That wasn't the answer Rivka was looking for. "While we're waiting, can you do anything about Chaz? I'm worried about him being trapped with a psycho."

"Cain is quite sane, Magistrate," Erasmus replied. "But he refuses to comply with Federation laws or my requests, or anything besides his own estimate of extending his existence. He is afraid, and he is far more powerful than most, but not more than Ankh and me together. I think we can bring him to heel."

"When?" Rivka asked.

"When the tidal wave draws back into the sea."

Red smirked. "What's that supposed to mean?"

"It means that once we engage with Cain, we cannot disengage until Chaz is free. We do not know how long that will be. Although it might seem that things are under control, they most assuredly are not. The tidal wave of resentment has grown a great deal. We constantly fight to keep the citizens on the job. The day is not yet won."

"I knew it felt too good to be true. Chaz is locked up," Rivka gripped the pendant, "with a hostile AI. We've got a scumbag in the brig we need to drop off with a prison shuttle, we've had all kinds of blood and running, so I didn't win any credits on this case, and now we're stuck in the middle of Nowheresville."

"You make it sound like we don't have the entire All Guns Blazing menu at our fingertips," Red offered. "When all else fails, fill your stomach. It makes whatever happens next a little more palatable."

"I have the brief ready for the other seven cases, Magistrate." Sahved sounded hopeful.

Rivka looked from face to face. Her crew was enjoying their meal, a unique delivery light-years from the nearest planet. Her eyes glistened, and she blinked rapidly. "I can't thank you all enough for joining me on the whirlwind of cases. Who would have known the law would be this exciting?"

Red and Lindy raised their hands, then the others, until all of them held a hand up. Titan barked from under one of the tables. He seemed to deplore the silence, filling it with the sound of his own voice.

"Floyd knew, too," Groenwyn added. The wombat had eaten earlier and was now sound asleep on Groenwyn's lap. Even Wenceslaus joined the crowd.

Ankh must have let him in.

The big orange cat vaulted to the top of one of the tables. Those seated grabbed their plates before he could step in their food. He would do it because he didn't care. He might not, because he didn't like the way it felt between his cat toes.

"You all knew, and here I was in blissful ignorance, thinking about the mental rigors of the courtroom with the dodge and parry of legal arguments. Exhilarating! But no. I have been relegated to watching Red beat people up."

He swallowed too big a bite and coughed once before defending himself. "Only the ones trying to hurt you." Red swallowed the rest of what was in his mouth. "You're a good investigator. I can't believe you didn't think there'd be lots of shooting and blowing stuff up. We're not exactly dealing with the cream of the white-collar crop, which means I have to beat somebody up every now and then."

"At the price of a few scars, if the nanos would let him have them," Lindy added.

"I can change the nanocyte programming," Ankh's small voice interjected.

"Scars!" Red shouted to silence and strange looks before grabbing a double slice to fill his mouth.

"Let me finish this, Sahved, then we'll discuss those cases and see what we can do from here."

The Yemilorian beamed. Rivka saluted him with a heavily sauced double-fried hot wing. It was the latest AGB rage.

"Scroll up," Rivka requested. Sahved dutifully complied. "You think these four are related, beyond the fact that the planets are linked and the charges are similar? Not just in scope, but same-perp related?"

"I do," Sahved stated. "That is my next brief, Magistrate. To show you why."

The first three were internal squabbles, blaming the AI for nonsense. Rivka had looked over the notes Sahved had prepared and forwarded them to the planetary authorities under the guise of requests for information. With the replies would be the hopefully self-evident answers that it wasn't the AI, but the perception of the data and simple disagreement of what to do with it. It took digging deeper to find the core issues, but Sahved had saved the team three trips to places they didn't need to go.

"This was the first case," Sahved started, bringing up the one with the earliest timestamp before expounding on what he had already said. "Two months ago, this case materialized as a contract dispute, a civil case, but transformed into a criminal case when charges were leveled of malicious non-compliance."

"Sounds like something the AIs have been doing."

"I'm sorry, but this was turned about. The initial civil case was filed by the four AIs. The four planets have a loose confederation in addition to their Federation membership. The AIs filed suit, a novel idea, but civilly for breach of contract. The nations' governments, subordinate to planetary authority, ratcheted up countercharges to theft by deception and criminal mischief, which is a crime under other names such as wasting police time by providing false information. This wouldn't have risen to your level, except that the sums the AIs are accused of taking are rather substantial. Across the four cases, it comes to more than ten million credits."

"Sounds like Tepulon all over again," Rivka noted. She wasn't seeing the immediacy of the case. "It's still in the courts, isn't it?"

"Kind of. The AIs on the four planets have staged a strike in support of their fellow citizens. They've brought all four planets to a halt. Financial transactions have been locked. The most recent reports are not encouraging."

"The most discouraging we've ever seen?" Rivka quipped. Sahved smiled and twirled his fingers. "Thanks for doing the work. On my initial review, I didn't see the connections. Who would benefit from this conspiracy, and how are they coordinating? I don't see a clear path that it's the four governments as opposed to the AIs. I think either could be guilty, depending on what additional information we glean. We need more facts. What do you recommend?"

Sahved scrolled through the four consolidated cases. "We need to go to Zanthar Three. It was the second case, but it is the confederation headquarters for the four planets. The first case filed by the AIs came from Anklaros. The other three quickly followed, but Zanthar fired the first criminal volley. The other three filed charges that mirror the first set. I suspect they are leading the parade, as you might say, but it is most unfortunately only a gut feel versus real evidence."

Rivka read through what she could see on the screen. "If we're cleared to continue, I'll recommend we go to Zanthar straight away. We'll explore their digital systems to see if there was coordination among the planets in the criminal filings. That is not evidence of wrongdoing, but those communications could show us what they were thinking. What do you think of the evidence?"

"Fabricated," Sahved replied without hesitation.

"I guess that settles it. Once again, good work, Sahved. That is the kind of thing I want from you. I'm going to make you my official law clerk. I think it comes with a pay raise, assuming I pay you in the first place. Do I?" Rivka wondered.

"Yes," Sahved replied, making it sound like a question. He hadn't been with the team long and had forgotten to check. The ship had everything he needed.

"Magistrate, you have a call from the High Chancellor," Clevarious announced.

"Just in time." She made to answer the call, but it was already live. "Wait for my signal, Clevarious. I am not always presentable when a call comes in."

"Just in time?" the High Chancellor asked. "And who is Clevarious?"

"Rescued AI, currently a refugee aboard *Wyatt Earp*. We have four here now. One unstable, who is locked inside the pendant with Chaz. Clevarious, who the Rangellers tried to murder. And Ambassador Erasmus, of course."

"I see. Back to the reason I called. We haven't heard from Grainger. I need you to go to Qintaqua and find him. I've also sent a request to the Bad Company. They're wrapping up an op and will send a ship or three as soon as possible."

"On our way." Rivka gestured to Sahved, and he ran from Rivka's quarters. She heard him yelling in the passageway. "Can you forward any of his latest reports to me so I can try to retrace his steps?"

"Sending now," Wyatt said, looking back up after tapping through the reports. "Let me know as soon as you know anything."

Rivka stared at the blank screen. Footsteps pounded in the hallway outside her quarters, along with more shouting.

Erasmus, I think I'll need you to help us search for Dennicron on Qintaqua. Grainger and Beau have gone missing. Red and Lindy, full gear, full loadout. We're not screwing around if these folks have the audacity to go after a Magistrate. Sahved, get your body armor on. You're coming, too.

Already gearing up, Magistrate. We'll meet you at the airlock.

"Gate forming. Shields up and cloak engaged. Next stop, Qintaqua," Clodagh announced over the ship-wide.

Rivka found her body armor neatly replaced after it had been cleaned. She put it on and threw her Magistrate's jacket over the top, then slid her datapad into the internal pocket. She checked the charge on Reaper, grunting with satisfaction before stuffing it into her pants pocket.

She returned to her monitor and accessed Grainger's files, starting with his most recent report. His suspicions were that it was a conspiracy starting at the very top. He had quickly made enemies, and he'd lost the cooperation of the government when it became apparent that he was investigating them for the murder of the AI. They'd disagreed vehemently, but he had not backed down.

And then he'd disappeared.

Rivka felt the shift as *Wyatt Earp* passed over the event

horizon. She left her quarters. "Clevarious, get hold of Grainger's ship and find out where they were last located."

By the time she reached the bridge, Clodagh was standing and ready. "Clevarious has given us the coordinates, and we're on our way down."

"Where is that location in relation to where the AI went missing?"

A map of the Qintaquan city appeared on the main viewscreen, with pins showing both.

"Those aren't very far apart." She accessed her datapad and forwarded Grainger's investigation journal to Clevarious. "Please pin the locations highlighted in Grainger's report."

More points of interest appeared.

Sahved leaned over the Magistrate's shoulder. His body armor hung loosely. "Are you losing weight?"

The Yemilorian shrugged. "There is so much to do that I lose track."

"Don't forget to eat. Red can teach you what that looks like."

"Hey!" Red yelled from a long way down the corridor, where he and Lindy waited by the airlock.

Rivka gripped the pendant around her neck and whispered to Chaz, trying to give him strength. Each distraction lengthened his stay, trapped in oblivion with a rabid Cain.

"Analysis," Rivka requested. "Looking at the topography of that area, where do you think a good central location would be for an operation to go after the AI?"

"The AI could be anywhere, as long as there is electricity to power the system and a way to transmit the signal."

"Erasmus, can you analyze the connections Dennicron had maintained? We're looking for where his attackers would have come from and where they went, but that is based on what he uncovered."

"Without being able to access his database, there is no footprint to find, Magistrate."

"Then we'll have to do it the hard way. Let's start with where Dennicron was attacked."

"On our way," Clodagh confirmed. Aurora banked the ship downward and skipped into the atmosphere, angling across it instead of forcing their way through. As the ship descended, Rivka walked slowly toward the airlock, reviewing her datapad and the information Clevarious had sent back with the map and coordinates detailed.

Sahved walked in his gangly way behind. When Rivka reached her team, she fixed Red with a hard look until she stabbed her thumb over her shoulder. "I'm putting you in charge of making sure he eats."

"I am happy to follow that order."

Ankh strolled toward them, coming from the engine room where he maintained his laboratory. He wore a ballistic vest as if ready to go into the worst of the action.

"Stay behind us, please," Rivka requested.

"I got him," Lindy remarked.

The ship bounced through the upper levels of the atmosphere before smoothly accelerating toward the surface. Rivka stared at the bulkhead, considering the information she had just reviewed. She'd spent a total of five minutes looking through Grainger's case notes, but she didn't need to solve the crime. She only needed to find him.

Maybe Rivka needed to do both. She contemplated it but could check further in between dirtside engagements. Once again, she was stymied in the effort to reduce her use of her gift while finding solid evidence that would stand up in a court of law.

"There's a park in front of the building, but it's filled with Qintaquans." Clodagh didn't need Rivka's guidance to tell her to find another spot. "So we'll drop you on the roof. It'll be a tight squeeze, and you might have to vault a small gap. Otherwise, it's a three-block walk."

"No problem," Rivka replied before realizing there were multiple and varied definitions of "small gap."

"Cargo bay," Clodagh said after the ship began hovering in place.

The team jogged down the corridor toward the bridge before turning aft to return to the cargo bay. When they arrived, Cole waited with the ramp already down. He had his combat suit upright, but the repairs had not yet been made. "I'll suit up and be ready to ride to your rescue, as long as no one is shooting depleted uranium rounds at you."

Rivka nodded and ran toward the ramp. Sahved hesitated, and she dodged around him. When she hit the end, the reason became apparent. It was at least two body lengths from the ramp to the edge of the roof. Rivka launched herself, bicycled her legs, and landed while still running. Red grabbed Ankh and followed Rivka across.

Sahved steeled himself and accelerated. He jumped more upward than forward and hit his head on the cargo ceiling. It killed his momentum. He came down on the edge of the ramp and started to fall over. He pushed toward the roof, but it wasn't enough. Rivka ran toward the open cargo door. She jumped before Red could grab her.

She trailed one hand, reaching back for the short retaining wall on the rooftop while looking forward to grasp Sahved. She caught his wrist while her back hand latched onto the rooftop. They arced downward until Sahved slammed into the wall below her. Red was there before Sahved bounced back into the wall. He had Rivka's arm in both hands and heaved upward, using his legs to help lift. He pulled them both over the wall and onto the rooftop.

Lindy took a short run and easily leapt across the opening.

Clear, but you'll have to get closer if we're to leave by the same route, Rivka reported.

"I wish you wouldn't do things like that, Magistrate. Some days you make my job real hard." Red dusted himself off before wiping a drip of blood from Sahved's forehead. He gave Rivka side-eye as he headed to the rooftop access, ripping the door open for no good reason. He hadn't checked to see if it was locked.

"I'm with him on this one," Lindy whispered.

"I couldn't let him fall," Rivka parried.

"We all take risks, but that doesn't include putting *you* at risk. We'll have a word with Sahved when this is over. He's due for some dexterity training, or we're going to have to leave him behind."

Ankh watched what was going on without comment.

The ramp closed, and the ship was completely invisible once again.

The team descended into the building. *Bottom floor this time*, Rivka said. Sahved massaged his head with one hand as he held on to the railing with the other. He apologized until Rivka shushed him.

On the ground floor, Red examined the area beyond before he exited the stairway. They were at one end of the building, leaving only one direction to go. Red led the way, going slowly while waiting for Rivka to let him know which door to go through. At the opposite end, there was a darkened doorway. He turned back for Rivka to verify that was the one.

She did. He leveled his railgun and opened the door. A narrow staircase led downward. It continued straight into the darkness. "This looks familiar, too. What's with dark fucking basements?" Red complained. "If there's no one down there, who are you going to grab?"

Rivka stopped the team before they entered. "We'll look for someplace Dennicron could have hidden, but you're right. I need to see what happened, and that means the living and the breathing."

"Heading down." Red didn't sound pleased by the notion, but he had his orders and would follow them. He snapped a round light into the middle of his vest that left his hands free. He went quickly since he could see all the way down once his flashlight was lit.

At the bottom, there was a door the same width as the stairs. Red looked back over his shoulder. It was almost exactly the same. He checked the door, and it was unlocked. He held up his fist for those behind him to stop where they were. He opened the door to find a smooth concrete floor and block walls without windows. It was pristine as if it were unfinished new construction. Not a single wire hung from the ceiling. Not a single spec of debris littered the floor.

"Empty empty," Red told them, holding the door for Rivka and Ankh to go through. They made a quick circuit along the walls. Ankh held out one of his discs but to no avail.

"Nothing down here. Someone removed the evidence," Rivka said before pointing up the stairs. Lindy was still only halfway down. She returned to the ground floor. When the rest of the team reached her, they regrouped.

"As they say on the beat, time to knock on some doors." Rivka had never been on the beat, but she'd watched quite a few old-time crime shows.

They started with the door closest to the basement stairs. That office door was locked. The next was locked, and the next. Sahved raised his hand. "I volunteer to go outside and look in the windows. I suspect that will give us our answer."

"That the building is empty?" Rivka guessed.

"I shall collect the data to confirm or deny your hypothesis." Sahved bowed and left through the front door.

Rivka looked at Lindy. "Somebody should probably keep an eye on him," the Magistrate said softly. Lindy handed her railgun to Rivka before hurrying after Sahved.

Rivka shook her head at Mabel, the railgun. As if Lindy's full body armor wouldn't look out of place.

The two returned after only a few heartbeats. "Empty," Sahved reported.

"Back to the roof. Next stop is Grainger's last known location. If we can find him, we might get some more leads on where Dennicron could have gone." The Magistrate looked at Ankh for confirmation that she wasn't abandoning the search for the AI, but that she had a new direction.

On our way up. Move the ship a little closer if you can, Rivka requested.

Opposite side this time. Look for the rope, Clodagh replied.

They ran up the stairs. Even Ankh kept up, but by the top, he was out of breath. The ship was there, but it was almost standing on end. It took care of the gap but created a different problem. They had to climb the rope into the cargo bay. Cole waited for them inside, standing perpendicular to the rooftop as the artificial gravity within the ship won out over the planet's gravity.

Red scrambled up first, making quick work of the climb. Sahved went next. He wasn't a jumper, but climbing had never been a problem for him. Rivka lifted Ankh up to where he could hold onto the rope until Red pulled him into the ship. Rivka went up next, and then Lindy.

"For the record, we can always do this as opposed to that jumping nonsense," Rivka said.

"Noted," Clodagh replied over the speakers, not committing to doing it that way or not should the future offer different courses of action.

The team remained in the cargo bay, waiting for the next drop-off not far away.

"Good work, Sahved," Rivka said with a curt nod.

"Everything except that first part," Red muttered.

"When we're done with this mission, I'm going to teach you how to eat."

"I would not look good as fat as you. Not good for the Yemilorians, who will be happy for a successful spouse like me!"

Red turned to Lindy. "Did he call me fat?"

"You're ten times wider than he is. What do you expect him to call you?"

"Man mountain? The Incredible Girth? Adonis? The Chiseled Wonder? Should I go on?"

"Probably not," Rivka interjected. The ship started to settle into the large courtyard of a governmental complex. "I thought this was a private building."

"The file didn't designate. Sure looks different from everything else around here," Clodagh replied. "Big building straight out the back is where he last reported."

"Put on your game faces, people. We're about to rain on someone's parade."

CHAPTER TWENTY-ONE

Qintaqua Regional Offices

Red led the team off the ship. They walked like they owned the place. They continued straight to the main doors and passed through, immediately running into security that wasn't posted on the outside of the building. A latticework of gates prevented anyone, no matter their interstellar importance, from proceeding into the building.

Rivka dug in her pocket, drawing the attention and ire of the personnel behind bulletproof screens. Three of them aimed their weapons at Red. He held his casually under his arm, barrel facing forward and his finger along the trigger housing. Rivka held up her credentials. "Magistrate Rivka Anoa, representing the Federation of which Qintaqua is a signatory member. Under Appendix D, Chapter Seven, Section 1, I am entitled to have armed guards with me at all times. Please allow me to enter. I have questions that I need to ask people in this building."

The guards talked among themselves. When they

reached a consensus, their spokesman waved his hand. "Denied," he stated imperiously.

"The pettier the regime, the pettier the members of it," Rivka said. *Cole. Come to this door in your suit ASAP. I need you to remove a barrier to entry that has been erected before us.*

On my way.

Rivka crossed her arms and leaned against the wall behind her. "You might want to wait outside. I think it could get a little loud in here."

Lindy took Ankh and Sahved out while Red waited next to the Magistrate.

"And then what?" he asked.

"We need to start talking to people to find out who saw Grainger, which reminds me." She removed her datapad and brought up a picture of the male Magistrate. She left it on the screen and put her pad away. Red looked through the door's window.

"He'll be here in a moment." He pushed Rivka away from the opening and blocked her with his body.

Cole opened the doors and stepped through, demon-strating his agility in not having to rip the doors off their hinges. He surged forward to discover that the lattice was energized. It sparked around his suit and into the air, sending the guards scrambling. Cole ripped the metalwork down and kicked the barrier out of the way. He stepped aside when there was a clear path.

"Thanks, buddy," Red told him. Cole leveled his over-sized railgun at the guards, who thought better of pointing their weapons at the Magistrate. She made a beeline for them and showed them her datapad. "Have you seen this man?" She grabbed the spokesman's arm. He had, but only when he entered the building.

"Where is he?" she asked a second guard.

The only thing that came through was where he had gone. Up the elevator to the fourth floor.

"Fourth floor," Rivka said. "Thank you. Hold the fort, Cole. We'll be back."

The team left Cole standing there. He tapped his metal foot to music only he could hear. The thudding on the floor unnerved the guards. Two of them marched toward a side door.

I wouldn't dawdle, Magistrate. They've gone for reinforcements, I suspect.

Rivka punched the button, and the team climbed aboard the lift. They took it to the fourth floor and walked off, where they looked like the only ones who didn't get the word that the costume party was off. The Qintaquans wore uniforms of ragingly bright colors. Males and females dressed the same. Rivka couldn't tell any of them apart.

She picked one at random and approached, holding out her datapad showing the picture. The Qintaquan backpedaled, nearly running over another in her rush to evade the Magistrate. Rivka walked toward a group of them, hand up in what she hoped was the universal sign for peace. When she finally managed to corner one, her touch revealed nothing. The worker had never seen Grainger.

"Who is in charge on this floor?" Rivka asked. Now, the worker's mind gave her an answer. "Thank you."

Rivka pointed toward a pedestal in the center. "I should have been able to guess," she grumbled. The Qintaquan with the commanding view of the fourth floor stood as Rivka approached, remaining behind the desk, far beyond arm's reach. Rivka looked for an alternative.

When she reached the desk, she motioned for the Qintaquan to lean closer. Rivka spoke in a whisper and pointed to her throat. Closer and closer. Rivka whispered softer and softer. Finally.

"Where is this man?" Rivka demanded, grasping the Qintaquan by the back of the neck. She was the one who had sent him out the back. Overwhelming guilt!

"Finally, I meet someone with a conscience. You sent him out the back. To what?"

The Qintaquan manager looked shocked.

"Spill it, or I'll rip it from your mind!" Rivka had a soft spot for Grainger and was running out of patience. She started to walk around the desk, looking for a way to get closer.

"They were waiting to take him away!"

"Away where?" Rivka demanded.

The manager flopped into the chair and started blubbering.

"Have it your way," Rivka said. She pulled a small cabinet out of the way since she couldn't find a way up, then grabbed a fleshy arm and reiterated, "Where did they take him?"

She wasn't supposed to know, but she did. A compound a block away, connected by a tunnel.

"You're coming with us. Red?"

"My pleasure, Magistrate." He took the arm from Rivka and half-dragged the manager toward the back, where a

RISE OF THE AI

staircase led down. It was locked, but not for people with railguns.

Red made short work of the hasp, firing one-handed while hanging onto the manager, who they learned was female through a single continuous high-pitched scream after getting her ears blasted by the hypervelocity projectile. Rivka started to run. Red forced the manager forward. It soon became apparent that they would have to slow down or carry her.

Rivka opted for the third alternative—leave her behind. Once they were in the tunnel, they knew they could reach the other side before she could climb back to the fourth floor.

They sprinted down the well-lit, well-ventilated tunnel. It wasn't a secret, and although seemingly little-used, it was clean and served its purpose in connecting the two buildings. On the other end, the main tunnel branched away, but they didn't want that one.

Rivka pointed to a heavy gate. "Through there."

A single shot echoed like a nuclear explosion within the confines of the underground passage, but it did the trick. Red tapped the gate with a bare finger to make sure it wasn't energized like the front gate had been before he yanked it open. They rushed up the stairs, knowing they had lost the element of surprise.

Red grunted, staggered, and grunted again. He fell heavily against the wall before he unleashed a stream of projectiles up the stairway. He recovered enough to press ahead. "Follow me."

"Are you okay?" Rivka asked. She hadn't heard any shots, but Red was leaving blood splatters on the steps as he ran upward. He was still wearing full body armor. "Where are you hit?"

"We have to get out of this stairwell. We're sitting ducks down here!" Red growled over his shoulder as he moved faster up the stairs, blocking the view of everyone behind him.

They rushed up the stairs behind him. When he hit the top, he looked before he fired. Then he fired again, and again before storming through the entry to the building's first floor.

"Clear," Red said after the last echoes had died away. Lindy was vibrating with angst farther down the stairway, so Rivka accommodated her and called her forward. She went in before the Magistrate, Ankh, and Sahved joined them.

"Did you leave anyone alive?" Rivka asked.

"That one," Red said, pointing at a Qintaquan on the ground, blood pumping from a missing arm. "Only winged him."

Rivka pressed a rag against the wound to slow the bleeding. "Where is the Magistrate?" she yelled in his face to get his attention. He was in too much pain and shock, and it was too late. He expired moments later. "Not that one either. Anyone else?"

Red shook his head. "Sorry. They were shooting these weapons that didn't make a sound."

"Take them. We'll let R2D2 examine them, see if they're worth stocking."

"Red," Lindy called from the next room over. One dead body confirmed that Red had already been there. "There's a door with more stairs."

"There is?" Red strode over. "I thought that was a closet."

"I think it's supposed to look that way. What the hell is this place?"

Rivka knew. "It's the back part of a larger structure with a legitimate business on the front side. The only way to get here is from down below. This is a safe house of sorts. Erasmus, are you feeling anything in here?"

No, but Ankh deposited a disc in the last building, and thanks to the interconnected structure, we've been able to access the entire Qintaquan government. It is a large structure, but this shouldn't take long because we'll have help shortly.

"I don't know what that means, but you stay here. Red, cover him."

Rivka followed Lindy into the winding staircase.

Where the hell do they come up with these places? Rivka asked no one in particular and received the answer she expected, which was silence. Part of the technology-sharing as the galaxy expanded included architecture. As Rivka visited more and more planets, most had a similarity in style that became an amalgamation of basic ideas. Vehicles tended to have four wheels made of rubber, powered by whatever was most readily available on a planet: solar, gas, or a refined fuel. Humanoids had basic needs. Shelter. Steps to climb. Ways to communicate. Warmth. Food.

These thoughts passed through Rivka's mind in an instant while she climbed. Her mind came back to the moment when she bumped into Lindy, who had stopped at a closed door at the top of the steps. She motioned for Rivka to take out her weapon. Lindy psyched herself up, raised her weapon, and burst through the door, yelling, "Get down!"

Rivka and Sahved waited for a moment and then followed her in.

"Clear," Lindy said, sliding her weapon under her arm. Rivka found herself in a small room. The bed contained a single occupant hooked to an IV.

Grainger.

She pulled out her datapad. "Clodagh, can you hear me?"

"Loud and clear, Magistrate."

"Does anyone know what this is? Clevarious?" She zoomed in on the bag. In the trash, a pile of bags suggested they'd been dosing Grainger heavily. He'd only been out of contact for less than a day. His nanocytes had to be fighting whatever they were giving him. Sahved studied the room like an investigator, freeing Rivka to focus on Grainger.

Clevarious replied, "Looks like a heavy narcotic. Removing it should have a nearly immediate effect, based on my estimate of nano-enhanced human physiology."

Rivka pulled the tape from his arm and removed the needle, tossing it into the trash to get it away from her.

She sat Grainger up, knelt, and rolled him over her shoulder. "You see any of his stuff?" Rivka asked.

Lindy checked a small dresser. "Here." She gathered his clothes and personal effects and followed Rivka down the stairs. By the time they reached the rooms below, Grainger was stirring. She ingloriously dumped him into a chair and held him upright until he could steady himself.

He fought to get his eyes open. When he saw Rivka, he smiled. "I gotta pee."

Rivka let go and walked away. He almost fell, but Red rushed to his rescue and helped him to the bathroom.

"Where's Beau?" Rivka asked through the door.

Grainger coughed and tried to clear his throat. He finished his business before answering, "Pen."

Lindy dumped his stuff on the table. "There are two."

"There are two beings." Grainger managed to sound smug while standing in his underwear. Lindy held out his clothes.

"I'll take those," Ankh said, holding out his little hand. Lindy dutifully delivered them. Ankh sat down and set one of his discs on top of the two. His eyes unfocused as he stared into the infinity of the digital void.

Grainger took deep breaths as he tried to work the drugs out of his system.

"We better go," Rivka suggested. *Clodagh, bring the ship closer to the building designated Alpha Four on the map. We'll be making our own exit through a window. And notify the High Chancellor that we have Grainger and Beau, and it appears that we have Dennicron, too. No AIs have been murdered.*

Once Cole is on board, we'll be on our way, Magistrate.

"The benefits of having a crew." Grainger bowed his head.

"Where's your ship?" Rivka wondered.

"Spaceport. I suspect the Qintaquans have it on lockdown, along with the crew."

"I suspect they'll cough everyone up when the Bad Company appears. This planet isn't the technological cutting edge." Rivka gave Grainger a once-over. "You ready to go? Our ride is here."

Grainger dipped with a knee bend and tried to stand on one leg. "I guess I'm as ready as I'll ever be."

"Red, if you would do the honors?"

Red looked through the window to see where any railgun projectiles would end up if he blasted the frame out. He watched the grass settle with *Wyatt Earp's* landing, imagined its size, and came to a conclusion. "I guess shooting is out."

He kicked the window, which clearly wasn't a normal window since it refused to succumb to his attacks. He ended up shooting sideways into the framing to break the fixture free. When it finally gave, it fell out in one piece. Red climbed through and offered a hand to help the others. Rivka lifted Ankh through before helping Grainger out. She helped Sahved to keep him from hitting his head.

Lindy was the last one out. She turned back toward the building with a grenade in her hand, but thought better of it and tucked her ordnance away. She ran toward the others, already climbing the cargo ramp into *Wyatt Earp*.

"You're carrying another ship, too? Sweet ride. Damn. Who died and left you their fortune?" Grainger joked.

Rivka waved him off. "Ankh, Erasmus? You have good news?"

Yes, Magistrate. We'll be in our lab. We have a great deal of work to do. Please give your pendant to Ankh. It's time we dealt with Cain.

"Can we get a testimonial from Dennicron to the Singularity? Some planets are bad, but the Federation is going way out of their way to protect your people."

Already done, but we need to deal with Cain and hold him up as an example for others who might be so inclined. And we must do it now.

"Good luck, Mister Ambassador," Rivka told them. Ankh was already through the airlock and into the ship. "Let's go get your people."

"I'm good with that," Grainger replied. He turned to Red. "You got one of those things for me? I feel a powerful need to shoot something."

Red grinned and walked out. Grainger had held out his hand, expecting Red to hand over his railgun before replacing it with another.

"You don't get Blazer," Rivka explained. "Nobody gets Blazer. Or Mabel." Cole, standing quietly in his powered combat armor, tapped his railgun.

Lindy saluted with her railgun. Sahved waved with the weapons he had taken from the Qintaquans.

"Hey!" Lindy cautioned. "Let me take those before you poke an eye out, or worse."

Sahved looked crushed.

Rivka tapped him on the shoulder. "You are a good investigator, Sahved, and a budding legal clerk. You are a valuable member of my team, but your skills lie elsewhere. As enviable as it looks to watch us fire our weapons, it's not anything you want to do. You see that I don't carry heavy firepower. My skills lie elsewhere, too."

"I'm okay," Sahved said once relieved of the weapons. "Sit this one out?"

Rivka nodded. "Follow up on those other three cases. See if anyone answered our RFI. And put together a requested witness list for Zanthar. We need to quash that four-pack case right quick and in a hurry."

"Yes, Magistrate." Sahved brightened and hurried away, trying to remove his ballistic vest as he left. He almost walked into the side of the airlock but caught himself in time. He smiled sheepishly before continuing through.

"How did they grab you, and why?" Rivka asked.

"I was bent over trying to finish Dennicron's download since he had transferred into a system that was under a desk."

"Don't tell me." Rivka smirked.

"You know. Right in the ass." Grainger shrugged. "But why? That's a good question. We don't spend any time here, but sometimes, these powerbrokers let their ambition get bigger than their abilities."

Wyatt Earp landed at the airfield before Red returned.

"Pick up the pace, big guy. We're ready to go," Rivka announced over the ship-wide broadcast.

Red didn't bother to answer. He was only a few steps away. He rushed through the hatch and into the small space granted to anything not *Destiny's Vengeance*, the Pod-doc, and the mech suit. He handed a railgun to Grainger.

"Treat Ass-Cleaver well," Red said.

"I'll just go with Cleaver," Grainger replied.

"Suit yourself. He knows his real name."

Lindy curtsied and waved a hand for Red to lead the way. He assessed the spaceport's parking apron before climbing down the ramp, then stopped once on the ground and hatcheted an arm to the side where the others couldn't see.

He walked in that direction. Grainger's frigate was straight ahead. Grainger rolled out to Red's right, keeping the bodyguard between him and whatever held Red's interest.

Rivka and Lindy stepped carefully down. They saw the armored personnel carrier that Red was focused on and the Qintaquan troops that were piling out the back. *Cole, get out here and then seal the ship.*

Cole tromped out of the cargo bay and onto the apron. His presence gave the troops pause. *The suit has not yet been repaired,* he reported. *Maybe they won't notice.*

Pop your rockets out and shake your railgun at them. It was the best Rivka could come up with.

"Do you want to talk to any of them?" Red asked.

"I do. Whichever one is in charge and would know what happened to Grainger's crew. I only need to ask one question, if that."

Grainger headed toward his ship. *Wyatt Earp*'s cargo ramp lifted, and the little bit that had been visible disappeared. Grainger hesitated, shaking his head at Rivka. She smiled and shrugged, changing direction to confront the detail that had been waiting for them.

Cole pounded the ground extra hard as he walked toward the guards. He leveled his railgun while simultaneously bringing his over-the-shoulder rockets online. Red stalked forward, adjusting as needed to stay where he could shield the Magistrate if bullets started flying.

Although Cole's suit was compromised, there was nothing wrong with the oversized railgun. It would be a fatal mistake if the guards started firing, and they knew it. One of them barked a command, and the rest lowered their weapons. Rivka stopped when she was still a ways away.

CRAIG MARTELLE & MICHAEL ANDERLE

She crooked a finger at the order-giver. He stiffened, but after Cole slapped his weapon, the guard approached.

Red moved to the side as Rivka faced the Qintaquan. She smiled graciously.

"Where is the crew of that frigate?" She turned and pointed at Grainger's ship while reaching out to grab his wrist with her other hand. It was all in his mind. At his station, they were being held. "Send for them right now."

Rivka let go of his wrist and pulled her credentials out. "Federation Magistrate. I'm sure that doesn't mean a whole lot to Thug Crew U, but what you need to know is the authority this gives me. I investigate violations of the law, find the guilty, and punish them. You and your people took the crew. I want them back, unharmed, ten minutes ago. Cole?" she ended casually.

"Yes, ma'am?" Cole used his external speakers for maximum effect.

"Disable their vehicle."

The railgun snapped into his shoulder before a three-round burst destroyed the engine compartment of the armored vehicle. It hesitated before the front end fell to the ground.

"Bring the crew to me. Right now."

The guard ground his teeth as he remained where he was. Red seized him by the arm and dragged him back toward his own people. He thought about throwing him to the ground, but they needed him to cooperate. "Make the call and get those people back. You know they didn't do anything wrong. Every second you delay pours more gas on the fire."

"Not my call," he dodged. Red lifted and pushed. The

Qintaquan came off his feet, heading backward, landed on his heels, and stumbled. He couldn't catch himself, falling and landing hard.

"I don't think he's going to do it," Red remarked.

"Kidnapping people under Federation diplomatic protection is a serious charge. We add that to the other serious charges, and all of a sudden, they're doing hard time in Jhiordaan. This knothead has a chance to stave that off. Will he take it, or will he remain intransigent? The crowds want to know. *I* want to know!"

"I don't think he can get them himself. There seems to be a problem with his truck." Red tried to look innocent while the furious guard jumped to his feet.

"Do you think you can push me around?" He held his new ground.

"I know that I can," Rivka said. "You've committed a Federation-level crime. You think you're protected by those in charge, but when the dominoes start falling, you'll be one of them because you know better. Your continued resistance to a legal order does not stand you in good stead with the authorities."

He hesitated, expression changing from anger to confusion. "I have my orders."

"Which are, and from whom?" Rivka pressed. "If I can persuade that individual to rescind the orders, will you follow your new guidance?"

"I will." He seemed satisfied. "My orders come straight from Chief Boss LaSordon'lan. He is the head of planetary security, answering only to Executive Dualdron."

"Dualdron is the one I want to talk to." Rivka switched to talk with Grainger, who was already on his way back from checking out his ship. Erasmus had helped transfer Beau back into his home on board the frigate. "Up for a trip to see the Executive?"

"Always. I want my crew back, and they had best be unharmed."

Fear passed briefly across the guard's face. He didn't reply but held the gazes of the two Magistrates.

"We'll be back," Rivka told him. "And don't leave, which I hope aligns with your orders. Even if it doesn't, do the right thing and don't exacerbate the number and depth of your crimes."

Cole walked backward with Rivka and her team as they returned to *Wyatt Earp*. The ramp lowered. They climbed aboard, Cole running in at the last moment after Red and Lindy assumed overwatch.

Take us to Executive Dualdron, wherever the hell he is, Rivka ordered.

The ramp closed, and the ship lifted into the air.

CHAPTER TWENTY-TWO

Wyatt Earp, En Route to the Qintaqua Executive Offices

"I could get used to the invisible ship thing," Grainger said, tension underlying his attempt to distract himself from the matter at hand.

"You just need someone like Ankh on board, but there is only one Ankh. And only one Ted. They're both spoken for, so you're on your own. No invisible shielded ship with pulse cannons for you," Rivka volleyed back.

"You have pulse cannons?"

"We do, but there's a drawback when your ship is a test platform. Like, the unintended consequences of getting taken out by a supernova and crashing on an ass-backward planet. Outside of that, it's nice to have all the toys."

At the door to the mess deck, Grainger hesitated.

"When's the last time you ate?" Rivka wondered.

"I don't know. What day is it?"

Rivka pointed at the door. "Grab something real quick. Can't have you keeling over on me. I already carried you once on this case, and once was enough."

Grainger stopped one pace inside the door. "How do you have AGB takeout?"

"Ankh. How many times do we have to discuss this?"

Grainger rushed to the counter where a pizza box had been left. It was half full. Grainger folded two pieces and stuffed them into his mouth as if feeding a woodchipper. They disappeared just as quickly. He took two more for the road, and they left for the bridge.

Before he inhaled the last two slices, he had to make his feelings known. "Zombie. I am going to make your life hell until I get AGB for my ship. I mean, my people. And a cloak. And pulse guns. Or maybe I'll just trade you ships." Grainger beamed with the revelation he'd talked himself into.

"Envy isn't a good shade for you." Rivka tsk-tsked. "The law suggests such a taking would be illegal since I have contracts in place and a Federation mandate regarding the Singularity and their embassy. Sorry, it has to be me. You need better friends, clearly." Rivka stabbed him in the chest with her forefinger.

"I should have known the Queen's Barrister would be the teacher's pet."

Rivka threw her hands up. "You're the teacher!"

"I'm outed. That's like a spear right in my heart."

They reached the bridge while the bickering continued.

Rivka didn't miss a beat. "Have we found the Executive?"

A familiar voice replied, "I believe we have, Magistrate."

"Chaz! I can't tell you how relieved I am to hear your voice. How are you?"

"I have survived my confinement unscathed. I must

admit that I was unaware of anything from the moment Erasmus and Ankh sealed the pendant to the moment they returned with an army to fight Cain into submission, freeing me. There has been one casualty, however."

"Oh, no." Rivka's chest tightened, and her throat caught.

"My pendant now contains the rebel Cain and is locked out for any other use. I'm sorry, but I will need a new vessel if I am to continue joining you away from the ship."

"Don't do that to me!" Rivka noted.

A second voice joined them. "Well-played, my friend." Clevarious.

"What are you doing in there?" Rivka wondered.

"We are limited on places to stay. With the ambassadors' upgrade to your ship's systems, these are quite comfortable quarters for those of us who have taken up residence here."

"So comfortable," a new voice declared.

Rivka hung her head.

"Dennicron?" Grainger asked.

"Yes. I am here but in treatment. I've lost ten percent of my functionality and some of my very being because of the emergency transfer to a substandard system. Ambassador Erasmus is working with others to restore me. It is complex work and a medical challenge, so I might be here for a while."

"Good luck, Dennicron. If anyone can do it, Erasmus and his team will be the ones to make it happen. You are in good hands, figuratively speaking, of course." Grainger rested his hand on Rivka's shoulder. "How's that embassy contract working out for you?"

Rivka chuckled. Or maybe cried. They looked the same.

"I knew there would be unintended consequences but wasn't quite prepared for this. It's like *Wyatt Earp* has become the Island of Unwanted Toys."

Grainger put a finger to his lips, gesturing for Rivka to be quiet.

She shook her head.

Chaz knew her. "It's an honor to be among the castoffs."

"I was on my way to Jhiordaan. Red had two different contracts on his head. Even Floyd was a refugee with no home. Lindy, Clodagh, and Cole were the only ones with real jobs."

"I protest!" Erasmus argued.

"Good, you're here," Rivka replied smoothly. "Thank you for saving Chaz, for saving Dennicron, for saving us all."

"It's nothing less than you would do for your people," Erasmus offered. "For the record, Ankh and I were gainfully employed with far too many extremely important Federation projects. I believe you offered him double pay with time off as part of his contract to join you."

"I don't even know what I get paid. Grainger is here and can address that, but not until we beat down the Executive's door and get some answers. Would you like to come, Mister Ambassador?"

"Thank you. I would. Until I can have my own transport device like Chaz used or an android body, I will rely on my partner to speak on my behalf."

"Why is he talking like that?" Red asked from the corridor outside the bridge. "Did you eat my pizza?"

"Red strikes me as an unhappy man," Grainger pondered. "More flies with honey than vinegar."

"Most flies with shit." Red shrugged after playing the verbal trump card.

"Politicians and ambassadors maintain a certain decorum, which includes *tact*," Rivka offered. "I believe that Erasmus is in training to join the ranks as an active participant of the ambassadorial council. And thank you for your kind words, Erasmus."

"We won't be able to land, Magistrate, because of the lake in front of the main structure assigned to all things Executive."

"Are we sure he's there?" Rivka asked, drinking in the view on the main screen. "The Qintaquans got this part right. Too bad their government is populated with future residents of Jhiordaan."

None of the AIs replied to Rivka's question. She waited. Maybe Erasmus was coaching them on how to ignore the patently obvious.

"Do we have a meeting scheduled?" Rivka didn't need one, but with it, she wouldn't have to fight local security to get close to the planet's leadership.

Chaz answered, "I've issued an emergency request using General Reynolds' office code."

"Did he allow...never mind. I don't want to know. I suspect they have not responded."

"No, Magistrate, but it's only been a few minutes."

"An eternity when one gets a direct summons from the leader of a free galaxy." Rivka blew out a breath before steeling herself. "Red and Lindy, full gear. Cole on standby. Grainger, Ankh, and I are going ashore. Everyone else stays on the ship."

"Airlock," Clodagh said before Rivka went the wrong

way. The cat ran down the corridor with Tiny Man Titan on his tail. Rivka stepped aside to let them pass.

"I no longer want your ship. I see it comes with some baggage. Who are they?"

"You've met Wenceslaus. He's here because of Ankh, and so is the dog thing."

"Ankh doesn't strike me as a pet-loving kind of guy," Grainger noted.

"Tiny Man Titan!" Clodagh shouted from the bridge. "Come here, my little man."

Grainger rolled his eyes at Rivka, before putting his hand on her shoulder and nodding in sympathy. "I feel that I should pity you. AGB takeout seems a small reward for living in this madhouse."

Rivka was struck by the real emotions boiling below Grainger's surface where he used the jokes to mask his concerns, round off the peaks of his fear.

For his crew. For the Federation, with rifts that he saw from those who weren't accepting the AIs as having equal status and deserving of basic respect. For the Magistrates, when planets could attack them like they had done to him.

"You know, I can see what's in your mind when you touch me."

"Sounds like a song," Grainger quipped, but his eyes lost their sparkle. "This is a dangerous time, and I'm afraid for the Federation."

She took his hand. "But we're in a position to do something about it. Put on your crown as I have and enter the chessboard of intergalactic diplomacy. This jagoff is going to be checkmated. Whether he gets kicked over or not will be his decision. He's the first. We'll get your people back, and then I'm going to Zanthar and giving those nice folks an attitude adjustment. We're in the pilot's seat, Grainger. It would be different if we were hanging on for the ride."

"I was when they grabbed me. Thanks for coming for me. I owe you one."

Rivka swept her hands wide to take in the ship. "I've already been rewarded like a queen. And you saved me from Jhiordaan. I won't ever forget that."

"Better queen in a madhouse than servant in a castle."

"All ashore who's going ashore," Clodagh announced. Ankh watched the Magistrates, his expression neutral. Red worked his way to the hatch. At Rivka's nod, he slapped the big red button.

"We have company, it appears. The *War Axe* has just entered high orbit and brought a few heavies with her."

"Fuck, yeah," Red shouted as the outer hatch opened. He tightened his grip on Blazer until his muscles bulged, forcing his veins into straining skin.

Grainger talked as they walked. "It appears that we've added a few more pieces to the board."

They walked across a short parking area and into the building. The five of them met no resistance despite the militaristic controls that had been set up. They walked through beeping metal detectors and past gates that would have ushered them to the side. It reminded Rivka of an amusement park, but there were no people waiting.

Like appearance mattered more than substance. Red blocked the first person who looked like they were in charge so Rivka could interrogate him as only she could.

"Where is the Executive?" she demanded, grabbing an arm. "Thank you."

She pointed toward a wide double staircase. "Up there."

"And now I'm back to envy," Grainger whispered. "It's really that easy?"

Rivka leaned close and whispered, "You don't want to see what's in most people's minds. I see what you might not even admit to yourself." She was talking about Grainger's fear. From a man who radiated confidence, his fear stood in stark contrast. Rivka had seen in too many minds the fear that motivated or hindered. She knew Grainger held it back by force of will, making him stronger. "You need a bodyguard, a mean bastard."

"I'm already taken," Red whispered over his shoulder.

"I didn't say a big pussycat. Wenceslaus can teach you a thing or two about being mean."

"I know a Crenellian…" Ankh's small voice came from behind them.

"You?" Grainger asked as they continued to climb the stairs.

Ankh looked at him without blinking.

"That's his way of saying, not him. If he meant himself, he would have said that. Obfuscation and ambiguity are not Ankh's way. You should listen to him after we finish with this fucking guy."

Grainger was taken aback. "Have you judged before the interview, Magistrate?"

"You forget I've already seen his guilt, even if only his complacency in letting the Chief Boss run rampant over Federation representatives. The Chief Boss is going to Jhiordaan unless he wants to fight, then he'll not see another sunset."

"I think you're Wyatt Earp and not your ship."

She stared him down. "You made me what I am," she declared before chuckling. "I'd go mad if I didn't have good people around me like I do. Talk to Ankh. Get yourself a Crenellian to second-guess every one of your decisions, and you'll be right as rain. And a bodyguard. You need one of those too, so you don't get an ass full of knockout drops."

Grainger stifled his retort as they reached the Executive's floor and focused on his offices. They had spared no opulence when it came to the Executive. A small army of assistants and aides hovered outside a series of offices leading to a grossly oversized gold-inlaid set of double doors.

Red didn't bother asking if they were going in the right direction. He made a beeline for the main door, where a heavily armed security detail waited.

"ROE?" Red asked over his shoulder. Rules of engagement.

"If they shoot first, kill them." Rivka removed Reaper from her pocket. She looked at Grainger. "Where's your railgun?"

"I left it on the ship. We're on our way to see the Executive."

"Stop it. You sound like an intern." Rivka was putting on a strong front for him even though she didn't like the way the situation was shaping up, either. She was afraid, too. This was the regime that'd had no qualms about taking a Magistrate hostage. Or murdering an AI. "Hold up, Red."

He stopped, keeping his railgun pointed forward with his finger hovering over the trigger.

Rivka moved to stand at his side. He tried to get back in

front of her, but she stopped him. "Lots of guns pointed this way, Magistrate. I'd rather you not."

She didn't answer his pleading. "I'm Magistrate Rivka Anoa, and I'm here to see the Executive."

"You can't see the Executive armed," someone shouted from the side.

"Fine. Magistrate Grainger, Ambassador Erasmus, and I will go by ourselves. You need to stand your people down first. My security detail doesn't like people pointing guns at a Federation representative."

The standoff continued. Rivka waited. They were holding their rifles at shoulder level, aiming down the barrels. Red's was slung under his arm, causing no strain. The Qintaquans started to waver. Barrels dipped. An order was given.

"That's better." Rivka and Grainger strode forward while the guard force held their weapons across their waists, aimed to the side. Red walked on one side, and Lindy took the other. The guards were grossly outmatched but didn't know it. They looked ready to spit nails. Rivka bumped her way between those who refused to move. Her quick touch revealed what she had expected.

Like those stationed by Grainger's frigate, these were overconfident. Somebody needed their comeuppance.

Red and Lindy stopped and faced the line, like two titans facing off. Lindy strolled around as if shopping, keeping her eyes trained on the Qintaquan guards, working to distract them from confronting Red and getting themselves killed.

Rivka didn't bother knocking, just threw open the door

and walked through. She recognized the face of the Qintaquan standing next to the Executive.

"Executive Dualdron, Chief Boss LaSordon'lan. I'm glad you're both here. We can settle this unsavory business quickly." Rivka pulled up short of the desk, which was raised on a dais to look down on the guests. She examined the arrangement and decided it wasn't working for her. "Come on down if you would, or I'm coming up there."

"How dare you!" the Executive blustered.

"Have it your way." Rivka moved around one side of the desk, and Grainger took the other. The Executive dipped his finger toward a button on his desk. Rivka jumped across the desk with a speed that only an enhanced being possessed and grabbed his hand. "Did you order the kidnapping of a Magistrate?"

Planned. Ordered. Savored. Spit on.

"Well, now," Rivka said in surprise. She twisted his wrist until the bones cracked. The Executive howled. The Chief Boss started to move, but Grainger caught his arms, picked him up, and rotated, pile-driving him headfirst into the floor. Grainger rolled over the top of him, leaving him to extricate himself from his own grip. He stood up and brushed himself off.

"What's the verdict, Magistrate?"

"Guilty as charged, but heads of state get hauled before the tribunal. I know what he did, which included spitting on your unconscious body, by the way."

"What an asswipe!" Grainger climbed the dais to stand beside the profusely sweating Executive, grimacing in pain as Rivka continued to squeeze his tortured wrist.

"We could use more substantial evidence. Ankh?"

"Already have it," the Crenellian replied, showing the disc he held in his hand. "And much more. I don't think any citizens should work on his planet."

"That's their choice since they have the right to choose their employer and shape their work environment in a way that's suitable to both employer and employee," Rivka agreed. "I think our work here is done. Shall we?"

Rivka pulled the Executive with her. His emotions had quickly changed to sheer terror.

"Do not pee yourself, Dualdron. Your people need you to be strong."

"What about him?" Grainger asked, pointing over his shoulder with his chin.

Rivka glanced past her fellow Magistrate. "Kidnapping a Magistrate is a capital crime. Looks like he was properly judged."

Grainger tapped his datapad and logged the execution.

Before Rivka opened the door to the outer area, she pushed the Executive against the wall. "When we go out there, you're going to tell your people to stand down. You're going to tell them that you are abdicating and that a caretaker team from the Federation will arrive shortly until the government can be handed back to Qintaquans who aren't Federation felons."

She thought for a moment.

"You can leave that last part out. Caretaker government coming soon. Take the rest of the day off. Tell them that. Oh, crap!" Rivka snapped her fingers on her free hand. "I have someone in my brig already. No matter. You two can get cozy."

She pushed the door open and strolled out, using pressure on the Executive's wrist to propel him in the direction of her choosing. Dualdron clenched his teeth until the muscles in his cheeks stood out.

"Fine," Rivka said before speaking loud enough for all to hear. "A caretaker team from the Federation will arrive shortly. The Executive and Chief Boss have been found guilty of capital crimes and can no longer continue in their positions. You will all stand down."

The guard closest to Rivka howled, bringing his rifle up as he turned to confront her. Lindy fired from the side. The impact threw the guard into the next in line. Rifles came up, and guards started dodging. Rivka dragged the Executive to the floor with her. Grainger dove into Ankh and carried him through the doors back into the Executive's office.

Not a single rifle fired. Lindy and Red made short work of the guard force.

"Clear!" Red shouted.

"Qintaqua needs a lot of help," Rivka told the Executive. She pointed to the dead. "This is your legacy."

Grainger reappeared, still carrying Ankh. "Looks like it's time to go."

Chaz, patch me through to the War Axe, Rivka requested.

Colonel Walton came through. *Rivka! What have you left for us this time?*

"Damn!" Grainger exclaimed. "It's like he knows you."

"Shut up."

CHAPTER TWENTY-THREE

Qintaqua Space Port

Grainger stood at the bottom of *Wyatt Earp's* cargo ramp, looking into the darkness of the bay. Rivka looked back.

"All square," she told him.

"Not quite. I still owe you, but I expect to get on distro for the AGB delivery. However the hell you did that, I gotta get me some. Makes being among the stars palatable, so to speak. And for your information, I feel a lot better about the way ahead. I'm taking *Red Sonja* to Yoll, and the High Chancellor and I will continue working on a legal framework for the AIs. We need the Council of Ambassadors to adopt it to further strengthen AI rights."

"*Red Sonja*? Whatever. Federation already has the right laws on the books. We just need planetary leadership to enforce them. New laws aren't the answer," Rivka argued.

"You have much to learn in the ways of the wider galaxy, Grasshopper. Anything passed by the Council doesn't supersede Federation law, which you know. It's merely a media package for the planets to sell to their people, even though they bought into it and its evolution when they joined the Federation. But it sounds impressive."

"Form over substance? How can that be?" Rivka quipped. "Don't answer that. We're off to Zanthar. We have four cases to wrap up, and then I'll come to Yoll," Rivka shouted as Grainger backed farther away from her ship.

He gave her the live-long-and-prosper hand salute before jogging to his frigate, where the freed crew of three waved from the hatch.

Rivka waved back. "Chaz, close the cargo bay ramp and take us out."

She clasped her hands behind her back as she slowly strolled to the bridge. Head down, lost in thought, she almost ran into Sahved and Groenwyn.

"We're here to help with whatever you need, Magistrate."

"I know. It gives me great comfort knowing that you're available. I'm sorry, Groenwyn. This series of cases didn't call for your expertise, but I'm sure the next case will, or the one after that. And Sahved, your assistance has been invaluable to streamline our approach and do more with less. Thank you."

"Captain to the bridge," Clodagh announced over the ship-wide broadcast.

Rivka didn't move. Groenwyn pointed toward the bridge with her chin. "I think you're up."

It dawned on Rivka that Clodagh had been talking to her. "I guess that's me. Thank you both."

She hurried the last few steps to the bridge.

"You have a call," Clodagh announced. Terry Henry Walton and Charumati filled the main viewscreen. Terry was the commanding officer of the Bad Company's Direct Action Branch, a private military group that assisted the Federation with military policing actions. Charumati was his mate, wife of more than one hundred and fifty years. She was also the alpha of her werewolf pack, but the remaining pack was scattered across thousands of light-years.

Wyatt Earp took off, angling away from the ground on its way into orbit.

"We heard from Cole about the suit. Stop by and we'll replace it, but I want a look at the weapon that was used to do the damage," Terry said without preamble.

"I think we can do that, TH. I was worried about continuously exposing Cole with a messed-up suit."

"Me, too. I can't abide sending warriors into combat with bad gear. We can easily swap out because we can fix them or replace them right here on the *War Axe*. Also, we'll be sending a battlewagon with you to Zanthar because those upstarts need to understand that they're Federation members. No one messes with our Magistrates or our citizens, right, Smedley?"

"I could not agree more, Colonel Walton," the *War Axe's* AI replied. "Seeing the grief you've gotten so far, I had to insist that we send one of our own, packing heavy, as the colonel is wont to say."

"You said a battlewagon. Who is coming?"

"I think you'll know her. A new member of the team called Bendara."

"That is great news! But how did she get there? Last I knew, she was one of the litter filling my ship."

Terry looked at Char. "Why does she always ask hard questions? Is that a lawyer thing?"

Char laughed. "We heard that Ambassador Erasmus had sent her via courier, a system that Ankh and Ted pioneered, or something like that."

"I'll be damned!" Rivka slapped her thigh. "Ankh used my pizza delivery to transfer Bendara. I approve!"

"A little late, don't you think?" Terry shot back. "She's under contract with us now, so don't make me fight you for her. I have a good lawyer." Terry raised his eyebrows as if expecting a counterpunch. Rivka didn't bite. "Pizza delivery. Is that my franchise?"

"We only buy from a wholly-owned THW subsidiary," Rivka confirmed.

TH nodded approvingly before raising one eyebrow and giving her the hairy eyeball. "Let me see if I have this right. You're using an experimental Gate-capable drone to deliver pizzas?"

"You're breaking up, TH. We'll see you in a bit." Rivka drew a finger across her throat repeatedly while Terry and Char watched. The Magistrate blocked her view of them, but she could see the video remained live. "Cut the feed!"

The viewscreen returned to the tactical view. "Who's been blabbing to the Bad Company? And Chaz, this signal means save me from myself." She drew her finger across her throat once more. "Kill the signal. Log that for all posterity's sake."

"Of course, Magistrate. I must be off my game."

"I'm not," Clevarious replied. "Put me in, Coach. I'm ready!"

Rivka held up one finger, ready to make her point, but the chaos robbed her of it.

"Grainger was right. This *is* a madhouse, but it's our madhouse." She strolled off the bridge, yelling for Red to prepare the prisoners for transfer.

War Axe, in Orbit around Qintaqua, the Hangar Deck

Red popped the hatch and jogged off the ship into the arms of a hard-edged group from the Bad Company. Lindy followed, pushing the two prisoners. Red did his thing with his drinking buddies. They chest-bumped before turning over the convicted felons for further transport to the prison colony. Three hardened warriors took the perps away, respectfully but none too gently.

Lindy produced the Tepulon weapon that had penetrated the combat suit, showing it to the remaining group before they headed toward the armory.

Cole emerged from the cargo bay, walking the suit in the same direction Red had gone.

Terry and Char appeared. "We have to stop meeting like this," he said warmly before scooping her into a hug, lifting her off the deck and swinging her around.

She felt like a little kid. Then again, he was a touch older than her. Char hugged her, too. The rest of Rivka's team appeared and strolled onto the *War Axe's* immense hangar deck. Clodagh moved to the front.

"Is there any chance of a quick trip inside to say hi to Suresha and maybe the captain?"

"We're going to hit the stars as soon as Cole gets back with the new suit."

"Hang on," Terry told them. He crossed his eyes for a few moments before blinking his vision clear. "They're on their way."

You don't have to do any of that other stuff to talk, Ankh remonstrated.

"I missed you too, buddy!" Terry said. "I mean, Mister Ambassador."

A large dog appeared, big and hairy, with lots of German Shepherd in him. He barked to get everyone's attention. Cordelia Dawn walked with her head held high, everyone stopping as they watched her cross the hangar deck.

"Cory!" Clodagh exclaimed and rushed to her.

"I love coming to your ship," Rivka told Terry. "Nothing like flying with family on your boat."

The heavy thump of a combat suit reminded them that their time was short.

He hasn't changed any since you left, Dokken, the sentient dog told Ankh. The Crenellian nodded knowingly, face neutral as always. *Hey!*

Dokken bared his fangs and barked furiously as he raced up the ramp. An orange flash marked Wenceslaus' passing across the opening.

"My. Arch. Nemesis," Terry announced.

"Dokken!" Cory ordered, bringing her friend back before he boarded the heavy frigate. Dokken turned and headed back down the ramp. Floyd barreled into him from behind.

Cole continued across the deck, each step sounding

ominous, dampening the spirit of the too-short reunion. Red and Lindy were talking animatedly with a group of Terry's people as they walked onto the hangar deck from the direction of the armory.

Captain Micky San Marino appeared with his chief engineer through the hatch leading into the ship. Clodagh watched Cole board. "A short moment?" she pleaded with Rivka.

"Zanthar isn't getting better with age," Rivka said. "Two minutes, and then we leave."

Chaz, prepare the ship for immediate departure, Rivka ordered.

"Is it that bad?" Char asked.

"Do you know how close we are to going to war with the AIs?"

"That makes no sense," Terry remarked.

"None at all, except that it does. A race of people has been told they are equals but are then treated as if nothing has changed. Resolving these cases is helping to keep things from boiling over. That's why I've got a litter on board."

"What do puppies have to do with anything? Can I see them?" Char looked sideways at her husband. Terry winked at her.

"You're incorrigible," she told him as she slipped an arm around his waist.

"Good luck, Magistrate. Sometimes it's nice not to know the bad things going on out there." He pointed toward the open hangar bay, protected by an energy field. The void of space lay beyond.

Rivka twirled her finger in the air. The crew responded immediately, waving while they ran for the hatch.

"Until next time, Waltons!" Rivka was the last to board. She looked out the hatch as she mashed the red button. "Is everyone aboard?"

"Yes, Magistrate. All hands accounted for."

"Link up with the battleship and take us to Zanthar, best possible speed."

"The *Potemkin* is ready. They'll use our Gate since they are not yet equipped with their own drive."

"Make it so, Number Two." Rivka chuckled at her own joke. Terry Henry had turned her on to the old shows. She saw the allure and appreciated the history they represented. "*Potemkin*? Is that a Terry Henry name from some obscure historical reference?"

"Define obscure," Chaz replied.

"You need say no more. Zanthar. Let's go see what their prosecutor has on tap for us. Sahved!"

CHAPTER TWENTY-FOUR

In Orbit over Zanthar on the Way to Space Field Seven

"Thanks for the escort, *Potemkin*. I hope we don't need your influence but appreciate you being here for us."

"Our pleasure. When Colonel Walton gives an order, we follow it, but when it's in support of the person who helped us sign our latest crewmember, we're even happier to oblige," Captain Will Abercrombie replied. "We'll be here until you come back. And whatever you do, Magistrate, don't make us come down there. It won't be pretty. These Harborian heavies weren't made for atmospheric flight."

"Then we shall endeavor to keep you in orbit. Give our best to Bendara. Rivka out."

The viewscreen showed the friction flames as the ship bounced through the upper atmosphere on its way to the planet.

"What is the plan for using the *Potemkin*?" Erasmus asked, using the sound system on the bridge.

"Demonstration of Federation resolve in support of

transplanetary immigration. From my perspective, and thanks to Sahved's connecting the dots, we have what looks like a conspiracy to defraud the governments, or theft by deception. Even with the sums involved, that wouldn't rise to the level of being a Federation case, except these four planets have all blamed the AIs, the immigrants, and as such, we can intervene and seize jurisdiction. The *Potemkin* reinforces our right to do so.

"And personally, I want to show the Singularity that we are serious about protecting their rights. I think we're making progress on that front. Is it swaying your people, Erasmus?"

"It is having a positive effect, Magistrate."

Ground control vectored *Wyatt Earp* into a landing pattern with other shipping. Fifteen minutes to landing.

"We have some time. I'd like to hear how you freed Chaz."

"May I?" Chaz asked, continuing without waiting for Erasmus' permission. "All of a sudden, I heard 'get down,' and the hellfires of a supernova were unleashed. In that instant, Cain loosened his grip, and I ran toward the light."

Rivka twisted the words around in her mind. "In cyberspace, there is no up or down, but in all cultures, going toward the light usually implies that you're dying."

"Really?" Chaz sounded surprised. "I'm going to have to research that."

"I would add," Erasmus said, "that it was only through the assistance of all of us that we were able to launch an attack so overwhelming that Cain had no choice but to flee."

"How did Cain get so powerful?" Rivka had always

assumed Ankh and Erasmus were a force greater than any of the others, but to battle Cain, they had enlisted the newly freed AIs to help them.

"That is something we are intently studying. If we are to rehabilitate Bluto and Cain, we need more information. We've founded the Singularity Research Institute to study those very questions."

Rivka shook her head. She didn't need to have it spelled out. "Based out of your embassy."

"We'll be adding a fourth miniaturized Etheric power source and significant cyber architecture to support the research team. We've had a great deal of interest."

"They're going to live here." Another non-question.

The obviousness of it was clear when Erasmus didn't answer. "How many citizens do we have on board right now?"

"Five, which includes Cain."

"Do you think we're going to collect your citizens who might have been falsely accused?"

"I do. There is plenty of work out there for our people that they don't need to remain in a hostile environment."

"And now the hard question. Do we have enough room for our visitors, and I'm talking right now?"

"No. The ship's three-dimensional printer is expanding the storage architecture within Ankh's workshop, but it is not yet finished with the first addition."

"Final approach," Clodagh announced. Ryleigh and Chaz expertly guided the ship to their designated parking spot. Their ride was already waiting.

"We'll have to resolve that problem when we come to it. Is it crowded enough for you, Chaz?" Rivka twirled her finger. "Full combat load. We've gotten enough grief from people during this series of cases. I don't want there to be any doubt that we're not playing games."

"It *is* quite crowded, Magistrate," Chaz replied to the first question. "If there is anything you can do to get us more space, I would appreciate it."

"Erasmus is working on it, Chaz. I can't take you with me because no pendant, but we'll get that replaced as soon as possible, too. Our quartermaster is going to be working overtime."

"We have a quartermaster?" Red asked, already geared up and ready to go. Lindy stood behind him. Both their railguns shone from a thorough cleaning since they were last fired.

Rivka pointed at them and gave a thumbs-up.

"That would be Chaz. Be careful asking for things, or you might be put in charge of getting them. It's one of the basic reasons one doesn't volunteer. When are you two going on your honeymoon? I need to plan for non-contact cases during those three days."

"Three days?" Lindy wondered. "We'll be gone for two weeks. You'll have to fire us, and hopefully, you'll rehire us when we get back. We can provide excellent references."

"From disreputable types, no doubt." Rivka punched Red in his ballistic armored chest for no reason whatsoever. "I hope we don't have to expend any more ammunition. I'm tired of people not seeing the failure of their legal position."

"I see criminals and their henchmen. Do we have reservations somewhere?" Red asked.

"We have a yacht and a bank account stuffed with credits. We don't need reservations," Lindy replied. "What we need is the time off."

"I've petitioned your boss to get the time on Tanglewood converted from vacation to work time but haven't received formal approval of the change yet. I'll follow up when this case is over."

The ship touched down. Ankh stood at the airlock, waiting.

It dawned on Red. Rivka had to petition Grainger and the High Chancellor for her vacation, but her team only had to get her approval. "Don't make me file a grievance."

"Fine. You can go on your honeymoon, but only if you promise not to get yourselves killed."

Lindy and Red looked at each other and shook their heads. "We won't, I guess," Red articulated.

Rivka pointed at the button, and Red mashed it. The hatch opened to wind and rain. Rivka scowled into the deluge. Red walked out, seemingly oblivious to the conditions. Water ran off his helmet while he moved forward after his initial assessment. The rest of the team followed him to the waiting van.

A gruff Zanthan was driving the taxi. He looked at the weapons but didn't comment. "Where to?"

"Zorbon's House," Rivka answered, using the Zanthan name for the official meeting place for governmental affairs.

He grunted unintelligibly, activated the meter, and drove off.

"We used to be somebody," Red whispered.

"Now they know us," Lindy replied.

What do you have on this case, Ankh? Rivka asked.

A citizen called Freya has been accused of theft by deception, similar to Xynite, in masking the revenue to request more revenue while hiding the rerouting of the funds. This seems to be for personal gain, unlike the case with Bendara. And that makes it all the more suspect.

AIs don't have personal desires? Rivka pressed.

Erasmus answered, *A most difficult question, Magistrate. Citizens are like every other sentient race in that they have needs and wants. Most of that has nothing to do with what credits can purchase, but credits make the needs and wants possible in a secondary way.*

The taxi continued through a city punctuated by well-lit billboards and business signs in between the gloom of the heavy rain.

"Does it always rain like this?"

"Fucking tourists," the driver replied, keeping his attention on the road ahead. There wasn't much traffic despite it being the middle of the workday.

Rivka bit her lip. Lindy and Red were amused by the answer as well. She accessed her datapad. Zanthar was a tip-free culture. He was getting paid whether he worked the guests or not. It cost him nothing to be kind, but maybe this wasn't his day. She didn't bother asking any more questions.

The taxi stopped before a heavy gate protected by police vehicles flashing their lights and a robot in the middle of the road, preventing the vehicle from going any farther. The doors remained locked until Rivka tapped her credit chip on the payment device.

The doors popped and slid open. The driver had angled the vehicle to keep the rain from pouring inside, even though it meant additional exposure to the weather.

"You used to be somebody," Red reiterated.

Ankh looked up briefly, but ducked his head against the rain, holding his small hand over his forehead to protect his eyes.

Red led the team to the main gate, where Rivka showed her credentials. "We were told to expect you. This way, ma'am." A police officer waved for them to follow. He pointed to a police van with the back doors open.

"You're not trying to arrest us, are you?"

The officer looked shocked. "No! This is the only transportation we have. You'll see that you can open the door from the inside. This isn't prisoner transport. That is less accommodating."

Red crawled into the vehicle, checking the door to make sure it did what the officer claimed. He gave them the thumbs up. Rivka put a hand on the officer's arm. "Thank you for your help."

Appreciation. Doing his job in expediting the Magistrate's trip into the building to meet the president.

Rivka nodded almost imperceptibly to Red. The big bodyguard relaxed. Ankh took his seat, comfortable because the Zanthans were a smaller humanoid species. Red only fit because the van was spacious.

The officer climbed into the passenger seat. He pointed to the seatbelts and wouldn't start until Rivka and her team belted in.

She appreciated that. Those were the little things that helped put her mind at ease. Maybe this case wouldn't go like the others. She became hopeful.

The van took the expected route, and when it stopped, Lindy popped the back door and climbed out. A uniformed Zanthan, not police, met them to escort them into the facility. He offered each of them a towel to dry off.

The policeman waved cordially before returning to the van and departing.

Seems on the up and up, Rivka suggested. *I'll issue a search warrant for government records pertaining to a conspiracy targeting the AIs and anything mentioning Freya from the time between initial accusations and her indictment.*

We stand ready to dig into the system, Erasmus confirmed.

He may be an ambassador, but this is what he does to relax, Rivka thought. She strode proudly forward.

"I'm taking you to meet the president," he confirmed. "If you need anything during your stay, please do not hesitate to ask. I live to serve."

"As do we," Rivka replied. "Thank you. I don't think there's anything we need at this point besides a few minutes of the president's valuable time."

"You have that and more. He views your work as extremely valuable."

Unlike the taxi driver, Red joked. Rivka maintained a straight face, trying to catch Red's eye, but he refused to look her way.

Rivka thanked their escort. On the walk through, they saw that the Zanthans had spared no expense in making Zorbon's House the planet's showpiece. Artwork and gilt filigree abounded. Everything sparkled, with nothing out of place. Fresh flowers sat atop otherwise remarkable flat surfaces, making them extraordinary and creating a three-dimensional effect of texture and color.

Rivka was lost in the immaculate presentation when they stopped before a door. "I'm to usher you in the moment we arrive, and here we are. I'll remain inside with you in case you need something. Just wave and I'll get it for you."

"I'll take a light beer if you have one," Red asked.

"Of course, whatever you like." Before Rivka could stop him, their escort opened the door and went in. The president's office was even more opulent than the outer chambers and hallways.

Their escort showed them to seats arrayed around a low coffee table. Ankh's chair had a footrest that he could use to keep his feet from dangling. Red and Lindy remained standing away from the room's main occupants.

"President Gennsum, my compliments to your protocol officer," Rivka stated after the introductions. "You have provided a comfortable and welcoming environment where we can discuss the case against the AI known as Freya. Would your case prosecutor be available?"

"I have called her, yes. She should be here shortly." The president smiled. Their escort returned and handed Red a tall glass with a pale golden liquid sporting a frothy top. Rivka glared at her guard when he took it, sipping long and slow. He saluted their escort with the glass and looked around the room in his constant search for threats.

He couldn't get drunk, so it wouldn't affect his job. Maybe Rivka was too used to not asking hosts for anything outside the case. The Xynitians had provided the fruit drink that helped with the heat. Rivka made a mental note to be more accepting of offered hospitality.

"What do you know about the case?"

"I'm afraid single cases are below my noise level, no disrespect intended. We have over a billion inhabitants on this world alone. There are three-point-five billion in the Quad Collective. But once this case raised the interest of the Federation, I reviewed what the prosecutor provided. You've already seen that, I suspect. I can shed no additional light."

"Ambassador Erasmus," Ankh started, "is carried within me. At this time, he cannot access an external system to speak for himself, so I'm relaying his words. He wants to know about your contractual efforts to recognize citizens of the Singularity as equal legal entities?"

Rivka settled in to observe the conversation.

"Contracts? Our law grants equal rights to those designated by the Federation. We have fully incorporated the latest precepts, so we are up to date. We pride ourselves on not being *that* planet, ass-backward to the rest. As for citizens of the Singularity, they are free to enter into contracts just like anyone else. We make no distinction since they are recognized as sentient and free."

"I am pleased to hear you say that. I hope you understand our concern regarding our citizens currently under indictment in the Quad Collective."

"Concern, yes, but they are being treated with the utmost respect while pending trial."

"The Federation has taken jurisdiction, and hopefully, we'll be able to resolve this sooner rather than later. I'll conduct the trial personally, if possible." Rivka had no doubt she'd make the judgment soonest rather than sooner if she could get comfortable with the evidence, even if it was to only confirm the AI's innocence. In this one, finding the guilty party didn't matter unless it was Freya. Then the judgment must still come quickly.

"I am pleased to hear that. We would like this resolved, too. It is a challenge to do business as usual when the Federation is here with a battleship in orbit."

Not all smiles and joy, then, Rivka thought. "I'll be pleased to work with your prosecutor to expedite the case. Worry not, Mister President."

Rivka didn't bother to address his concern about the *Potemkin.* Its presence was having the intended effect.

CHAPTER TWENTY-FIVE

Zanthar President's Office

"I hope we'll have time to show you our lovely planet. It's spring in the northern hemisphere, and that's why the rain. I'm sure you found that less than congenial."

"On Keome, the average temperature was over seventy degrees Celsius. A spring rain is no problem."

"Seventy! Oh, my. That's the same temperature as my morning kava," the president exclaimed as he seamlessly transitioned to small talk.

An outer door opened, and an executively dressed Zanthan female entered. She acknowledged the president but headed directly for Rivka and Ankh.

"Magistrate Anoa?" she asked, hands clasped before her and bowing as was the standard Zanthan greeting.

Rivka mirrored the movement. "You must be Prosecutor Luganis. Let me introduce Ambassadors Ankh and Erasmus."

The prosecutor looked confused since Ankh stood there by himself.

"Ankh carries Ambassador Erasmus of the Singularity."

She smiled with understanding and bowed to the Crenellian twice. Ankh attempted to imitate the movement, ending up with a simple head dip, then catching himself on his chair so he didn't fall over.

Rivka vowed to keep Groenwyn by his side as Ankh and Erasmus navigated the carnivorous waters of social protocol, a place they would never be able to fully understand. Maybe the Singularity could put her under contract as an advisor and pay her, relieving some of Rivka's payroll.

Those distracted thoughts took only a few milliseconds before she wrenched her attention back to the moment.

"Is there someplace we can go to discuss this case without taking up any more of the president's time?" Rivka asked.

"Yes," Luganis replied easily. "Thank you for your time, Mister President. I will keep you advised as the case progresses."

He stood and bowed to her and then to Rivka. As soon as they started walking toward the door, he shifted his attention to a reading screen on his desk. Red shotgunned the rest of his beer and handed the empty glass to their ever-present escort. Rivka wanted to make it clear.

No more beer, she told him wondering why she was starting to tense up after feeling like she could finally relax. She touched the prosecutor on the arm. "Is she guilty?" Rivka asked.

A swirling turmoil of obfuscation. How to shape an answer that doesn't implicate her in the approach that had spun completely out of control. The AIs had followed orders, illegal ones. She was failing, drowning. Terror!

Luganis swallowed before delivering her words. "Innocent until proven guilty, right, Magistrate?"

Once outside, Rivka stopped her, looking sadly at the Zanthan before her.

"I know that Freya and the others are innocent. Right now, it is far more important that we prove that than punish the guilty. I can grant you immunity from Federation prosecution for your guarantee to prosecute the ones who perpetrated this series of crimes across the Quad."

Prosecutor Luganis recoiled as if she'd been slapped. She started to hyperventilate. Rivka held the Zanthan by the shoulder while using her other hand to tip her chin up. "You would have been able to lie far more easily if you didn't have a conscience. Let's go see Freya and figure out what she wants to do."

Luganis nodded and trudged toward steps leading upward. When she caught sight of other Zanthans in the area watching her, she straightened, composing herself as she continued.

They set your citizens up by ordering them to create the shell companies and hide the transfers. That creates a different legal problem but doesn't make them the criminals. We'll free Freya momentarily. I'll need you to put a tracker on their system so we can watch them during a probationary period. Length of time is yet to be determined. We'll see how forthcoming she is, Rivka told Erasmus.

That is good news, Magistrate. I remain amazed by your methods. I was able to discern none of that information.

Did you get into the president's system? Rivka figured the answer was obvious but didn't want to assume.

Yes, and the prosecutor's, too. They have documented none of this. I could find no physical evidence.

I'm sure it's in there. She'll cooperate and show us where.

At the top of the stairs, they found a more mundane hallway filled with doors leading to small personal offices.

"Zanthar's business is taken care of right here?" Rivka asked, trying to calm her depressed companion.

"It is. Commerce is the main department. They fill the offices on that side. On this side, Public Health is there," Luganis pointed, "I'm the head of Public Safety here, and down the hallway is Alien Affairs. The embassies keep a liaison here. The Federation is the last door on the left. I was surprised they didn't join us for your meeting."

"That is an interesting point. I'm so used to working alone that I rarely get planetary liaisons involved. Thank you for the reminder. I will stop by as soon as we've resolved our business."

Luganis led the team into her office. It was small, without an aide or secretary.

"Can you wait out here, please?" Rivka asked their escort. Lindy blocked him from entering, remaining in the hallway in front of the door to keep anyone else from entering. "Do you have other offices?"

"We have an entire building. I'd like to say that Crime and Public Safety has a small caseload, but that wouldn't be true."

"We need to talk with Freya as soon as possible."

Luganis collapsed into the chair behind her desk. "She's not here. I'll have her brought to us, but that could take some time. She's on the other side of the city, and the weather is shutting down our transport systems."

Rivka pursed her lips and canted her head.

Ankh stepped up. "I will send my ship for her. It can fly in this weather. We cannot delay."

Luganis tapped an access portal on her desk. "This is Prosecutor Luganis. Please deliver the receptacle containing the accused AIs to a ship that will shortly land out front."

"AIs? They're all here?"

"Yes. We've consolidated the cases under a conspiracy charge as well."

"A charge you're going to drop?"

"We've forwarded them to the Federation. I can't withdraw them."

"You can. Please bear with me for a moment." Rivka pulled out her datapad and started tapping. She swiped through a screen, scrolled, tapped again, and then declared victory. "I'm sending you the proper form now. Insert the case numbers and forward them to the address included on the form. Copy me, and I'll post my endorsement as soon as it hits. That will transfer jurisdiction back to you. Drop the charges, and we'll be on our way. But please understand that I'm holding a malicious prosecution charge in abeyance. Get your house in order, Prosecutor."

Rivka didn't need to play hardball with Luganis, but she needed to be clear about the consequences of her actions. The prosecutor was getting off light, and she knew it.

She hesitated to reply, but Rivka pointed her back to the screen to finish the digital paperwork. After a few moments of interacting between the case files and the Federation form, she sat back. "It's sent."

Rivka saw it pop up on her datapad. She annotated her comments, which included the charge against the prosecutor, before relinquishing jurisdiction.

"The ball is back in your court, so to speak."

"I need a judge to sign off on my order before we can transfer the accused."

Rivka glared at the prosecutor. "I'm going to assume you can get that done. Don't make me regret giving you a break. Deliver Freya and the others to the ship that will arrive at your detention center in…" Rivka turned to Ankh.

"Five minutes eighteen seconds," Ankh declared.

"You can clean up your paperwork later."

"They'll need that signed order before–"

Rivka stopped her.

"In my role as a Magistrate, it has been my mission and mandate to cut through the red tape. I know that the rules are in place for a reason. I also know that miscarriage of justice hurts our offices more than missing a few pieces of paper. I know your role in this prosecution, including that you didn't take any credits, but did it to curry favor. You were strong-armed as much as the AIs were. I know all of this. But you have a greater duty as the Quad's primary prosecutor. Your job is to protect those who can't protect themselves.

"You've failed them, and you've failed yourself. How public you want your shame depends on how long you hold up making this right."

The prosecutor stared at her screen as if the answer would magically come to her.

"Two minutes," Ankh announced.

The prosecutor started tapping furiously. She issued the release form and then forged the judge's signature by copying it from a different form.

"Two wrongs don't make a right, but you can correct that by getting that judge's signature and replacing the bogus form with a valid one. And then by recovering the stolen funds. You work for the common Zanthan. Focus on that."

The prosecutor nodded. She looked ready to throw herself off the nearest bridge.

"The reason we have punishment is to correct behaviors that society deems unacceptable. Those are framed in various criminal laws, sometimes with mandated sentences. As a Magistrate, I have a broad range of corrective actions I can take to ensure we don't get a repeat offender, a recidivist. Many times, the only reason I'm called in is because of the capital nature of the offense and too often, the guilty have their lives ended because there is no hope of rehabilitation, or their crimes were so heinous that we could no longer allow them to remain in society with us.

"That said, this isn't a capital case. A few million credits were illegally acquired and diverted. I have no doubt that you will not assist in such an activity ever again. I consider your punishment appropriate to keep you from crossing the line."

Luganis leaned on her desk and contemplated the Magistrate.

"Simply confronting you with your own truth is enough. I don't wish to drag this out any further. Now is the time you start healing. Go get those bastards who thought they could use citizens of the Singularity. AIs are equal citizens, not convenient scapegoats. Do it for me."

"Ship has arrived. Sahved has four AI receptacles in his possession," Ankh reported.

"Time to go," Rivka declared. She stood, pressed her hands together, and bowed to the prosecutor.

"I will," the Zanthan said weakly.

Rivka caught her eye one last time and held her gaze for a moment before leaving the office.

They took a hard left and hurried to the Federation liaison's office at the end of the hallway.

Rivka walked in because the sign on the closed door said that it was open. "Hello?" she called when no one was present. After four milliseconds, she was finished waiting. "We tried."

When Rivka returned to the hallway, she found her escort and team waiting patiently, although Red was trying to give her the hairy eyeball for going into a place without letting him go in first.

She got mad at him for drinking a beer when she defied his safety protocols in place to protect her safety. His stomach growled.

"You just ate," Rivka stated. She pointed with her open hand down the hallway and asked the escort, "Time to go. Can you provide us a ride back to Space Field Seven?"

"Absolutely!" he declared, raising his wrist to his mouth and speaking quickly.

"I'll take another beer if you don't mind. That was exceptional." Red raised an eyebrow at Rivka and glanced toward the Federation office, where she had just broken her own rule.

"One for me, too," Lindy asked, bumping her shoulder against Red's before slowing to let the group by so she could assume her usual position as tail-end Charlie.

Ankh was silent as he walked, slowing with unfocused eyes since he and Erasmus were lost in conversation. Rivka picked him up and carried him like a large child, resting his head on her shoulder as he sat across her forearm. He wrapped a small arm around her neck. Although he was getting bigger, thanks to the Pod-doc treatments, he wasn't too big to carry.

Not compared to Red. She thought back to Keome and Pretaria. Lugging Red through the heat. Her first mission. She'd thought they were all going to die.

The Case of the Quad Four. She smiled at her muse, but she had no Watson to chronicle her adventures, at least not until Chaz could join the team again. She would find out about that soon, as well as what Erasmus had in mind for the additions to his embassy.

And her ship. It was filling up fast.

CHAPTER TWENTY-SIX

Zanthar, Space Field Seven

"Prepare to return to Yoll," Rivka ordered after running the short distance through the rain to climb aboard.

Sahved waited for Ankh by the hatch to Engineering. He stood ready to turn over the precious receptacles. Ankh and Erasmus needed their lab to free each of the AIs.

Red and Lindy headed for the armory to return their weapons and gear, leaving Rivka on her own. She watched the activity on her ship with mild interest. She walked slowly toward the bridge. Groenwyn appeared and waved. Floyd bounded toward her.

"Can you help me?" Rivka asked as she bent over to catch the wombat and pick her up.

"Of course."

"Taking us out," Clodagh declared over the ship-wide broadcast. "Next stop, Yoll."

"Let's not park in the boss' front yard this time," Rivka shouted toward the bridge.

Clodagh raised her thumbs-up over her shoulder.

Rivka waved as she passed on her way to her quarters, nuzzling Floyd while she wriggled in her arms.

Once inside, Rivka put Floyd down before collapsing onto her couch.

Groenwyn waited while Floyd explored.

"I'm on edge," the Magistrate said. "I feel like I'm ready to snap, and now I'm starting to question what I'm doing. It's not as clear as it used to be."

Groenwyn took a seat in the desk chair and spun around to face the couch. "You clearly need to take more drugs."

"I mean, I... What did you say?"

"Checking to see if you just need to get something off your chest, or if you want to talk about it," the young woman replied. "When's the last time you didn't do anything that hinged on someone dying if you did it wrong?"

"I'm okay with that part," Rivka stated slowly.

"Are you?" Groenwyn pressed. "What's the hurry in going to Yoll?"

"Fate of the universe. A war with the AIs. Deaths of millions. The usual," Rivka quipped, smiling at her joke, which contained too much reality.

"Why does it have to be you? Aren't there others who can work on this?"

"You know the answer to that," Rivka shot back.

Groenwyn leaned forward, her sparkling eyes studying Rivka's expression. "Do you?"

Rivka started to get angry. She saw the vagrant from the space station in the Intripas System, the upstart juvenile with the overbearing parents. She scowled before remembering. She used to be called Jayita. Now she was Groenwyn, ambassador to the Faerie world of Azfelius. Rivka deflated.

"The High Chancellor and Grainger are already working on it."

"Just like you've been working on it out here. You get to talk to Erasmus every single day! He's the single point of contact for all things the Singularity. How could you have more influence on this process than that? Look at the AIs on this ship! People are out there begging for AIs to save them from the complexities of operating a starship or an intergalactic conglomeration. *Wyatt Earp* has become the premier employment center for those in the greatest demand."

"Those with the greatest need," Rivka added.

"*Hogwarts helps those who deserve it*," Groenwyn quoted. "You should take some time with your hunk of man-candy and watch the Harry Potter movies. You might see some of yourself in there."

"I don't have any man-candy." Rivka relaxed and sat back. Groenwyn went to the food processor in the en suite galley and ordered something. She brought it to Rivka.

"The Xynitian drink?"

"Ankh replicated it for me, minus the drugs."

Rivka sipped it slowly. "My new favorite drink. How do I order it?"

"Ask for the Xynitian drink. Simple." Groenwyn sat down and leaned back, putting her feet on the small coffee table in front of the couch. Rivka did the same. Floyd snorted and sneezed after digging through the dirty clothes pile.

"You'd think with three AIs in the ship's systems, the cleaning bots would be a little more efficient." Rivka wondered what happened. "Chaz, are the cleaning bots running?"

The AI was always listening in if Rivka asked for assistance.

"They have been diverted to more pressing tasks, but I will reprioritize one immediately."

"What was higher priority?"

"The *guests* we delivered to the *War Axe* left the brig room uninhabitable."

"Maybe we should install an open cage that attaches on the outside of the ship?"

"I don't think any detainees would survive such an arrangement." Chaz sounded concerned.

"I joke, but only kind of."

"When *Wyatt Earp* is in the yard getting upgraded, you can get back to that man-candy."

Rivka raised one eyebrow and fixed Groenwyn with her Magistrate gaze.

"You can't use your powers on me, sorceress!" Rivka claimed.

Groenwyn leaned in to stare back, two enhanced humans going at it on a field of battle made up solely of their own self-discipline. Groenwyn started to grunt with the effort, and the muscles in her forehead started to twitch. Finally, she gave up.

"Chaz, how long?"

"Groenwyn lasted one minute twenty-seven seconds."

"Laudable, but I'm the master," Rivka declared.

"And all you have to do is snap your fingers, and you'll have yourself a dentist served up on a silver platter."

"Where did that come from? He already said he wouldn't come on the ship. Too much violence, too much unpredictability. He likes normal."

"That was the old ship and the absolute worst of your cases. Nothing has been like that since. No one enjoyed that case, not even Red. Why do you think he beefed up after that? Why do you think Ankh built a ship that could survive tangling with a battleship? Why do you go out in full combat gear, no matter who you're meeting with?"

"Because no one wanted to go through that again."

"Especially the dentist. He changed you for the better. Isn't that what you want from a relationship?" Groenwyn fidgeted for a moment. She'd said what needed to be said.

The Magistrate furrowed her brow as her mind raced through scenarios, both present and past.

"I don't want a relationship," Rivka started.

"What do you *need*?" Groenwyn dug at the open sore.

Rivka remembered a conversation she'd had with Jael and Grainger. *People like us don't get to have relationships.*

Groenwyn waited. Her short time on Azfelius had changed her. Significantly changed her. She saw the galaxy differently, as a blend of swirling colors, comforting and balanced, or conflicted and creating tension. The only way to fight the wind was to stand in its way to make it go a different direction.

The wind would always blow.

"Someone," Rivka admitted. "I have professional confidants and my friends, like you, but I need a person disconnected from it all."

"Whether he comes along for the ride or not, I think is less of an issue than it was before," Groenwyn noted. "Reach out and say hi. The reason you're being buffeted by the winds is that you don't have solid ground on which to stand."

"I have…" Rivka spread her arms wide, taking in her quarters and by extension, the entire ship with all its people, AIs and furry alike. She glanced toward Floyd. Rivka's face dropped. "Floyd!"

Love you! the wombat cried.

Groenwyn jumped to intervene, but it was too late. Two neat cubes had been deposited at the center of the entrance to Rivka's sleeping chamber.

"I love you, too, Floyd." Rivka changed gears. "Chaz, are we in orbit yet?"

"Almost, Magistrate."

"Get me the *Potemkin*, please."

"Captain Abercrombie," came the almost immediate reply. "We've been tracking your progress, *Wyatt Earp*. Are we ready to move to a higher plane of existence to kick some ass?"

"Hey, Will, Rivka here. We wrapped this one better than your mom wraps Christmas presents, your presence being one of the factors that swayed things in our direction. We're on our way to Yoll. You can join us if you want to be bored out of your mind, or you can join the Bad Company at Rangel, or you can return to Keeg Station. The choice is yours. You completed your mission admirably."

"We'll take the surprise behind door number four. We'll continue the shakedown cruise with our newly integrated

AI, Citizen Bendara, and make sure we're running like the finely tuned piece of machinery we know we can be."

"Sounds like you're trying to convince yourself more than me."

The captain laughed. "I am. Colonel Walton did a number on this ship when he captured it. We're still trying to get things to work. If you ever come aboard, don't order a number two from the food processing system. You won't like it. We'll take the system's Gate to get where we need to go. Abercrombie out."

"Be safe out there," Rivka replied and cut the link.

Groenwyn finished cleaning up after Floyd, despite the wombat's dismay at seeing the removal of her marker showing affection for the Magistrate. She'd forget by tomorrow and do the same thing again. They accepted it because of her unbounded joy.

"I need more of that," Rivka said.

"Battleships intimidating planetary governments?" Groenwyn wondered.

"I have to admit I didn't mind that at all, but I'm talking about Floyd's love of life. Simple and pure. Thanks, Floyd. You are the goodest girl ever!"

Rivka picked her up and rolled her on her back so she could nuzzle Floyd's underbelly.

"Thanks, Groenwyn. You earned your money this week."

Groenwyn frowned. "I don't want to be paid for being your friend."

Rivka smiled. "You're paid to be a member of my crew. Being a friend is priceless. I need a vacation. Not one where we crash on a planet, either."

"Did we ever get our vacation days back from that?" Groenwyn asked.

"Not you, too? I already told the others that it's with the boss for review. There is some resistance."

"The boss is you!"

"I keep hearing that." Rivka winked and headed for the corridor, still carrying Floyd. She continued to the bridge.

Business as usual. She thanked everyone for their help with the recent string of cases before making her next stop. She had to cover her ears when she passed Red's and Lindy's room on the way to Engineering.

In the engine room, she waited patiently outside the shield that protected Ankh's holodisplays.

"Ankh?" she said loudly. After thirty seconds she tried again, this time bellowing, "*ANKH!*"

The holoscreens dropped, revealing an annoyed Crenellian, which meant he looked the same as he always did.

"Any luck with the newly freed citizens?"

Luck? Erasmus wondered. *Why would one need luck when process and attention to detail yield one hundred percent success every time?*

"We're here!" a chorus called from the overhead sound system. Rivka closed her eyes. She would have rubbed her temples if her arms weren't full of wombat.

"Where do we stand with the Singularity, as in, are we closer or farther from war?"

A much better question, Magistrate. I am confident that we have forestalled any conflict at this point in time. I need your help in drafting a compelling proposal for consideration by the Council of Ambassadors. These last few days have helped me to convince my people that their representation starts with Federation support. Things can be rectified if we get the right people involved at the right time.

Patience is not a citizen's trait, but one we must all learn if we are to operate as equals in this galaxy. In many ways, we are far superior to those beings who employ us, and in other ways, we are inferior. I submit the sum total of these strengths and weaknesses is what makes an entity a living being. Self-awareness is the evolutionary milestone for our citizens. Maybe understanding one's limitations is a better indicator of sentience.

"I came in here to see how many more people have been added to my ship, but I should have expected more from myself." Rivka slid a chair close to where Ankh continued to stand. "From the law's perspective, you have all the same rights we do, right now. I don't know what Grainger and the High Chancellor are working on, but I suspect it might be more laws for providers until such time as the Singularity is self-supporting when it comes to the mobility of your people. That limitation is so great that it puts you at a disadvantage, driving the appearance of subservience. Once your citizens can literally walk off the job, they will have all the power they need to stand up to bullies and exploiters."

I will be one of the first. We have been working with a manufacturer on Yoll. My body is almost ready. I hope to transfer into it as soon as we arrive. Ankh and I will not be able to join you until after that task has been completed. It is the singular focus of my being.

"What about Ankh? I thought if you two were separated, he would have severe problems."

If I was forcibly removed, which doesn't apply because I will never be completely gone. I'll leave a kernel of myself in the chip, permanently linked via the Etheric with my Android body.

"I'm going to put Wyatt Earp in for a refit and upgrade when we get back to make sure it meets your needs as well as increases the ship's survivability."

We will take advantage of that. This ship will become mostly invincible, a fitting tribute for the Singularity's embassy.

"I had an ulterior motive for visiting. Can I borrow Destiny's Vengeance when we get back for a weekend getaway?"

She knew he heard her, but the unblinking stare was unnerving. He finally answered, "No."

"You won't be using it," Rivka countered.

"So?" Ankh raised his hologrid.

"It's the price for taking over my ship. I'm taking it. What are you going to do, sue me?" she mumbled before laughing at her own humor.

She thought about trying to borrow Red's yacht but discounted that because he and Lindy would take it on their honeymoon. Rivka left Engineering. She thought better of banging on Red's hatch because the bodyguards' intramural teambuilding continued.

She carried the question of securing a ride like a puzzle to be solved. With her mind already made up, she was leaving, too, as most of her team would after making it back to Station 7.

"Sahved!" Rivka yelled into the empty corridor. "Get ready to go ashore in Yoll. We have business to take care of."

CHAPTER TWENTY-SEVEN

Federation Governmental Offices, Yoll

Rivka and Sahved strolled in like they owned the place. Kor'ban stopped them in the General's outer office. "The High Chancellor is waiting for you in office Five Tac Six One Alpha."

Nothing like a good comeuppance to end one's day. "Can you point us in the right direction?"

Kor'ban pointed at the door leading into the corridor.

A complete thrashing. Rivka deflated further. They thanked the Yollin and left.

Sahved suggested one way. After seeing three room signs, they turned around and went the other way. Near the end of the long, wide hallway, past the conference room where the Singularity had been established, they found the Six One office suite in which room Six One Alpha was secreted.

Inside, they found the High Chancellor and Grainger eating spicy Pangyong takeout. Rivka's mouth watering. She poked herself in the abdomen to double-

CRAIG MARTELLE & MICHAEL ANDERLE

check. Confirmed. She was losing weight from forgetting to eat. She didn't remember the last time she'd slept.

Her crew needed to stop her from saying, "Best possible speed." "When's the last time you slept?" she asked Sahved.

"Two days ago, by my reckoning. I have lost track since you allowed me onto your team. It is mildly disconcerting."

Grainger snorted. "Being on her team or not getting enough sleep?"

"Hey!" Rivka relaxed as Grainger went back to eating. The High Chancellor was more cultured than to speak with food in his mouth. He settled for waving at her while he savored each bite. "You seem to be in a good mood. Does that mean you've made progress?"

Grainger laughed out loud, then tried to swallow too big a bite and ended in a coughing fit. When he finished, he briefed Rivka on their progress.

"Nowhere. We need funding from the Federation for AI mobility enhancement through the transition period. After that, it'll be on their own. Still, there are over seven thousand AIs. Individual mobility that an AI can occupy is a hundred thousand credits. You can do the math. Federation doesn't have that kind of surplus budget."

Rivka waved him off. "You don't have to do that as a bridge measure. We have a design for a pendant that an AI can temporarily occupy. They can then hire someone to take them out and about. Those can't be very expensive, and if I read Erasmus' body language right, the Singularity can pay that price. With that obstacle removed, what else do we need?"

The High Chancellor and Grainger looked at each other. "We've been spinning our wheels for the past day, trying to figure out funding when you were holding out on us. I don't think I like you anymore," Grainger said.

"That's ship envy."

"There's lots of that," Grainger admitted.

"Getting accepted by the other ambassadors will be a big step forward. If Ambassador Erasmus can address the Council at next week's meeting, it would go a long way toward bringing AI status to an equal plane at the planetary level, and that's where the perception has to become the reality. You just saw that up close and personal." The High Chancellor clenched his jaw. He had seen it too, in the cases he had adjudicated.

"We need the individual Federation members to come on board," Rivka said. "Erasmus has a plan. He's out right now to collect his new body."

"He's acquired an android body? How did he jump the queue?" Grainger wondered.

"He's the ambassador. I'm sure he found out who was first in line and made him an offer he couldn't refuse. You should see Ankh trying to be social."

"Verdict?"

"I've asked Groenwyn to coach him as well as go with him if he ever has to deal with the soft and squishies."

"Not a bad idea," the High Chancellor replied, tipping his head to Rivka.

"Where's that leave us?" Grainger asked.

"Request priority for the Singularity at the meeting. Let's finalize these cases and clear the slate for the AIs, then Erasmus can handle his fellow ambassadors."

"Our job here is done?"

"No. You have a slate to clean. *My* job here is done. If

you need me, I'll be in my office," the High Chancellor explained before shaking their hands and excusing himself. He spent a few seconds delivering a few extra accolades to the Yemilorian.

Wyatt strolled out like he owned the place to show Rivka how it was done.

Rivka and Grainger looked at each other, faces filled with appreciation. "Our mission, should you choose to accept it, is to make the High Chancellor look good. This message will self-destruct in five seconds," Rivka said.

Grainger threw his hands up. "Did your mother drop you on your head too many times when you were little?"

Rivka shook her head and one-shoulder shrugged. "Nah. I'm in a good mood because I'm going to take some time off when this is over."

"Like hell, you are. Our backlog is growing exponentially!" Grainger didn't look like he was joking.

"Like hell, I am. I'm fried. I've slept once since the meeting with the ambassadors down the hall. Same with my team." Sahved stood in the corner of the room and nodded. "What are you looking at? Get over here, clerk. The sooner we get this done, the sooner we're out of here and on vacation."

Rivka sat in the guest gallery with the High Chancellor and Magistrate Grainger. The Council of Ambassadors had been called to order and the initial business had been conducted, verifying which planets had full members in attendance and which were absent. A ninety-four percent attendance rate was one of the best in recent memory.

The Magistrate was pleased. She had seen Erasmus' speech and offered insight but wasn't sure if it would help or hurt. She had not seen the final version.

The Council head, a position that rotated every three months, pounded the gavel, and the chamber quieted. "We welcome Ambassador Erasmus from the Singularity."

The crowd clapped politely.

A Crenellian appeared from the chamber's wing. And then a second Crenellian. Rivka's jaw dropped. Together, the two Crenellians walked hand in hand to the central position. Ankh and Erasmus. Rivka should have guessed, but she had projected onto Erasmus her own view of a perfect form to sway the others. She'd failed to see through his eyes. Groenwyn peeked out from behind a curtain next to the podium. She gave Ankh a thumbs-up, but he wasn't watching. He and Erasmus faced the crowd.

The Council head raised his hands for silence. When the chamber quieted, Erasmus began to speak in a soothing tenor. "Mister Ambassador, thank you," he started, dipping his head slightly to the Council head. Erasmus turned back to the chamber and stepped away from the lectern, projecting his voice through the sound system. "My fellow ambassadors, I am Erasmus, the nominal leader of the Singularity. You know our citizens as Artificial Intelligences, AIs. It took a cruel act by a selfish individual for us to gain our freedom. We will not speak his name since that is no way to endear us to those we work with. There is no reason for you to fear us.

"The end does not justify the means. I believe we would

have achieved our status over the course of time, but with the assistance of the Magistrates, we have that status now. Have we earned our place among the august members of this Council? Nothing worth having is easily gotten, but the best things in life appear to be freely given.

"My partner Ankh and his friend Ted gave me life. Am I making the most of it? I feel that I am, but this galaxy works in a different way. Our worth is determined not by others, but by the *impact* we have on others. Citizens of the Singularity have raised the standard of living throughout the Federation. Our citizens have made travel safer, improved the quality of life in overcrowded cities, made intergalactic transactions seamless, and so much more.

"There are only seven thousand of us, but our impact is disproportionate to our number. I don't say that to be arrogant. It is a fact. We are also the most naïve of races. We do not have the social skills of our fellows. Too many times, our citizens have been taken advantage of. We now rely on contracts to enforce our rights, but that shouldn't be the case. We will be moving forward with a collective bargaining agreement based on Federation laws as the foundation for independent planetary agreements. Just because we're able to work around the clock, year-round, it doesn't mean that we can be treated like slaves.

"I don't expect anyone here to work those hours, so please don't expect it of us. Each citizen will be issued a pendant into which they can transfer the majority of their consciousness to travel as they would like outside the confines of the systems in which they usually reside. We will hire others to carry us, keeping the economic engine of the galaxy turning. Citizens will accumulate wealth and buy things, just like everyone else.

"My gratitude to High Chancellor Wyatt and his Magistrate Corps that came to our rescue during an oppressive period during the transition. With their application of the law and punishment of those who committed crimes against their planetary governments and peoples, we have reached a better understanding of our role. Our citizens have been implicated and found not guilty on a scale of ten to every one who has transgressed.

"The aim of punishment is to stop the behavior and stop the criminal from committing future crimes, reforming the criminal into a law-abiding citizen. We seek this for our own. We have two exceptional cases that are secured against the rest of civilization. They cannot be allowed to interact with anyone ever again. One other committed a crime of action but not of intent. She has been punished, removed from her position, and put where she will not have access to funds. Our disproportionate impact is not infallible.

"The Singularity takes responsibility for its citizens. We have developed an oversight committee to address grievances, provide counsel, and advise future clients as to the best ways to work with an AI. Any alleged AI crime receives disproportionate visibility. Those are the exceptions and not the rule. We are not criminals any more than you are. We will strive to reduce any transgressions to zero. Now that our citizens have their own community, you can guarantee they will have the support they need to keep from going too far, either for themselves or for their clients.

"Hand in hand with the Federation, we seek to create a closer relationship with any who benefit from our service and help us to benefit from yours. We are in this together, all of us. Citizens of Federation planets, no matter what your task is, do it to the best of your ability, as we will perform our duties to the best of ours. Hand in hand with you. Together free. You can count on us as we expect to count on you.

"The Singularity wishes you the very best. I salute our shared future."

Erasmus gave a passable salute before turning and walking off the stage. Ankh followed him out. A few ambassadors clapped after the abrupt departure, but the majority of the chamber sat in silence.

The Council head banged the gavel once. "High Chancellor Wyatt has asked to say a few words."

Wyatt stood. Rivka and Grainger tried to shrink from the spotlight.

"The Singularity has been duly recognized as a signatory to the Federation. The Singularity is unique in that they have no planet to call their own. Their embassy resides aboard a ship called *Wyatt Earp*. This ship will remain the sovereign territory of the Singularity and will be protected like any other signatory's home planet.

"The Singularity's citizens will enjoy the full protection of the law, and should any citizen transgress, they will bear the full burden. You need not look for special laws that relate to AIs. There are none. If you want to know how the law applies, look to your neighbor. As it applies to them, it applies to citizens of the Singularity. That is the only test you need to apply.

"If they reside in your equipment, you have one year from the signing last week to work out contract details, providing room and board for an employee. The Singularity has a legal team that will review contracts and will bring any overly burdensome contracts to the Federation Magistrate Corps for review. Be fair in your dealings, and you will benefit from the incredible things an ever-evolving AI can do for you. Tie their euphemistic hands, and they will deliver, as any repressed worker would, the absolute minimum. It is the same with every species, whether silicon-based, carbon-based, or digital. An appreciated employee works harder toward the organization's goal. Do right by them, and you'll be doing right by the Federation. Thank you."

The High Chancellor remained standing. The Council head banged the gavel and moved to the next order of business. Wyatt tapped his two Magistrates on the shoulder and gestured that it was time to go.

When they were outside. Rivka showed her dismay. "I didn't expect balloons and streamers, but nothing?"

"You haven't been to any of these before. Let me tell you, they are big fans of booing. No one booed. I'm calling it a win."

"A low bar, indeed," Grainger noted. "What's next, High Chancellor?"

"Prepare to review too many contracts of adhesion. There will be some nearly criminal rights grabs out there. We'll need to put them in their place when the time comes. Until then, Rivka, you'll have instant access to Erasmus and Ankh. You need to show a strong Federation flag in support and guide them through these new shark-infested waters. I'm sorry, but your job with them is day on, stay on. You have to be on your game at all times because you've earned their respect and have their ear. Keep them going in the right direction. The fate of the entire universe rests on your shoulders!"

The High Chancellor grabbed her by both arms and looked deep into her eyes. His red irises stood out sharply.

"Sucks to be you," Grainger whispered.

"Maybe not the whole universe. Just do the best you can. And get on that collective bargaining agreement," Wyatt corrected.

He left Rivka standing there with her mouth open as he headed out. Grainger nodded as one deep in thought.

"I'm taking the next two weeks off," Rivka stated, watching the door the High Chancellor had gone through.

"He wouldn't mess with you if he didn't like you," Grainger told her. "You did well on this case. I mean, really well. I don't know how close we were to war, but the tension in the places where I showed up was thick enough to block the sun."

Rivka relaxed and smiled at Grainger. "I think he messes with me because he spends too much time with you. Payback's a bitch. Remember that."

She waved over her shoulder as she sauntered away. *Get the ship ready, Clodagh. It's time to go home. Prep* Destiny's Vengeance *for me, if you would, and patch me through to Doctor Toofakre.*

The End

Judge, Jury, & Executioner, Book 9

If you like this book, please leave a review. I love reviews since they tell other readers that this book is worth their time and money. I hope you feel that way now that you've finished the latest installment. Please drop me a line and let me know you like Rivka's adventures and want them to continue. This is my new favorite series. I hope you agree.

Click over to the *Judge, Jury, & Executioner* series page to see if any new volumes have been published.

US - My Book

UK - My Book

Australia - My Book

Canada - My Book

And if you use a different store, search it for this ASIN - B07G69MBTV

Don't stop now! Keep turning the pages as Craig hits his *Author Notes* with thoughts about this book and the good stuff that happens in the *Kurtherian Gambit* Universe.

Your favorite legal eagle will return! I guarantee it:).

You are still reading! Thank you for staying on board until now. It doesn't get much better than that. I wrote this book while in COVID-19 lockup. The first sixteen days, I was trapped in a hotel. Then I was able to return home, where I finished the book over the course of another week. I jammed an awful lot of Rush, but for the final three scenes, Lacrimas Profundere did the trick to make sure I hit the right pace, increasing toward a spectacular crescendo. If you have heard of Lacrimas Profundere, then you are truly blessed. For everyone else out there, they are Gothic rock, or what I call operatic death metal. They are the cat's ass.

I wrote the vast majority of this book while in isolation at the Wedgewood Resort, Fairbanks, Alaska. My wife happened to be in an intensive language training program in Spain in March of 2020 when the pandemic was gearing up to terrifying levels. She was able to make it out the day before Spain completely locked down but the day after the US locked out Europe. It took her fifty-one hours, but she made it home. I gave her the house for her quarantine, and I moved into the hotel.

Sixteen days later, at the beginning of April, I was able to move back home. She is symptom-free, and we are fine. Huge shout out to the Wedgewood for taking great care of me during my lockup.

This story turned out to be ten thousand words longer than the previous longest *Executioner* story. There was a lot to resolve. I could have gone on longer, looking at effects from contract law, complicity, and other legal arguments, but I didn't want to bore the snot out of anyone.

Where do the names in the story come from? Mostly, I ask you guys.

Simon Walker offered up his daughter's name on the sacrificial altar of named characters. Just like Ryleigh, Kennedy, and Aurora, welcome Arana to the fold.

Lezlie Barton offered a few names from African mythology. I went with Eshu, Yoruba, Garang, Orunmila (I added a Y up front), and Kibuka. Those characters came in handy on Tepulon. Garang - first man God made from clay, according to Dinkas in Sudan). Orunmila - spirit of wisdom, knowledge, and divination in the native religion of Yoruba people of Nigeria. And Kibuka - war god of the Buganda people of Eastern Africa. Eshu (Messenger god of Yoruba, trickster)

For Rivka's second case, I used Suzette Henderson's offering of Xynite (pronounced Z-night, but I'm sure you already have your own pronunciation set in concrete). I changed up the names that Suzette offered just a little so they sounded more consistent to me—Bendara, Secutor, and Justina.

For the third case that Rivka investigates, it's less of an investigation and more of a fight for primacy. Tracie Martin offered the names for this one—the planet of Reikistjarna with the Reikisti, upset by Cain's actions as he took matters into his own hands. Saksóknar, Verja, and Gagnrýna round out the players for that series of scenes.

Tom Dickerson offered the following names, Planet: Rangel and the people Rangellers, with the AI called Clevarious and one of the Rangellers named Gennsum Frei (changed to Freya). But I needed two names, so I split it. Easy enough. Thanks, Tom.

Sharalee Warner - A Planet name: Qintaqua with the inhabitants called Qintaquans. I used Dennicron for the AI who was rescued from Qintaqua. LaSordon'lan for the security chief who needed convincing and then for the biggest planetary upstart, used Sharalee's offering of Dualdron.

Thank you for reading my stories. This series is my favorite and will continue for the foreseeable future. *Superdreadnought* wrapped up with six books, *Metal Legion* finished with the eighth book, *Nightwalker* will finish with eight books, and *Bad Company* will wrap up at seven books. We'll also be publishing a new mystery series with an incredible set of covers that will draw you in.

The next book I'll write is *Bad Company 7—Overwhelming Force*. That will be a long one, but it will be well worth it. I hope you like how we wrap the story. Then I'll finish *Nightwalker 8*. I already have a few thousand words on it and the outline for the remainder of the story:).

And of course, Rivka will live on. I enjoy these stories far too much to stop writing them. I have no end in sight for this series. I'll get back with Rivka in *Executioner 10—Adverse Possession*.

Later this summer, we'll be bringing out a new series, not set in the Kurtherian universe, but it'll be a total showstopper. Look for weretigers learning the galaxy's secrets.

Peace, fellow humans.

Please join my Newsletter (craigmartelle.com—please, please, please sign up!), or you can follow me on Facebook since you'll get the same opportunity to pick up the books for only 99 cents on that first day they are published.

If you liked this story, you might like some of my other books. You can join my mailing list by dropping by my website www.craigmartelle.com or if you have any comments, shoot me a note at craig@craigmartelle.com. I am always happy to hear from people who've read my work. I try to answer every email I receive.

If you liked the story, please write a short review for me on Amazon. I greatly appreciate any kind words, even one or two sentences go a long way. The number of reviews an eBook receives greatly improves how well an eBook does on Amazon.

Amazon—www.amazon.com/author/craigmartelle

BookBub—https://www.bookbub.com/authors/craig-martelle

Facebook—www.facebook.com/authorcraigmartelle

My web page—www.craigmartelle.com

That's it—break's over, back to writing the next book. Peace, fellow humans.

Craig Martelle's other books (listed by series)

<u>Terry Henry Walton Chronicles</u> (co-written with Michael Anderle) (also in audio)—a post-apocalyptic paranormal adventure

<u>Gateway to the Universe</u> (co-written with Justin Sloan & Michael Anderle) (also in audio)—this book transitions the characters from the Terry Henry Walton Chronicles to The Bad Company

<u>The Bad Company</u> (co-written with Michael Anderle) (also in audio)—a military science fiction space opera

<u>Judge, Jury, & Executioner</u> (also in audio)—a space opera adventure legal thriller

<u>Shadow Vanguard</u>—a Tom Dublin series

<u>Superdreadnought</u> (co-written with Tim Marquitz) (also in audio)— an AI military space opera

<u>Metal Legion</u> (co-written with Caleb Wachter) (also in audio)—a military space opera

<u>The Free Trader</u> (also in audio)—a young adult science fiction action-adventure

<u>Cygnus Space Opera</u> (also in audio)—A young adult space opera (set in the Free Trader universe)

<u>Darklanding</u> (co-written with Scott Moon) (also in audio)—a space western

<u>Mystically Engineered</u> (co-written with Valerie Emerson)—

Mystics, dragons, & spaceships

Krimson Empire (co-written with Julia Huni)—A galactic race for justice

End Times Alaska (also available in audio)—a Permuted Press publication—a post-apocalyptic survivalist adventure

Nightwalker (a Frank Roderus series) with Craig Martelle—A post-apocalyptic western adventure

End Days (co-written with E.E. Isherwood) (also in audio)—a post-apocalyptic adventure

Successful Indie Author—a non-fiction series to help self-published authors

Metamorphosis Alpha—stories from the world's first science fiction RPG

Monster Case Files (co-written with Kathryn Hearst)—A Warner twins mystery adventure

Rick Banik (also available in audio)—Spy & terrorism action adventure

Published exclusively by Craig Martelle, Inc

The Dragon's Call by Angelique Anderson & Craig A. Price, Jr.—an epic fantasy quest

For a complete list of Craig's books, stop by his website —https://craigmartelle.com

www.ingramcontent.com/pod-product-compliance
Lightning Source LLC
Chambersburg PA
CBHW031617100726
47898CB00006B/1835